The Touch

Also by Daniel Keyes

FLOWERS FOR ALGERNON

Daniel Keyes

The Touch

HARCOURT, BRACE & WORLD, INC., NEW YORK

*The author wishes to express
his gratitude to Yaddo, to the
MacDowell Colony, and to
Ohio University for their support.*

For Aurea,

with love

*Remember, I beseech thee, that
thou hast made me as the clay;
and wilt thou bring me into dust
again?*

Job 10:9

The Touch

June

1

At first he thought he heard someone moving around in the bedroom and he listened: the whirr of the electric clock, his wife breathing regularly beside him, his own heart beating. That was all. He suspected the dream had awakened him with a solution; all he had to do now was recognize it.

Karen groaned and rolled over. She had been in it, beautiful as ever, but different, possessing qualities that belonged to her sister. Was that the answer? Could he merge the two without Karen knowing he had changed her? Closing his eyes, letting his mind go blank, he invited the dream to return. But it was gone.

Barney Stark opened his eyes and lay awake staring at the glowing hands of the clock. He had awakened several times during the restless night, and each time the hands seemed less distinct. At ten of two they had been bright upraised arms; now they hung limply. Five-forty.

He strained to see the little window on the clock where the date would show, wondering if today was red or black, but the cycle calendar wasn't luminous. The manufacturers should have thought of that—especially on a Fertility Clock. What would primitive people, seeking supernatural guidance and intervention of the gods for bountiful crops and families, make of such a device? Probably use it to make rain. Perhaps he should pray for a thundershower. He was annoyed that Karen hadn't been able to take the whole thing in better humor. He had been so careful to be offhand, joking about it when he brought it home, not wanting it to seem, as things always seemed to her these days, a reproach. Still, he should have known she would be repelled by the practicality of it, as she had been by Dr. Leroy's tests, calendars, and thermometers.

She would rather go on thinking that babies just happened, would rather conceive of them as the culmination of romantic love and moonlit passion, without thinking, planning, knowing; would have preferred, he was sure, the stork purity of her childhood beliefs to the stark computation (she'd have swatted him for a pun like that so early in the morning!) of the monthly cycles and body heat. She hadn't at all seen the fun in the primitive Earth Mother he had sculptured, with pendant breasts and swollen belly, as a fertility offering to the gods; had actually cried when he playfully put it out on the lawn during the last full moon.

Though she wanted a child as much as he did, she had resisted the medical examinations for several months, even after he had gone first. She would have preferred, he knew, to go on hoping, praying, dreaming, without ever finding out for sure, and even though the tests showed them both capable of conceiving, she was embarrassed at the need to think about it. She went through the motions of taking her temperature, charting her cycle, planning the days, but her irregularity was astonishing, as if her very body rebelled at the idea of consistency, and in the beginning there had been so many heartbreaking false alarms, that he suspected she was doing it all wrong and had lost all faith in her fertility bookkeeping.

The crisis came when she began visiting gypsies for readings, consulting dime-store horoscopes for astral signs, searching her dreams for psychic promises; which was why, when he had read about it in the newspaper, he went out and invested the $17.95 in the Fertility Clock.

The woman had looked at him oddly, as if surprised to have the husband buy it, but she explained how it worked. It was a bedroom clock (naturally!) with a mechanism to count and register probable fertile and infertile days, and once his wife fed into it the information about her longest and shortest periodic cycles, it would thereafter reveal, in that small window on the face, a continuing calendar with numbers—coming up red on probable days of fertility.

"Astounding!" he had roared. "Baby roulette."

She had laughed at that (would have to tell it to the girls!), but Karen had cried.

As if she sensed he was thinking about her, she rolled back and sighed, her black hair fanned out on the pillow, one arm flung back, the other on her abdomen, as if to feel if anything was there yet. He wondered if her beauty was too strong to change—lashes like Japanese brushwork against whiteness; cheekbones high, but not protruding, under perfect skin. Even in the dim light he could tell there were few wrinkles. But she was the type who would take it hard when the body changes came.

Somewhere in that thought was the idea he had been

struggling with in his dream. To change her face, the tilt of her head, perhaps even the way she held her hand. But the changes would have to come from her sister, Myra, as he had last seen her four years ago, before he and Karen were married. Was it possible to blend the best of each without Karen knowing?

Sleep was out of the question now, though it was barely daylight. He got out of bed and dressed. Coffee first, and then he would try it. He hadn't touched the "Rising Venus" for a long time, and he hadn't planned to now that things were so hectic at the Center. But he couldn't put a good idea aside. Inspiration didn't come that often these days. As he started out of the bedroom, he saw her head was to one side now, left arm under the pillow, right hand still on her stomach. If she conceived after all this time, he would have to do the face differently, add something to it. A woman expecting a baby lived for the future rather than in the past.

He turned on the light in the kitchen and knew he had made a mistake. The sink was filled with dirty dishes; the table hadn't been cleared. Why hadn't she just piled them all in the dishwasher? Don't get angry, he told himself. When you lose your lousy temper it drives everything else out of your mind.

He started to take the electric coffee maker to the basement, but the cover was nowhere to be found. He looked for instant coffee, but the jar was empty. He turned off the light and hurried downstairs.

Taking the damp cloth off the life-size figure, he looked at his work. Unquestionably, Karen was beautiful enough to be his model; firm, classical body, delicate right hand touching her thigh, left hand cupped with slender fingers to her breast, eyes modestly down, full lips sad. But of course it was all wrong, and he knew why. During the past three years, the figure (begun, put aside, destroyed, begun again) had changed almost imperceptibly into a more romantic, distant Venus than he had intended. All that was missing was the shell, and the Zephyrs, and Spring about

to cover her. But it wasn't his own vision at all: nothing
but a trite, three-dimensionalized version of Botticelli's
"Birth of Venus."

In this morning's dream the "Rising Venus" had been
finished, and while he was making the plaster mold, she
had come alive and offered herself to him. But when he
embraced her, she became violent and resisting, until the
clay cracked and crumbled in his arms. The face had been
Myra's. Apart from the obvious sexuality and fear in his
dream, there was an insight, he realized: the idea of adding
to Karen's face some of the things he recalled about her
sister, giving it the individuality it lacked, and in a way
returning to his original vision. He knew the determined
line to give her lips, and how to change her eyes. He
could feel in his fingertips how the clay would work. But
not too anxious now, not rushing it, or he might lose
her. There had always been a strength and excitement behind the beauty of Myra that had been lacking in Karen.
How to show it . . . ?

Four years ago in college: bubbling, exciting, impossibly
alive. Always at the center of things: in the midst of every
student strike or fund-raising campaign; to challenge for-
eign policy; to fight for student rights, faculty rights, minor-
ity rights; to protest for the dispossessed, the disenfran-
chised, the poor. And you could be certain, if there was a
demonstration, a civil-rights sit-in or teach-in or sleep-in,
or a march against war or poverty, Myra would be there
to help plan and lead it, surrounded by admiring males
who would have followed her anywhere.

He remembered her laugh, saw her hand gesture when
she argued (palm up, fingers straining to grasp an idea—
like Rodin's "St. John the Baptist Preaching") and the
intense gaze of blue eyes that captured everyone who came
close to her and swept them up in her zeal. He had followed with the rest, adoring from a distance at first, and
then closer. But always there had been too many admirers.
Until finally he contented himself with the dream of Myra
as a model for a full-life nude he would call the "Rising

Venus." He had started it from the memory of her one
summer in a bathing suit, never telling her about it, began
and stopped so many times he feared it would haunt
him for the rest of his life. Looking at the figure now, he
realized it had been a mistake to change his original conception—that hope of adding a new note to the Venuses
sculptured through the centuries by suggesting the struggle
between masculine and feminine qualities in the Goddess
of Love. He had intended a Venus whose beauty would
be heightened by strength and determination, using the
fire of Myra's eyes, the excitement of her arched neck, the
taut way she held her hand. And through her he would
reveal the tensions of modern woman caught in her own
psychic crossfire.

He realized now that his own frustration, his inability
to finish it, was because Karen was wrong for it. She was
beautiful enough, but her beauty was too romantic, sentimental, maternal.

He had met Karen at several of Myra's protest-letter-writ-
ing-and-envelope-stuffing sessions at the huge Bradley house,
and though she never scoffed at Myra's causes (even
helped at times when posters had to be painted or hand-
bills distributed), she never really became involved. She
studied modern dance and acting, and she explained to
him once, when he teased her about it, that the stage was
more real to her than the picket line. Barney had paid
little attention to Karen until after Myra shocked Elgin
City by running off with her middle-aged assistant professor
of sociology (to Southern California, to help organize a
union of migrant workers and Mexican fruit pickers), leaving her worshipers to wonder what had become of their
goddess.

With Myra gone, Karen had bloomed, become lovelier,
more desirable. He began to delight in her naïve romanti-
cism, began to see her as someone to be cared for and
loved, and later, when they were married, he decided to
use her as his model for a more tender, romantic Venus.
By the time they had been married three years, he had

modeled her body several times, but had never been able to finish the head, dimly aware that the very passive unworldliness that had charmed him now interfered. Try as he might, he couldn't satisfy himself with her dreamy eyes and petulant lips. In her own way, she was as elusive as Myra.

This morning his dream had shown him that to finish it he needed to add something of Myra—blending the two sisters into one. He worked quickly. It was getting light outside, and he wanted at least an hour of modeling before he went to work at the Center. He hadn't worked on the Venus seriously in months, but now it excited him and he hated to stop. Even a little of his own sculpting would make it easier to work, during the day, on clay auto models.

He became absorbed in the changing expression of the face: just the slightest furrow in her brow to suggest Myra's impatience; the firmer, almost boyish chin; that look of haunted expectation in her eyes. Another time he would change the hand gesture: right palm upturned, fingers cupped as if holding a flower. But even as he began to work it out it occurred to him that Karen would recognize either the expression or the hand gesture, and it would hurt her. He stopped, with his hands still touching the slick clay. No need to decide yet. Come back and look at it again; or—even better—have Karen pose a few times and let her see it developing slowly to get used to it. He would watch to see if she suspected anything. If she did, they would have to talk it out. He dampened the cloth again, draped it over the figure, covered the tub of clay, and put out the lights.

He would get his own breakfast and let her sleep. Working this morning had been good, but she might sense it and ask questions. She was incredibly perceptive, could tell at times not only what he was thinking, but also when he was trying not to think, and she would know something was wrong.

He had forgotten about the mess in the kitchen, and for a moment felt the anger rising. But he calmed himself and searched in the dishwasher for the cover to the electric coffee maker. Then he understood why the sink was filled with dishes; there was no room in the dishwasher. Who but Karen would fill up a dishwasher and forget to set it washing?

He found the cover for the drip coffee maker in the dish-rack on the drainboard, and set the water to boil. But on his second try for a cup and saucer, a glass shattered into the sink.

"Oh, the hell with it!" he said, and smashed the cup and saucer after it.

In half-sleep Karen had felt him leave the bed to go downstairs. She struggled to open her eyes. It was barely light. Why was he up so early? Several times during the night he had awakened her with his restless tossing and turning; something was bothering him. She wondered dimly if she should get up and make him breakfast and lifted her head to peer at the clock. Only ten to six. She stared at the sweeping second hand and wished that by an act of will she could freeze it and herself in this instant of time between dreams and waking. Horrible enough to sleep and wake by the clock—but making love! She dropped back to the pillow and closed her eyes. The doctor's suggestion to go off on a second honeymoon two months ago and stop trying so hard had been the first intelligent advice she'd heard since this whole conception campaign had begun.

She had never imagined it would be so difficult to have a baby. When you read of all the unwed mothers who had to give theirs away, and remembered your parents' warnings, you believed the first time you did it you would become pregnant. She smiled when she remembered the times she and Myra had talked in the dark of their room long after bedtime for girls nine and eleven and finally figured out that babies came from kissing, a theory reinforced when she heard a precocious girl at school boast about deep kissing ("soul kissing," the girl had called it), and though Myra

said it was disgusting, Karen thought how beautiful that
the kissing of two souls should create life. But a year later
Myra triumphantly reported, on the advice of an older girl
who was taking a sex-education course, that there was more
to it, something about going to bed and having a man spill
invisible seeds into the place where you urinated. Karen
had been confused at first (arguing with ten-year-old logic
that it didn't make sense, because when you peed it would
wash out), but Myra was disgusted that their mother and
father went to bed and did the thing that the bolder girls
called laying and screwing that sounded so dirty that Myra
made it look horrible in her imagination. But later she tried
to tell Myra of the novels she read in which people *made
love* and were transported in flights of ecstasy and passion,
and how it could be beautiful if two lovers didn't think
about what happened after the soul kissing and were possessed by passion while it was being done.

That was how she dreamed it would be with her and
Barney from the first time she saw him. She had never met
a sculptor before, and she studied him secretly when he
came to the house with the others on Myra's committee—
Seniors for Student Action. Tall, with big hands and long
fingers, his sandy hair curling full at the neck, his eyes
pale blue with flecks of brown, his fair skin as smooth as
a girl's. It was the troubled look in his eyes that attracted
her. He was an artist, lonely, moody, from a poor family
in Hamtramck, and she tried to imagine what he was like
when he was off by himself creating beautiful, monumental
sculptures. She could never understand why an artist would
be as infatuated with Myra as the sociology and political
science majors (who followed her as if she were Joan of
Arc in their war against society), but still she was pleased
that he was shyer than the others. And when he came with
them to the house to write letters, address envelopes, or
make posters, she found herself drawn only to him, wondering if their eyes would meet and something would happen.
But she had never tried to attract his attention. Not as long
as he belonged to Myra.

That was something which had been clear between herself and Myra since childhood. She never resented Myra's hand-me-downs (even when the dresses had been mended and the toys worn or broken) as long as she was sure Myra was really done with them. She had learned her lesson once (how old had she been—five, six?) with Cindy, the wetting doll with missing arms, chipped nose, shredding hair. She had wanted it because it was hurt and unloved, and—since Myra never played with it—she had adopted it as her very own baby. Then one day, when Aunt Lucy, on a committee to get Christmas presents for the orphanage, had mentioned the need for dolls, Myra had gone to their room and brought out all her dolls including Cindy and donated them to the orphan children. Everyone had been so proud of Myra, but Karen had been so heartbroken she begged to be allowed to keep it. This was her own, her true baby, she told them. She would give a different one in its place. But her father had said, "Don't be such a selfish child. You would do well to learn from Myra," and she was so ashamed she didn't come to dinner but hid in the basement until bedtime. From that time she never used anything that still belonged to Myra.

So she was secretly glad when Myra went away with the professor. She would never forget the look on Barney's face when she met him on campus one morning and he asked her if it was true. When she told him it was, he said in a kind of silly daze, "We made a date three weeks ago, to go to the movies tonight." She wouldn't have dared be so forward but for the desperate look in his eyes (wanted to tease him and say, it serves you right for making a date for the movies three weeks in advance), and without thinking she had blurted out, "Why not take me instead?"

She could still recall his stare, as if he were seeing her for the first time. When he didn't answer right away, she felt the tips of her ears hot and her face flushed, and she wanted to die. But she laughed and said, "I was only joking," and ran, with tears burning, all the way to her drama class.

That evening he called and apologized. He hadn't meant to be rude, he said. He just wasn't the kind of person who could respond so quickly to the unexpected. Of course he wanted to take her to the movies. She had toyed with the idea of saying she had a date, of putting him off until next week, but she was afraid of starting off their relationship with falseness, and was secretly terrified that someone might take him away from her in the meantime. Several times during the movie she saw out of the corner of her eye that he was watching her, and she knew that with Myra gone he was finally aware of her.

She heard him moving around in the kitchen, opening drawers and closets. What in the world was he looking for at this hour? She opened her eyes again to see what time it was. Six-fifteen. Too early to go down and make breakfast. But she should get up and clear the kitchen. Right now he was probably upset because the dinner dishes were still in the sink. Her body resisted the thought of getting out of bed. It was too early. She watched the second hand sweeping time away. Strange how time seemed to stop when you slept, but kept going for others—for him in whatever he was doing and thinking downstairs—passing you by stealthily, leaving you behind. Time was sneaky.

She frowned at the Fertility Clock. At least she knew that what happened that night of their third date hadn't been planned for, prepared for. It was one impulsive moment shared without thought for the future. She had re-lived that beautiful night a hundred times, conjured it up secretly in the past three months of making love on days regulated by the Fertility Clock. She listened for a moment for sounds of him moving around downstairs, then rolled over and embraced the pillow. It was after they had left a dull party early, and he took her home, she had suddenly, without thinking, whispered to him: "Let's go inside. My folks won't be back until very late." She had led him upstairs to show him the room she had shared with Myra. There he kissed her, tentatively at first, and then deeply, caressing her arms, face, breasts as if he were molding her flesh, and then—as she wanted him to—he laid her back on the bed and began to undress her.

"Not this bed," she had whispered, frightened at the sound of her own voice. "This is Myra's bed."

He looked at her, confused for a moment, and then he carried her over to hers and set her down gently, and turned out the light. He fumbled around with his clothes, and it seemed it took a long time for him to get undressed to join her; and when he finally got into the bed he was nervous and awkward and she couldn't help crying out with the pain. When he discovered she was a virgin, he became sweet and apologetic for not being more gentle, and held her tenderly in his muscular arms and told her he loved her. When he fell asleep beside her, cradling her head against his shoulder, she thought: Now he is mine.

They awoke to the sound of her parents at the front door. Barney started up from bed, but she put her finger to his lips. They lay there quietly while her parents got ready for bed, and when the house was silent again he dressed and went quietly downstairs and out the back door. Moments later she heard a pebble against her window. He was standing in the moonlight and he threw her a kiss. She wept with happiness when he did that, and she lay awake most of the night thinking, Now his seed is moving inside me to create a new life. And she lay very still, afraid to move, whispering over and over: No one will take either of them away.

How naïve she had been. It wasn't that easy at all. At least not for her. She looked at the clock—seven-fifteen. The number in the window was eight, and red. She wanted his children more than anything in the world, but why couldn't he see how it embarrassed her to make love so clinically, on schedule. This premeditated, scientific copulation, like breeding farm animals or horses or laboratory specimens, was too much. Perhaps Myra could have accepted it. Myra might have caught the spirit of the thing, gone off to libraries, attended medical conventions to hear about the latest gynecological discoveries, and probably ended up working for birth control and planned parenthood. Well, she wasn't Myra, and she didn't want to become like Myra. It would happen when it was destined to happen. (Perhaps it had happened already, because she had willed it so hard that night at Torch Lake, in the romantic lakeside cabin—but when she told Barney she had felt herself conceive, he had explained, as if to a child, that it was something you couldn't feel. Why did thinking of it make her want to cry?)

She heard the sound of a glass or dish breaking, and then another one, and she sat up. What was he doing now? She dried her eyes and got out of bed. The thought of going into that kitchen nauseated her, but she fought the feeling. He would be scornful of what he called her "psychosomatic symptoms." She'd had them before. Well, she could control them. She fumbled with her robe and slippers and headed downstairs. She would get his breakfast and see him off to work. The last thing she wanted this morning was a quarrel.

As he was putting on his jacket, he heard her coming downstairs. She paused at the entrance to the kitchen, pushing back strands of black hair, yawned, and stretched the sleep out of her back and arms, but he saw she had been crying again.

"Sorry. I forgot it was your day to drive," she said. "I slept so soundly." She looked at the sink and table. "Oh, Barney, I meant to do them last night after I got back, but I— Here, let me make you some instant coffee."

"I don't have time to wait. I've got to pick up Max. And besides, there's none left."

"It'll only take a minute," she insisted, setting the water to boil again. "You've got to have something."

He wanted to walk out but checked himself. He'd been rough on her lately, last Monday because she couldn't find her car keys, and the argument yesterday about mislaying the department-store credit card made her cry. He had to let up on her. She really tried, but lifelong habits were difficult to change. He watched in astonishment as she removed a jar of instant coffee from the rear of the breadbox.

"Okay, just juice and coffee."

"I didn't mean to wake you last night when I got in," she said. "I had no idea it was so late."

"Past one. Did you accomplish anything?"

She set the cup of coffee in front of him, and started searching in the refrigerator for the juice. "Can't I make you some scrambled eggs or French toast?"

"I don't have time, and I'm not really hungry."

"Well," she said, sitting down to join him with an ill-concealed sigh of relief, "we've decided tentatively on *Hedda Gabler*."

"*You're* going to play Hedda Gabler?"

"What do you mean by that?"

He finished his coffee before she poured the juice for him, and though he had told her a hundred times he couldn't stand unsweetened grapefruit juice, he drank it.

"Why shouldn't I play Hedda Gabler?"

"What I meant was, why are they doing Ibsen again?"

"Don't you think I can play her? Everyone said I was good in *A Doll's House* last summer. You said so yourself."

"The role of Nora suited you."

She frowned and pulled her housecoat tighter and looked around her. "I see," her voice trembling. "You're probably right."

"That's not what I meant." But he knew he had said too much already.

She shrugged. "Anyway it was Dale Wexler's suggestion, and the committee likes the idea. But we need the approval of the whole company next week."

"Look, whatever they do you'll be good. When you married me, Broadway lost a great comedienne."

She laughed and tried to pinch him, but he escaped and grabbed his jacket, pretending it was a bullfighter's cape. She chased him, fingers curved upward at her forehead, to gore him, but he spun away and finally caught her in his arms and kissed her.

"I love you," she said.

He held her tightly. "I love you too."

He bent to pick up his jacket from where it had fallen to the floor, and she gasped.

"What's the matter?" he shouted.

"I just remembered something."

"Well, God, don't do that! You frightened me."

"I almost forgot to tell you that Lila and Dale are having some of the cast over tonight and they want us to stop in after dinner."

He stared at her. "How can we? The Winters are coming for bridge."

She looked at him in wild terror.

He groaned. "It was all arranged when we played at their place last month, after we came back from Torch Lake. Don't you remember?"

"Of course I remember. What makes you think I don't remember? I thought it was tomorrow, that's all."

"That's all? Well, you should have made a memo of it somewhere. That's exactly what I mean."

"What do you mean, that's exactly what you mean?"

"I mean you should have marked it down on your calendar. Is that too much to ask?"

"Yes it is," she snapped. "My calendar is too damned marked up as it is."

"Have a good day," he mumbled, heading for the door. "I've got to go."

"We'll have to break up the bridge game early tonight," she taunted. "Today is the eighth—a red-number day on your Fertility Clock."

As he left the house, he saw her watching him through the dining-room window and it angered him that their lives should be torn by one minor crisis after another, turning everything inside out because she resented the very idea of keeping track of anything. The result this time was predictable. She would calm down once he was gone and work like hell to get ready for this evening, and the house— on the surface, at least—would be spotless. The junk would be piled into drawers and closets, shoes hidden under beds, newspapers and magazines crammed behind the couch. If she felt like making up before the Winters came, there would be a couple of Martinis with glasses properly frosted, and candlelight in the dining room. And then for two or three days everything would be comfortable between them, as the air is dried out after a storm. For a few days she would even keep her appointments on time. But the change, as always, would be temporary, and after a while it would all be the same as before.

Watching him back the car out of the garage and then drive out of sight, she felt angry and lonely. She hated herself for having forgotten about tonight. She turned on the radio, but the throbbing beat made her think of TV headache commercials, and she turned it off. She hadn't wanted him to find the place in such a mess. She should have done the dishes last night, no matter how tired. She sighed and rested her head on the table.

Before their marriage, it had seemed like a wonderful life: keeping house while he sculpted, bringing his food, shielding him from distractions, watching him shape dreams into clay, and helping him cast them into permanence. At first, she had thought they would move to Greenwich Village or to the artists' quarter in San Francisco, where they would find friends who were painters and sculptors and struggling young theater people. If they ran out of money she could work as a fashion model and help him through the difficult years until he became recognized.

But he had convinced her it would be better to stay in Michigan, where their roots were, away from the phonies and the poseurs. Sensible, of course, just as it was sensible for him to take the job her father had gotten him at National Motors. Working with other people's ideas and forms, he had explained, was good discipline for a sculptor. And besides, there would be a decent income for a home and the children they both wanted. They could buy this lovely house, and he could have a studio in the basement to do his own work evenings and weekends. The best of both worlds.

But he had been kidding himself. In the last two years he had completed only two small abstractions that had meant nothing to her (pieces he had started during his graduate fellowship at college). And when she asked him to explain them he got angry and sulked for weeks afterward. The terrible thing was her fear that in some way she was to blame for his inability to create. If only she were different: practical enough to take everyday problems off his hands, fertile enough to give him a child without all this fussing and worrying that strained both of them. She stared at the sinkful of dishes, struggling against her revulsion. She had to change. Be efficient, she commanded herself. Organize! Get started. Have someone come in to clean the house for tonight and work at keeping it orderly. Keep the temperature charts carefully, and watch the little window on the clock.

If only she could force herself out of this chair, she'd get started. But her body refused to obey. She sat struggling for several minutes and then with supreme effort got up. She started the dishwasher, forced herself over to the sink, shook in the detergent as she turned on the water, and plunged her hands into the soaking pile of dishes.

She didn't know she had cut herself until the stain spread quickly through the soapy water, tinting dishes and the back of the sink with droplets of red. She stared, dazed, at the cut palm and fingers of her left hand, watched the threads of blood, and then screaming and crying, she smashed dish after dish into the sink.

Damn him for not picking up the broken cup and saucer! Leaving it all for her! She wasn't ready to change and be a housewife, cooking and washing and cleaning and every damned thing else on demand! She wasn't Nora in *A Doll's House* to be picked up and put down whenever it pleased him. She was herself. Why did she have to be changed into someone else?

She wanted to talk to someone. She wrapped a towel around her hand and started toward the phone to call her mother. Then she remembered that the company had sent her father to California to settle some lawsuits out of court for National Motors. She wished they were back already, and wondered if they would try to find Myra while they were out there. She hoped not, and then felt ashamed of the thought.

When the blood soaked through the towel, she wrapped another around it, pressing tightly against the wound, and lay down on the couch. Exhausted and limp, she nevertheless smiled. That took care of tonight's bridge game. She'd call Helen Winters and cancel for that evening. Barney would be concerned about her when he came home. He'd apologize, be gallant and attentive and affectionate, and they'd have a wonderful evening. She'd plan something special. And she would pretend today wasn't either on Dr. Leroy's calendar or in red on that stupid clock.

At that thought, she smiled and closed her eyes to sleep.

2

Max Prager was waiting on the sidewalk in front of his house when Barney stopped to pick him up. "S'matter, Barney?" he said, his pink round face unmercifully jolly as he slipped in and slammed the car door. "You look like a guy that's got troubles."

Barney grunted his apology for being late and sank into

silence. He decided that the ten-mile drive to the Center would be an ordeal. The car pool originally had five members who could talk among themselves. Then one had been transferred to Toledo, and another had moved to the West Side. For a while, Max Prager from Research and Collins from Safety Engineering had a great deal to talk about—technical things—and Barney had been content to listen. But Collins had retired three months ago, and now the two of them were alone in the car pool.

Prager was an odd combination. A refugee from the Nazis, he had been brought to Brooklyn at the age of ten. Embedded in his Brooklynese was the trace of a German accent. About fifteen years ago, at the age of forty, he had moved from the Brooklyn Navy Yard to the Research and Development Center at National Motors. Only once, in the three years Barney had known him, had he seen Prager really upset, when they promoted two younger men over him. The resentment had ended the following day, when Prager joked to Collins that he now had to clean up after newcomers still wet behind their Ph.D.'s, men who didn't know half of what he had forgotten about tracer technology.

"Hey, I see by the *Newsletter* you boys at Styling are having another art exhibition. Maybe you'll win another prize this year."

Barney grunted.

"I remember that piece of yours took first prize last year. What was it? 'Weeping Boy'? I never seen a piece I liked so much. Real talent. You know what I thought? I thought, That Barney'll be a famous sculptor someday."

"I did it in college, a long time ago," said Barney.

"Ah, but this year you'll have something new, hah? Bet you take first prize again. What's it called?"

"I'm not exhibiting this year."

Prager pursed his lips and raised his eyebrows.

"Haven't done much work of my own since I started here," Barney explained. "I've begun dozens of pieces but nothing I'm satisfied with."

"I guess it must be tough to spend the whole day modeling clay and then go home and work with the same stuff evenings or weekends. If it was me, I'd get sick of handling the same stuff day and night. I mean, how can you be creative?"

The old boy was perceptive all right. It was hard to think of a tracer technologist having insight into an artist's world.

"In fact," said Prager, "if you'll forgive my saying so, for the past few months you been looking like a man with a problem. I don't mean to pry, but maybe you've reached what they call an artistic crisis—where the creative talent is fighting the man. I knew a guy once—young fella like you—rewrite man on the Detroit *Times* who went through something like that—working with words all day, and he goes home to his family at night and tries to write a novel in his spare time. He tells me he started lots of novels, but he can never finish one, because after a day at the paper he's so tired of words he's got no creative energy left."

Barney looked at him quickly and then back to the highway where he soon had to turn off into the Center. "There was a time in high school and later in college when I had no trouble finishing whatever I started. Those were the days when sculpting brought me great joy. Not the awards and recognition, but the work itself. The real happiness is when you're so committed to a piece of sculpture that you're absorbed in the making of it."

Prager was nodding.

Usually he felt embarrassed about talking out his feelings, but he was still elated with the morning's work. "Even the sad moment when you stand back and know it's complete and right, and you have nothing to do with it any more—it must be like knowing your children are ready to leave you for the world—is a natural human sadness that comes from love. But, God, not being able to finish something you've committed yourself to is terrible. Instead of a joy, it becomes like a bone you can't get out of your throat. I don't understand what's happened to me. I never had trouble finishing things before."

Max nodded. "I always had you pegged as that kind of

person. That's the way this guy was too. You'd have liked
him. Well, let me tell you—he reads about the life of Gau-
guin, and what do you know? One day he leaves his wife
and three kids and goes off to Spain to write."

"What happened? Did he finish his novel?"

Prager shrugged. "Wish I knew myself how it worked out,
but we never heard from him again. Maybe after he got
rid of all his responsibilities and attachments he was able
to create. Maybe not. Who knows if it really makes a difference?"

They slowed down at the wrought-iron gateway with its
incongruous futuristic sign: NATIONAL MOTORS RESEARCH
AND DEVELOPMENT CENTER, in blue plastic on silver, beside
the entrance. Barney nodded to the security guard who,
seeing the Styling Division sticker on the windshield, waved
them in. He drove slowly around the traffic circle and
stopped to let Prager off in front of the Research building
before swinging around to his own parking space behind
the Styling building.

He turned off the ignition and stared at the building, like
an enormous igloo with a gold dome at one end for a
showroom (windowless, to seal it against unauthorized eyes)
which, at times, when he was driving to or from the Center,
caught the sun and blinded him. The entrance to the lobby
and executive offices, by contrast, were glass and transpar-
ent plastic, as if to reassure visiting executives, politicians,
and guided tour groups that National Motors had nothing
to hide.

Barney walked quickly through the lobby, frowning at
the orange and yellow plastic contour chairs set on blue
carpeting, and at the absurd dream-car designs framed
and suspended mysteriously in space. The keynote—as in
body styling—was power and thrust; swirling, reaching lines
and forced planes, imitating the severe functionalism of the
forties, contaminated by phony-futuristic gimmickry. To be
expected. Originality might not appeal to the styling chiefs
as having *go*, so the designers and stylists gave them recognizable *went*. It served. And they were probably right,

Barney told himself, because the people who bought the expensive cars wanted the old-and-familiar disguised as the
new-and-exciting. And what was more familiar than Buck
Rogers–futuristic? Go-go spaceman illusions for the earth-
bound millions who did their countdown, blast-off, and
retro-firing on the highways.

He nodded at the new receptionist, amazed that, as always, Personnel had come up with the right combination
of sweet-girl-next-door and youthful sexuality to excite and
cause guilt feelings. Blond hair flashed out and bounced
when she turned, as on TV commercials. Again, the wedding of opposites: safety, security, stability, spiced with reck-
less pleasure. Violent thrust, and then guilty awareness
you had passed the limit and had better slow down. "Danger—Curves" followed by "Children Crossing."

Nat Winters caught up to him at the security guard who
checked their identification tags. "Barney, hey! I've been
wanting to ask you, what's this I heard the other day about
you not submitting anything for the exhibition? Hell, it's
going to look funny for last year's prize winner not to
show something. Anderson's going to wonder."

"If he asks, tell him I'm giving the company all my creative energy and inspiration, and there's none left over to
waste on my own stuff. Tell him I'm a company man first
and a sculptor second. He ought to appreciate that."

"Come on, Barney. You don't mean that. It's going to
look very peculiar."

"I can't help it, Nat. I haven't been able to work. I
haven't finished anything I could submit, and I won't force
it just to exhibit."

"Okay. I give you a lot of credit," said Winters. "Really.
I wish I had your guts. All right, forget the exhibition.
Something else I've been wanting to ask you, privately, because I know you've got this kind of integrity. From an
artistic point of view—as a sculptor—what do you really
think of that wind-split on the fenders? You think it's okay?
I mean, you know how I value your opinion."

"You've got to stop worrying about it," said Barney.

"The track makes the body look lower than it really is. Once they get her out onto the showroom platform, or out on the proving grounds, it'll look right. Especially after we get the bumpers chromed. Stop worrying. It's a great body."

"Okay, Barney. I have faith in you. Let's get it out of the way so I can concentrate on my bridge tonight. Your place, right?"

"Of course."

"Good. Helen and I have been looking forward to winning back some of that money. Your wife's wild luck can't hold forever."

The rest of the day Barney worked under Nat Winters' direction, finishing up the model for its first executive showing at the end of the week in the gold-domed showroom. They had been working on it for nearly two and a half months, but now that the time had come to take it out of the studio and dress it up for judging, Winters hovered over it, on the verge of hysteria.

"Shouldn't we take off a little more? Scallop it deeper under the backlight?"

Barney had worked on Winters' designs often enough to know he had to be humored. He made a couple of imaginary passes at the brown plasticine clay under the rear-window line and stood back to admire the results. When Winters finally agreed they were finished, Barney quickly called one of the junior modelers to cover it with a sheet. But a few minutes later Winters was grumbling.

"Damned sheet makes it look like a dead elephant. Let me see it again. Maybe we ought to work on it a bit more."

And so it went the rest of the day. Twice Winters had them uncover the Panther II and made slight changes. Barney tried to control himself as he saw the work being botched. The lines had been clean, with the wind-split on the fenders creating the illusion of thrust—what the vice-president from Sales had described as the car body they wanted for the young-at-heart market in two or three years. Something youthful, bold, assertive, and all the other adjectives adding up to the promise of Potency behind the wheel. The young executive had assured them at the styling meeting that the concept had been developed by motivation specialists who knew what people could be made to want. This was to be a production model for the year after next, and the year after next Naked Thrust would be *in* again. In those terms, Winters had come up with a bold design, but now in his fear he was undercutting for ornateness, weakening the forward line he had achieved. When he was done, it was safely closer to the models that had been accepted for the last two years.

Barney tried not to let the compromise upset him. He tried to convince himself that he was not the artist here, but a craftsman, shaping, modeling to order, changing line, form, texture at the whim of the designers. But it did upset him, because seeing Nat Winters like this he had a vision of himself in ten or fifteen years. Insecurity was catching, and he had the notion that he was highly susceptible to the disease.

After work, Barney headed over to the Research building to pick up Max Prager, but the side street where he had dropped him off that morning was blocked by a barricade, and in front of the building were several company-police cars. He got out of his car and walked over, but as he started up the steps an elderly guard—one he had seen often around the grounds—came toward him, waving.

"Nobody allowed through!"

"But I'm supposed to meet somebody."

"Area's sealed off."

"What's going on?"

"Security reasons. Accident in one of the labs. I got to see nobody goes in or out."

"Well, I'm supposed to pick up one of the men who works here—Max Prager—we drive in together."

"Prager? Oh, I guess he won't be out for a while yet. He'll probably get a ride from someone else—or a cab."

Barney stood there for a few moments, and the guard,

lighting his pipe, said, "Yep, he'll probably have to stick around for a good while yet and get a checking over. You can't be too careful with this here radioactive stuff. No sir, you've got to be mighty careful."

"Radioactive?" Barney looked at him blankly, and then at the Research building. "You mean there's been an accident involving radioactivity?"

The guard looked around carefully and whispered, "Long as you work for the company, I guess I can tell you. One of the inside guards, friend of mine, heard the switchboard operator call for the Radiation Safety Officer. Seems—now keep this under your hat, will you?—seems they had a spill in the hot lab and a couple of them fellas got exposed to the stuff. Someone said that fella Prager was pretty near a hero, and if not for him the stuff would of got out and contaminated the whole damn town. Yes sir, so I don't guess he'll have to worry about getting a ride home. But, like I said, don't let on I told you. And don't tell no one else."

Barney thanked him and went back to his car, a bit dazed at the news. He had no idea Prager was working with such dangerous stuff. He had never spoken about it that Barney could recall. All he'd ever mentioned were "tracers" and "tracer technology." Then Barney recalled the word "isotope" in several of Prager's discussions with Collins. "Radioactive isotopes"—he'd heard that before, but he had no idea what they were. He would have to ask Prager about it.

As he passed Max Prager's house, one like all the rest in a row of neat houses owned by junior executives, it occurred to him that everyone in Elgin City was in some way connected with the automobile industry or depended on someone who did. He had thought often, when he let Prager off after work and watched the old guy trudge down the walk, how strange it was for him to live on alone in that big house so many years after his wife died. And it bothered him now that Prager had never accepted an invitation to dinner or to drop in for a drink. He was friendly enough in the car, but without ever saying so he made it clear that he wanted to be left alone. The last guy in the world you could think of as a hero.

3

When Barney got home he went in the side door through the kitchen, pulling off his tie. He wanted to shower and change before dinner, to relax until Nat and Helen Winters came. But there was no sign of Karen or dinner, and the place was as it had been this morning when he left. He called out, and she answered him from upstairs.

"What the hell is the matter?" he stormed. "Don't you realize Nat and Helen are coming over and the place looks like a—"

She held up her bandaged hand to silence him.

"What happened?"

"You didn't bother to tell me you broke dishes in the sink." Her voice quavered as she told him, and he knew she had nursed not only the hand, but also anger, all day, waiting to confront him with it.

"I'd better call Nat and tell them it's off," he said.

"I called Helen this afternoon," she said. "Don't you think I was capable of figuring that out for myself?"

"I'm sorry. It was thoughtless of me to leave the broken glass in the sink."

"Unusual for you. You must have a lot on your mind."

"I do," he snapped.

"Well, at least you won't have to face them across the bridge table until next month. July twentieth. You'd better put it down in your little pocket datebook."

"All right."

"I've already written it on my calendar. That turns

out to be one of my *off* days. You won't have to worry about breaking up the game too early."

"I said all right! Now that's enough!"

"What if I haven't had enough?" she shouted.

He clenched his fists. "I said, shut up!"

"Oh? Would you hit me? Would you finally give in to an impulse and hit me? Go ahead. Or do you have to think out the consequences first?"

He tried to control himself. That was his father's temper coming out in him. He had seen his father hit his mother— more than once—and he had cursed the old man for it. Now he knew there was a thin line separating the crazy, instinctive reaction and his awareness of what it would mean. Words could be taken back, quarrels smoothed over. She might tease him about his self-control, but if he ever lost it and hit her, that would be the end.

"You know I wouldn't hit you."

"You want to."

"I want to do a lot of things I don't do. Don't push me into actions you can't see the consequences of."

She met his eyes defiantly, and then looked down as the tears came.

"Do you have to bawl about it?"

"Yes, I do."

"You have an unfair advantage."

"Who's stopping you from crying? It would do you a lot of good."

"I don't cry. If you think you can reduce me to that, you'd better forget it. That's one lesson my old man taught me very well. If you don't mind, I'll shower before dinner. A cold shower to cool me off."

The phone rang as he was getting out of the tub, and Karen answered it. "It's Max Prager," she shouted. "Shall I tell him you'll call back?"

"No, I want to talk to him." He came out with the bath towel wrapped around him, and took the phone. "Max, hello. Hey, what was all that about?"

"Sorry I didn't get a chance to call you at the Center,"

said Max. "We had a little accident—nothing serious—and I had to stay late. I'll pick you up tomorrow."

"But what's this about you being a hero?"

"Who told you that?"

"Word gets around. I mean, is it true? And any chance of that stuff spreading?"

There was a short silence, and then Prager said, "Look, Barney, like I said, it was nothing serious. A small spill, and all taken care of with routine procedures. What's in real danger of spreading is rumors. People panic when they hear *radioactivity*. Take my word, everything was cleared up. Nobody got hurt, and none of it leaked out of the building. Little accidents like this happen all the time wherever isotopes are used. Okay? I'll tell you all about it tomorrow."

Karen looked at him questioningly when he hung up. "Hero?"

"A small accident in the Research building," he said. He decided not to mention the radioactivity for fear her imagination would get carried away. "Max says it wasn't much. Now what about important matters, like dinner? I'm starved. Should we go out?"

"I had some food delivered from the Chinese restaurant," she said. "Chow mein, egg rolls, and barbecued spareribs. The Martinis are in the refrigerator, already mixed, and the glasses are being iced in the freezer."

She looked up at him, softened now. During their honeymoon they had locked themselves away in a motel room with Chinese food and Martinis and had a drunken picnic. She was sentimental about it, and he knew it was a peace offering. He went down to get the drinks, and poured one for each of them.

"I'm sorry, baby," he said, clinking their glasses in a toast. "To us."

"So am I. To us."

He sat down beside her on the bed and kissed her.

"What are you doing?" She pushed him away. "Put that towel back around you."

"What's the matter now?"

"It's not me you're interested in. You're just a compulsive gambler."

"What are you talking about?"

"It's that clock. All you're interested in is baby roulette. Not me."

"Oh, come on now, this is absurd. I love you. The clock has absolutely nothing to do with it."

"How can I be sure?"

He thought about it a moment and then reached out and turned the clock's face to the wall. "What clock are you talking about?" he said, looking around. "I don't see any clock."

She squealed with pleasure. "That's better. There are no clocks or calendars. There is no such thing as time when we're together."

He reached for her and she pushed him away again.

"Now what?"

"The food. You were starved."

"Not any more."

"You'll need to keep up your strength."

He pretended to be shocked. "Mygawd, what did you have in mind?"

She threw a pillow at him and he hugged it. "Ah, Myrtle dear, my wife has thrown us together—thrown you into my arms—"

She shrieked and pulled the pillow away from him and threw it across the room. "My best friend too," she shouted. "It's always your closest friend—the one you trust."

He embraced her and she grew quiet.

"Oh, Barney, I'll try to change for you," she whispered. "Really I will. I'll be whatever you want. I love you."

He kissed her fiercely and tried to arouse her, but she knew it was forced. He was thinking about something else. She sensed it. Whatever it was, it left her cold with the feeling that another wedge had driven them yet farther apart.

4

The next morning, Karen shouted that there was a news bulletin on TV about the accident at the Center. He got there in time to see Max Prager shaking hands with the president of National Motors.

". . . and thanks to Mr. Prager's quick thinking and prompt actions, what might have been an accident of major proportions was quickly controlled. I want to assure the citizens of Elgin City and our neighbors in Detroit that none of the radioactive material escaped from the laboratory. Mr. Prager put the safety of others before his own. In exposing himself to an overdose of radiation to prevent the spread of radioactive material, he averted a catastrophe. We repeat: None of the radioactive dust escaped from the laboratory. The spill was immediately and thoroughly decontaminated by the specialists at the Center. There is no danger whatsoever. . . ."

"I hope they do something for the old guy," said Barney. "He was plenty hurt when they promoted those Ph.D.'s over his head."

"So that's what that hero business was about on the phone. You didn't tell me about the radioactivity. You always keep things from me."

"I don't keep things from you. It wasn't important. I didn't want to frighten you."

"Does that mean he's dangerous to be near? Is he radioactive?"

"Do you think the president of National Motors would shake hands with him if he were?"

"Barney, do you have to drive in with him?"

"Of course I do. See? That's exactly what I mean. You

have no idea of what's going on around you. These things are all worked out. This stuff can be checked and measured; they have all the instruments and they know all the safety levels. He wouldn't be picking me up for work as usual if there was any danger."

"I don't know. They don't tell you everything. I had no idea there was anything like that around here. I thought it was only in atomic plants, where it was all sealed off and protected."

"Well, I'm sure it's safe now. Trained technologists like Max Prager know enough about what they're doing to take proper precautions."

"Yes, but with all their *precautions* there was still an accident." Then suddenly, vehemently, "You men always know enough to take precautions, don't you?"

"Now what is that supposed to mean?"

She turned away. "I don't want to talk about it."

"Oh, God, can't I ever leave this house in the morning without a scene? Look, I don't know what's wrong, and I don't have time to find out. He'll be picking me up in a few minutes. If it's something I've done, I'm sorry."

She grudgingly let him kiss her on the cheek, and he nodded. "Thank you very much, although it's hardly enough to see me through this long day."

Prager pulled up to the curb just as Barney came out, and by the look on his face, Barney suspected he had seen himself on television.

"How does it feel to be a hero?"

"Aw, you know those TV things." But obviously he felt like talking about it.

"You said you'd tell me what happened."

"You really want to hear?" When Barney nodded, Prager seemed pleased. He always liked to talk while he was driving. "Well, damned close call. Never had one like that before—"

"Excuse me, before you go into it. There's one thing I don't understand. How come National Motors uses radioactive material? What do they use it for?"

"These are isotopes. Used as tracers. Soft gamma radiation is used for lots of things: everything from tracing the paint flow and the thickness of it on the body, to checking for flaws in the castings—radiography."

"I never knew that before. Go on."

"Well, I was taking one of the new technicians through the hot lab. That's kind of a double room—a hot cell and then two lead-lined walls—with us working the controls from between the two. Like we're in a sandwich, separated from the hot cell by one wall and from the safety exit by the other wall, and the only way out is up the ladder and over."

"But how do you get into the hot cell?"

"Oh, hell, we don't go in there. We handle the isotopes with remotes, 'slave hands,' we call them, like two giant dentists' drill arms with clamps at the ends. Well, now, I bring this guy in, and we're watching one of our bright Ph.D.'s extracting a capsule from its lead container. The capsule is only about two inches long, mind you, and it holds three pellets of Iridium 192. Three radioactive peas in an aluminum pod, packed nice and snug with aluminum powder.

"All this fellow had to do was cut open that capsule on a clearly marked line, remove the pellets, and shove them into the storage wall on the other side—our little 'hot bank,' we call it. Simple? So we're standing alongside watching him work the slaves through the hot box. Nothing to it. Man has a pair of hands and he can reach so far; his brain makes an extension and there's no limit to how far he can reach. I'm explaining to the new man how it's got to be cut open, like delivering a baby by Caesarean (only we get triplets every time).

"We watch him lower a precision rotary blade, and, like I told the Radiation Safety Officer later, I saw with my own eyes, the blade was right on the line. No doubt about it; I wouldn't blame that boy. One of the pellets must have been defective, and that's the fault of Tracer Control—the outfit that supplies the isotope. The blade bites into the capsule, out comes the aluminum dust packing and the three pellets, and then all of a sudden the new kid shouts, 'The Jordan Meter!' And damned if the needle isn't jumping five hundred. The kid at the control panel freezes. 'What do I do?' he yells. I tell him, 'There's no time to give lessons,' and I take over, working the slaves fast to get those pellets into the storage wall. I had one in, and two to go, when the new guy yells again, and I see the red warning light from the air monitor flashing overhead. And that means the dust is spilling over the first wall right into our trench."

"Jesus Christ," Barney said. "What did you do?"

"I shout for them to get over the safety wall and hit the showers, figuring I've got a couple of seconds to get those pellets stashed away. I couldn't just leave the little bastards there. But I tell you, Barney, it's a spooky feeling with that hot stuff coming over the wall and you can't see or feel it. I got the other pellets in, and then I barreled up the ladder and came down the other side, jumping the last five or six rungs. I tore the respirator off my face, stripped off the coveralls, and went into the showers behind the other two guys underwear and all, scrubbing like never before in my life, digging my skin until there were welts. All I could think of was that radioactive dust was all over me. Man, oh man! I'll never forget that sight in my life when the needle hit the top. That lab was hot! And can you imagine, all that bastard Safety Officer cared about was could we handle the cleanup without calling in Tracer Control. Boy, did I get pissed off. Not that I blame him for wanting to avoid a panic. Hell, we had the thing under control, and no one got a bad dose. But you'd think he'd worry about us instead."

"How do you know how much of a dose you got, if you can't see it?"

"Our film badges. And I carry a pencil meter. The doc had us in the infirmary in five minutes and checked us out.

The coveralls and respirators cut down our exposure, and nobody inhaled any. The only thing left was for the others to clean up whatever we carried out of the hot lab. What the hell, that's routine procedure. Companies do it every day."

"So they didn't have to call in Tracer—?"

"Tracer Control? Not for a little spill like this. You need them when the spill is out of hand, like when a reactor goes, or if it gets out of the lab and threatens to contaminate a whole city. Not for this. Luckily, we kept it all in the hot lab. Hell, an hour after the accident, the Radiation Safety Officer checked out every inch of the place; the safety chamber, the decontamination rooms we passed through to get to the showers; even my little office next to the lab. And they'll give the place a thorough going over—the whole area, just to be sure. But let me tell you, Barney. It was a close one."

He let Barney out at the Styling building, and Barney watched as he drove away, shaken by the idea that, as Karen had pointed out, with all their knowledge and safeguards, all their planning and precautions, something could *spill* unpredictably, at the wrong time and place, and affect their lives. And the damned upsetting thing was that it had been there, so close by all along, and he had never even known it.

July

1

Two days after the Fourth of July back-yard barbecue, Barney was sure he had eaten something that was making him sick. For the second morning in a row he had awakened with a headache and a rash on his right arm that seemed to be spreading. It occurred to him he ought to see a doctor, but he decided to see if he felt better later in the day. He dressed quietly in order not to awaken Karen and went down to get his own breakfast. The place was clean, most of the dishes washed. She was trying so hard to change.

Each time he decided to tell her he wanted a separation something interfered. First his grandfather's funeral and seeing his parents again, then her rehearsals, and now this. And during the past few weeks it seemed as if she sensed his intentions and was trying to change. Things had become easier since he stopped working on the Venus. He hadn't even gone downstairs since the funeral.

He put a salve and a light gauze on his reddened arm, and slipped gingerly into his shirt, thinking no more of it as he dressed and went out to where Prager would pick him up. As they drove off, Barney sensed that the old guy was unusually preoccupied.

"Something wrong?"

Prager shook his head, but then Barney noticed his hands on the steering wheel. "Burn yourself?"

"Started swelling a couple of days ago," said Prager.

"Looks like a bad burn." Barney stared at the hands, quite delicate for Prager's short, stocky build, fingers long and bony where one would have expected stubby fingers. There were blisters above the knuckles.

"Probably allergic to something," said Prager. "I'll see my doctor."

"Funny thing," said Barney. "I've got a rash on my arm. Itches like hell. I've been thinking of going to a doctor too."

Prager frowned. "When did you first notice it?"

"Few days ago. Thought I burned myself without knowing it. Then I thought maybe it was something I ate at the cookout we had."

Prager nodded, but his face was slack, and he hunched over the wheel as if he had to summon his strength to control the car.

"You okay?"

"Yeah, just a little nauseous. Look, I'm not going in to work. I'll drop you off at the Center and get myself to a doctor. I'll let you know as soon as I find out what it is. If it's something we both ate at the company cafeteria, we'll sue the hell out of them." He smiled weakly, and Barney watched as he drove off.

During the day, Barney felt nauseous, but he ignored it. It wasn't until later that evening, when the rash seemed to be getting worse, that he remembered Prager had gone to a doctor and might know what it was. At seven-thirty he called Prager's home, but a man who identified himself as Al Bendix said Prager had been taken to the Elgin City Memorial Hospital less than an hour earlier.

"What's the matter with him? What is it?"

"Sorry, I've been instructed not to give out any information to the newspapers or anyone—"

"I'm not the newspapers. What the hell is going on? He was going to call me when he got back from his doctor. I have the same—" But the man had hung up, saying, "Look, we're busy here. Call the hospital."

"What the hell!" snorted Barney as Karen walked in at the end of the conversation. "He had burns like mine."

"What burns?"

"On his hands, red splotches on the backs of his hands, and his fingers were swollen. I've got a rash breaking out on my arm too—itches like hell. First I thought it was a burn, but I didn't remember . . ." He saw her staring at his arm strangely where he had rolled his sleeve back to look at it. It had gotten worse, blistering like Prager's hands.

"I didn't know you had that," she said in a frightened whisper. "Look at this." She opened her blouse and pulled her left bra strap down to show him the red splotches on her breast. "And this . . ." lifting her skirt to show him another like it on her right thigh.

"When did you get those?"

She stared at the rash on her breast as if someone had put a snake into her bosom. "I don't remember. A few days ago. It started getting a little red, and I thought it was a reaction to those hormones I started last week. But yesterday when I noticed the same thing on my thigh I called Dr. Leroy and he said it might be a side effect and to stop taking them. But, Barney, mine are getting worse too."

They stared at each other, and then she whispered what was already on his mind. "Call the hospital and ask them what's the matter with him."

The nurse would say only that Max Prager was doing well, but could have no calls or visitors. Barney insisted on talking to one of the doctors. When the doctor finally got on the phone, Barney said, "Look, I've got a reason for being so insistent. My wife and I seem to have the same kind of rash Prager had on his hands."

"Did Mr. Prager come into your home during the past few weeks?"

"No, he's never been to my home, but—"

"Either of you work in the Research building?"

"No, I'm in Styling."

"Then I wouldn't worry about it."

"But why can't you tell me what's wrong with him? What's the mystery about? Just in case he has something contagious, I ought to know. I'm in a car pool with him. We drive in together."

There was a silence, and Barney was sure the doctor had covered the mouthpiece to talk to someone. "Look, it's nothing contagious," the doctor said finally. "No disease. Give me your name and address and someone will come over to check you out. Don't let anyone else in until our men get there."

Barney gave him the information, and before he could ask any other questions, the doctor had hung up. Ten minutes later someone from the company health office called to say that the hospital had contacted them and that a Mr. Garson and his men were on their way over for a routine check.

But it was more than an hour later when they arrived. Karen was still in the kitchen when Barney heard a car pulling into the driveway and through the open window saw a second car park at the curb in front of the house. It was too dark to make out anything except two pairs of headlights, but when their lights went off, he saw a white panel truck in the light from the porch, and at that angle he could see, in red against the white background, the name: TRACER CONTROL.

Two men in white coveralls and hoods with visors got out of the truck and moved slowly up the walk. One held the light and the other carried a small suitcase. Barney started toward the door to greet them, but through the window he heard the rattler-warning and somehow he knew it was a Geiger counter. But why was Tracer Control here, and why were two men in white coveralls using a Geiger counter on his front lawn? He called out, "What's going on?"

"Just a minute, Mr. Stark. Better stay where you are. We'll explain in a minute."

When they finally reached the door, he thought they were going to ring the doorbell, but the one with the box had a short rod in his hand and was passing it over the steps, the porch railing, the doorknobs, and the moldings alongside the door. The clicking slowed and then chattered before dropping off again. The odd thing, he realized later, was his knowing it was a Geiger counter, and at the same time feeling it was all wrong. Not sure how, or why, but knowing that in this orderly, scientific world, radioactivity should be confined to the laboratory, the X-ray room, fallout from bomb tests conducted by enemies (and some friends), but by no common sense or logic should those two white-clad, visored men be at his front door with a clicking Geiger counter. His mind would not probe to think what it meant. How could it, when he knew nothing about radioactivity or the equipment that produced or identified it? Suddenly he wished he knew more.

The bell chimed. Karen came into the room as he opened the door. She hadn't seen them coming, as he had, through the window, and at the sight of them—white, hooded, peering at her through visors—she screamed.

"I should have warned you," said Barney, trying to calm her. "They're the men the health office called about."

"Oh, my!" she exclaimed. "I couldn't imagine . . ."

"Did you think they were from Mars?"

"I don't know what I thought." She laughed. "But I wasn't going to let them in."

Barney opened the screen door. "Well, come inside," he said. "Mr. Garson?"

The one with the Geiger counter pointed the tube in the direction of the car at the curb. "I'm Al Bendix. This is Gus MacNight. But you and Mrs. Stark better stay right here in the foyer while we check you. Then we'll work our way slowly into the house."

Barney tried to think of something to ask, but there was nothing, because suddenly that little black box, whispering of radioactivity in a language he didn't understand, was the most powerful instrument in the world.

Karen, just inside the living room, gasped. "What's happening, Barney?" He knew she had heard enough about radioactivity and contamination and fallout shelters to understand what a Geiger counter was. Then she tried to explain to them, "Not here. There wouldn't be any radioactivity here in our house. It was built just two years ago, and we've only lived here a year."

The one with the flashlight was apologetic: "You've got it on your garage door, the front walk, the steps, the railing, and the doorknob. We'll check both of you first, and then inside the house."

"Us?" They both said the word at the same time, and Karen looked at Barney and drew back as if waiting for him to back her up—to deny it.

"But how—?" Barney choked. "You mean that accident at the radiation lab? But everybody said—"

The one with the Geiger counter—Bendix—gestured impatiently with the tube. "If you'll let us check you, Mr. Garson will explain everything. Your car is hot. Radioactive dust. So both of you are probably contaminated. I don't want to alarm you, but every minute counts. You'd better let us get to this quickly."

Radioactive dust. The words flung in his face choked him, clogged his throat and nostrils. Karen hung back. It was absurd, she whimpered. There couldn't be any radioactivity on her or in her house. When Barney, at their insistence, finally stepped forward to let them check him, she glared as if, in admitting the possibility, he had betrayed her.

Slowly, Bendix passed the tube over him, and the clicking increased as it neared his jacket. Barney tore it off. And then his shirt and undershirt—each suddenly seeming hot to his touch. When MacNight saw the trousers would have to come off too, and that the skin on his upper arms and shoulders showed traces of radioactivity, he tried to be reassuring. "Don't worry about it, Mr. Stark. We know how to handle this stuff," and he went to the truck to get a pump tank and two plastic bags. When he returned, he paused for a moment, and, seeing neighbors watching through their windows, he said, "We'd better go out to the garage because we'll have to hose you down. Got a light there?"

Barney nodded dully, and they both followed. Karen automatically switched on the light, while MacNight unreeled the thin plastic hose and started the pump, explaining patiently (very softly, it seemed to Barney), "This chemical agent will wash the particles off your skin, if they're not embedded too deep. No, don't touch it! You might rub it in. Now, just turn around and let me get your back. That's right. Now, gently, squeegee the solution off. Fine. Now we'll do it again."

Barney washed his arms off in the lukewarm stream and let himself be hosed down, both arms and legs, and each time Bendix passed the tube over him and it clicked faster, Barney's neck skin tightened and prickled as if things were crawling over him. Finally, after what seemed a very long time, Bendix's tube was satisfied that he was free of contamination.

"How did this damned stuff get here?" asked Barney.

Bendix shrugged, too busy to talk, but MacNight explained that Prager had carried it out of his little office in the research laboratory on his shoes and clothes after the accident.

"But how? My God, he told me it was all cleared up.

They said on the radio and TV that there was no danger from—"

"Look," said Bendix impatiently, "Mr. Garson'll explain it all when we're—"

"There was a leak," explained MacNight, "through a connecting ventilator duct. When they started up the air conditioning about three weeks ago it spread to his office, and he carried it out, to a few places, including his car and yours."

The words hung in the warm night air before they exploded into meaning. Karen shivered, and Barney, feeling the coldness in his own chest, understood why. MacNight carefully peeled the tape off one of the plastic bags and pulled out a hospital-type kimono for Barney to put on.

"And now, Mrs. Stark, would you please . . ." said MacNight, still soft and apologetic.

She was frightened, but Barney didn't know how to make it easier for her. Bendix motioned her forward with the tube of the Geiger counter. "The dress," he said, pointing to the gauge.

"But I just bought it," she gasped. "My beautiful dress! How could it—?"

"From your hands, or his, or from other clothes in the closet."

"But I haven't hung it in my closet yet. I just took it out of the box."

Bendix shrugged, but MacNight came forward again. "Sorry, Mrs. Stark, but we have to do this. I know how you feel, but it's for your own safety. Please . . ."

She yielded to his voice, took off first her dress and then her slip. Barney was about to protest, but MacNight, seeing that her brassière registered radioactivity, apologized again. "We don't have a woman along for the job. It was an emergency call—"

"They're all emergency calls," Bendix grunted.

"Don't mind him. We've been close to thirty-six hours without a break. Right from another job in Cleveland to Mr. Prager's house this afternoon, and pulled off that to

come here. I'll tell you, what we can do, Mr. Stark, is:
You hold the Geiger counter—she'll have to take off the
rest of her clothes too—and just pass it all around her body."

"That won't be necessary." Karen's voice turned so brittle
they all stared at her. She fumbled with the bra clasp, freed
it, and stood trembling defiantly in the yellow light. The
counter revealed traces on both breasts and thighs. Despite
her defiant casualness, both men looked away as she washed
herself. Barney moved to help her, but she drew away.

"Leave me alone. Don't come near me."

When she finished, they checked her again. The instrument ticked the normal sad throb of background radiation.
It had all come off, none of it buried in her skin. Then
Bendix pointed the tube at her head. "Better check your
hair."

She backed away. "There couldn't be anything. I brush
it every morning and night."

"It's so microscopic you couldn't be sure it brushed out,"
said MacNight. "We can't take a chance, Mrs. Stark. You
know we wouldn't insist if it wasn't absolutely necessary."

There were radioactive traces at two spots. One halfway
down, the other at the front of her scalp. When she heard
the rattle, her hand went to touch her hair, but MacNight
stopped her.

"Better not. You'll spread it."

"We'll have to cut it, Mrs. Stark." Bendix produced a
pair of shears from a pocket in his coveralls.

"I'll wash it out. If I can't brush it, I can wash it out,
can't I?"

MacNight shook his head. "You won't be able to wash
it out. And there's no time. We'd better cut it."

"And you might as well know the worst," said Bendix.
"The rest will probably fall out soon anyway."

MacNight faced him, visor to visor. "That wasn't necessary right now."

"She'll find out sooner or later. She might as well be
prepared that it ain't going to be no picnic."

She shuddered as if slapped, and the tension made her

shake. Barney wanted to reassure her, but there was no way to come close to her now. She could have taken almost anything but her hair.

"I'm really sorry," said MacNight, taking the shears from Bendix, "but this'll be the last of it."

He bent her head forward and, using the counter to guide him, cut carefully. "I'm trying not to take off any more than necessary," he explained.

But it was difficult, and by the time the counter registered normal, almost a fourth of her hair lay in the paper he had spread to catch it. Some had fallen on her shoulders and on her breasts, and MacNight had to check to see if any of it was radioactive. Then he stepped back and took the second kimono out of its pliofilm wrapping, peeled the outer tape away carefully, and held the garment out for her.

She slipped into it and pulled it tightly around her, and only then did she look at Barney.

"All right," said Bendix, "if you'll both come down to the car—be careful to walk along the grass where I've marked it with white powder."

She looked at Barney without moving, and he could see her beginning to heave as if she were going to throw up, but it was only the sobs she could no longer hold back. He put his arm around her, and she clung to him now, as he helped her to the car, openly weeping and fingering the ragged edges of her hair. "What did you do to us, Barney? What did you do?"

She wept against his shoulder as they got into the maroon sedan that had been parked at the curb. Mr. Garson introduced himself, but she made no attempt to look up. Barney nodded at the greeting and slipped into the back of the car alongside her.

Barney only half heard as Mr. Garson explained that they were going to the hospital for observation, and by the time they were released the house would be completely decontaminated. He felt her stiffen against him and sit erect. "The house?"

Mr. Garson, up front beside the driver, turned to her and nodded. He was distinguished, greying, with a clipped military manner. The gruffness Barney had noticed over the phone was magnified in the car, as in the dim light he gave them only his profile. "Afraid so, Mrs. Stark. It will take the DS—ah, the decontamination squad—four or five days to monitor and clean it out."

"All my lovely things!"

"Of course, you'll be reimbursed for damages. Mr. Engstrom asked me to reassure you that National Motors will also cover all expenses while you're at the hospital and all during the decontamination proceedings."

Barney realized it had to be done. Things they'd used or touched, or merely brushed against, had become contaminated. In with the dust she hadn't cleaned up would be radioactive dust, and it would swirl up in a breeze to land on the couch or the coffee tables or the lamp shades or the rugs.

"What happened?" asked Barney. "Max Prager said the radioactivity was confined to the hot lab. He said it was all cleaned up. How did it get out to his office?"

"They cleaned up after the accident," explained Garson. "They didn't call us, they did it themselves—which is perfectly all right, mind you—but no one thought to check out the ventilator system, which had an outlet between the safety area of the hot lab and Mr. Prager's little adjoining office. When the weather turned warm a week after the accident, and they started up the air conditioning, the ventilator served as a conduit for the dust particles and spread them from the duct in the safety area to Mr. Prager's room. He carried it from there—a week later, as I say, when no one was checking any more—to his own car and home, and to your car as well. And each time he entered your car he brought new traces with him, and each time you entered his you picked up more. Of course, he called us directly as soon as he discovered it," explained Garson. "He's in rather bad shape, I'm afraid. You two are lucky. Your secondary contamination seems far less than the dose he received. And of course, he has had an earlier accumulation of exposure."

"Barney, we're never going to be the same."

And Barney realized she had seen headlines and articles, but until now bomb testing, fallout, strontium 90, iodine contaminating children's milk, defective color TV sets, lost radium needles, even lurid stories of mutations born to victims of radiation exposure, had all been remote. The experts had always been there to assure them that everything was safely below the danger levels.

But they never mentioned the possibility of mistakes until it was too late.

He knew little about the effects of radiation on human beings.

Stories of radiation accidents rarely made the headlines, and now he could see why. The details would be kept secret until after everything had been cleaned up and National Motors and the Nuclear Energy Commission decided to let the public know. Then it would be a half-column in the Detroit *Times*, referring to something in an industrial suburb of Detroit that had been cleaned up five or six months earlier. Only the people of Elgin City would worry about it. To the rest of the world it would be (as it had always been to them) stale news.

He had a vague memory of radiation sickness from what he had read of Hiroshima, but, as he recalled it, first there would be the burns, the falling hair, and then a worsening of symptoms that had already started but that he had foolishly misunderstood (nausea, weakness and tiredness, burns), then, months from now, perhaps cataracts, and years from now, leukemia or cancer. For a time, perhaps sterility or mutations to miscarry. It hadn't been a big enough dose to kill them, perhaps, but always there would be the weakness, the emptiness. And the thought struck him: With a future like that to look forward to, what was the point of living?

"You'll have to direct us, of course," Garson was saying.

"I'm just hoping neither of you spent much time in crowds."

He turned his profile again, as if he had only a good right ear and wanted the answer directed toward it. "Did you?"

"Crowds? What do you mean?"

"Your movements—ever since the accident. We'll need you to help us retrace your steps. Everywhere you went, anyone you saw during the past month. You must have spread the contamination to a great many people and places. We've got a big job ahead, and I'd like to have you along for as much of it as possible—while you're able, that is. As I said, Tracer Control has been retained by National Motors to check on every possible leak, and we'll need your help. Of course, you'll remain on the company payroll, all the while."

"Of course." But his mind was flickering back across the past few weeks, to the trail of contamination he had left behind. It would all have to be gone over now. He was amused momentarily to think that even suicide was denied him—at least until he had walked back across every step of ground, and looked into every face. Everything and everyone he had touched would have to be Geiger-counted and cleansed as Karen and he had been this evening. It wasn't at all funny, and he knew they must be wondering why he was laughing.

2

For Karen, the five days at the hospital were imprisonment without trial, a nightmare in which she was a collaborator whose rendezvous with the enemy had contaminated her and for which they stripped her naked and cut her hair.

They hadn't cut it all off, but the tufts, where they had shorn it, angered her, and on the third day she grabbed the scissors and cut the rest short. It annoyed her that Barney stupidly pretended it looked better that way. After she cut it she was sorry, and sat in front of the mirror for hours staring at the stranger she would be to herself from now on. She had never in her life had short hair, as Myra often had worn hers, and for some reason it made her feel guilty.

"What's going to happen to us?" she asked him finally.

"They should be through by tomorrow," he said. "We can go home, see what's to be done, pick up the pieces. The place will probably be a mess. There'll be a lot to do."

"You know what I mean!" she snapped. "Don't patronize me. I mean what's going to *happen?*"

"I wasn't patronizing. For God's sake, stop being so touchy."

He infuriated her when he spoke that way, and though she realized it was as hard for him as for herself, she couldn't help it. "Sure I'm touchy. All you do is stand around and do nothing."

"What do you want me to do?"

"Anything. I'm frightened. To feel perfectly normal and healthy and yet know something's happening to you. Inside you . . ." She couldn't control her crying, and when he put his arm around her, she clung to him. "We're not going to be normal and healthy any more, are we? I mean, there are going to be effects from the radiation."

Neither of them had spoken of it before, but she had to make it real by putting it into words.

"Depends," he said, avoiding her eyes, "on how much we were exposed to."

She felt he was worried, trying to shield her, and she wanted to make it easier for him, but she didn't know how. "You had more of it than I did, didn't you?"

He nodded, and she waited, not sure if it was right to talk about it. Uncertainty was worse than knowing, and yet she was afraid to know. If she could be sure he knew, it would be all right. She wouldn't be afraid to deceive herself as long as someone was there to watch the danger.

"Do you know the effects?" she asked.

"No one knows for sure. But I've read about some of those other accidents—"

"Don't tell me. As long as you know what they'll do."

"We'll be under observation. There'll be tests—"

She shuddered, and when he touched her she flinched.

"Sorry," he said, "I didn't mean to—"

"Will it be like Hiroshima? The burns and the . . . other things?"

"Nothing like that. It's better if you don't think about it."

"I can't help remembering those pictures of Japanese women and children with their faces burned away and their heads all . . ." And then she remembered what the man with the Geiger counter had said. "When will my hair fall out?"

"Garson says three or four weeks after the radiation dose, but it'll start to grow back in about six months. Try not to think about it."

She buried her face in her hands. She didn't want to cry. It was unfair to torment him, but she wanted him to feel her anguish too. All the time they were at the hospital she had wanted to get back home, but now, knowing it was tomorrow was terrifying. Several times they quarreled about little things: the food, crumpled newspapers, a misunderstood tone of voice. When Mr. Garson came to take them home, she didn't want to go.

Garson nodded understandingly, as if he had been through all this before, and he spoke crisply and authoritatively about how safe the house was now. He assured them that Geiger-counter readings in every corner and crack of the place were normal now—nothing above the level of background radiation.

"What's that?" she demanded.

"Even if there had been no accident," he explained, looking around as if to find a blackboard and chalk to draw a diagram, "the Geiger reading wouldn't be zero. There is radiation around us all the time, some of it natural, a great deal more added to the atmosphere by the fallout from nuclear testing. But as for the dust carried out of the lab from the radioactive source material, our technicians have cleaned it out thoroughly. And quite a house-cleaning job it was. It included not only the house and your husband's studio, but also the garage and grounds to the street level."

He smiled as if he took personal pride in the scope of the job. "We even checked your neighbors. There was a trace on the Petersons' dog—two houses down?—luckily, not much. Mr. Peterson was rather upset since his wife is expecting another child in October. And the people next door, the Dillons, who were at your barbecue on the Fourth of July, had some on that thermos jug you borrowed. But you don't seem to have much to do with your other neighbors. The rest of the neighborhood seems clean."

Karen blushed at how much they knew about her life now, and at the thought that these men had been through her house, gone through her closets, touched her personal possessions, her letters, her underthings, had seen how sloppy a housekeeper she was. For a moment she felt as undressed as she had been in the garage, but she put it out of her mind as she had done then, shook off her embarrassment, and looked into Garson's eyes. "All right," she said crisply. "Let's go."

As they drove back to the house, Barney asked how they could be so sure there wasn't some trace hidden where they couldn't get at it. How could they go through everything?

"By doing precisely that," Garson assured him. "By going through everything. Your house was, as you will see, divided into sections and each section systematically checked, decontaminated, and rechecked. The men work with swabs, sponges, and whenever the counter shows the presence of radioactivity, they carefully swab and pick up the contaminated trace. We use not only Geigers—both the standard Geiger-Müller and some new ones—but also the improved Scintillation Survey Meter, which lets us sweep over broad distances. Standard procedure. Tracer Control knows its business. Most of our men got their experience as decontamination specialists in the army. I was in decontamination in the marines, on our overseas atomic installations. Radia-

tion spill is something we fight twenty-four hours a day
here at home as well. There are quite a few outfits like
ours, you know. Tracerlab in Boston. Nuclear Chicago in
Chicago. Others in the South and on the West Coast."

Then he paused and looked at Barney. "Think you'll be
up to giving us a little of your time starting Monday? I'd
like you to take Bendix and MacNight along the routes
you remember, places you visited after the accident. The
sooner we get to it, the more chance we have to control
the spread. And you too, of course, Mrs. Stark. I've sent for
several additional teams, and as we check out each place,
they'll follow up and fan out to do the decontaminating."

Barney said quickly it would be fine with him, and it
seemed to Karen he was embarrassed. He was avoiding her
eyes, and she sank deep into the seat and into herself, thinking that it no longer mattered to her where he'd been, or
with whom, during these past weeks. She couldn't tell him
now (there was enough pain to hold them both for a while),
but the things that had been driving them apart, that widen-
ing split between them had been wedged deeper than he
could ever know. She knew it was irrational to blame him
for what had happened, but when he touched her she knew
they would never again belong to each other.

She saw, when they arrived at the house, that the decontamination team, as Garson called it, was just finishing
the garage. In daylight the men in white coveralls and hoods
didn't look as ominous as they had that evening (was it only
a week ago?) when she saw them through the screen door
and nearly fainted. They were getting their things together
—Garson called it their "gear"—as they got out of the car
and walked up the driveway. She held back at first, unsure of
the reality. Men she had begun to believe were part of the
nightmares were finishing their everyday work and loading
their trucks.

She looked away as they carried out the huge drums
labeled CAUTION: RADIOACTIVE MATERIAL! In the driveway, the area around the car was roped off, and there were
stickers on the windshield and a tag on the door handle,

DANGER: RADIOACTIVE! with the lavender three-bladed design against the yellow background that she had come to know as the symbol for radiation.

"Outside of the car is clean," Garson was saying, "but the inside is too hot to work on, and it doesn't pay. We've locked it. The tow truck is on the way."

She had thought that once the men were gone she would be able to forget they had ever existed, but the inside of the house bore scars of decontamination. The foyer, living room, and what she could see of the kitchen from the doorway were marked with a crosshatch of red crayon lines. It was like seeing everything laid out on a graph.

Garson apologized. "Sorry about the mess. They try to be careful, but . . ." He shrugged. "You'll have a bit of tidying up to do."

Against the background of red squares the furniture looked strangely out of place. Some pieces were missing (the brocaded gold-patterned chairs her parents had given them) and in their places on the floor, to show where they had stood, were crayoned ovals.

"They were badly radioactive," said Garson, clearing his throat. "Impossible to clean. But National Motors will pay for anything lost or damaged as a result of radioactivity. I've been told to assure you the company will be most generous."

He had, she discovered, been correctly informed. In less than an hour from the time he and the decontamination squad left, Mr. Waycroft, from the legal department of National Motors, arrived with authorization, he said, to use his discretion in compensating them for loss or damage to their property.

Mr. Waycroft, with his short quick steps and long bowing pauses, did a silent ballet across the grid-chalked floors, and Barney and Karen followed. He looked at damages and at tags indicating removal of objects, and would sing out, "Oh, dear. Hole in the back of the sofa. How much?" tapping his pen against the yellow legal-size tally pad to show he was prepared to accept any named amount.

The figures they gave him were obviously too low, out-
rageously low, he made it clear by his expressions. But Karen
felt strongly against profiting from this. When she studied
the dining-room drapes, which had several holes cut out of
one of the pairs, trying to decide what it would cost to
have the single panel replaced, Mr. Waycroft lost his pa-
tience.

"Now, Mrs. Stark, it is obviously impossible to match
these other panels exactly. A new set is obviously called
for." With this he scribbled the notation "dining-room
drapes—$200," and showed it to her with a flourish. "Fair, I
think. You're entitled to it. The company wants you to be
compensated generously for any loss you've suffered as a result of this unfortunate accident."

"How will you compensate me for the sentimental value,
for the memories connected with the things we've lost?" she
asked. But that seemed to confuse him and threatened to
slow the proceedings, and she told him to forget it.

So it went with the furniture, draperies, linens, clothing,
and everything else the decontamination team had been
forced to remove or destroy. When it came to the car, Waycroft insisted on replacing their Pacemaker Rover with a new
Pacemaker Custom II. "After all, it wouldn't be fair, obviously, to ask you to take a secondhand car, which might
be in worse condition than your own. And anyway, as an
employee of National Motors you would have been entitled to a discount."

"Obviously," said Barney, and she felt like pinching him.

When it came time to check the studio in the basement,
she could see Barney didn't want to go down until Waycroft insisted that the house be checked "from stem to
stern" to make sure everything was "Bristol fashion!" She
realized it was the nautical turn that made Barney yield.
Behind Waycroft's back he pretended to hitch his trousers
front and back like a seaman about to dance a jig, and
winked at her. It was all she could do to keep from laughing. Waycroft in his own way was making this endurable.

It upset her to see Barney's studio through the grid of

red lines. All his pieces were set up against the far wall. A yellow tag indicated where some of his wiping rags had been removed, and there was a tag and mark where a tub of clay had been standing. She hadn't known he'd been working downstairs recently.

"Just to keep my hand in." He shrugged. "Nothing important."

But there was a tag on the cloth covering of the Venus.

"You realize we won't be able to set an artistic value on something you've been working on," said Waycroft, worried for the first time. "You'll have to set a fair price in terms of materials and labor. I mean as a work of art we couldn't, obviously—"

"Don't bother about it," said Barney. "I don't want to be paid for it. Leave it alone."

But Waycroft was already pulling off the covering cloth, and Barney was too late to stop him. "Oh, I'm sorry. I didn't realize . . ." He stood back, embarrassed before the life-size nude, unfinished but recognizable, blushing as if he had come upon her undressed in the bedroom. "I beg your pardon."

"That's all right," she assured him. "When he finishes it, people from all over the world may be looking at it. Like the nude in front of the Gas Building in Detroit." Turning to Barney, she pursed her lips. "But I thought you hadn't touched it since last month."

She could see he was annoyed.

"I worked on it a bit. Few ideas I wanted to try out."

There were marks in the clay, a circle where part of her arm had been scraped away to remove the radioactive dust, her lips seemed chewed, and part of her right thigh between her legs was removed as if with an ice-cream scoop. She trembled when she saw what had been done to her likeness.

Then, suddenly, she saw, even through the mutilation, there was something different about the face from the last time she had seen it. The eyes weren't hers, and the neck, arched at a new angle, gave her an oddly masculine quality.

It was still herself, but changed in a way that was vaguely familiar and disturbing.

Barney covered it quickly with the sheet and went to get some water to spray it. She had never thought of it before, but covered that way it looked like a corpse standing up.

"Don't bother putting any of this down," said Barney, wetting the cloth. "I don't want to be paid for anything down here. It's only clay, and I can repair the damage."

"But the company insists on making reparations for—"

"Don't be foolish!" he snapped, his face reddening. "Sculpture is worthless until it's finished. Until I say it's done—something outside myself, worth so much and so much—it's nothing. I've begun and destroyed thousands of things, and beginnings without endings are nothings. Pay me eight bucks for the clay they took away, but nothing else."

She followed Waycroft as they went upstairs, knowing by the look Barney had given her when he spoke that he wanted her to understand and approve, but again she couldn't help him. What he and they had done to the clay model of herself had upset her more than she could account for.

Two hours and four thousand dollars later, after Waycroft and Garson had gone, they were left standing in the center of their red-lined living room. A check, Waycroft had assured them, would be in their hands within the week. Now the markers and tags were tangible evidence of where the radioactive dust had been, and seeing the fabric cut out of Barney's favorite wing chair, and holes in his tweed jacket and her housecoat, gave it a more horrible reality than even the Geiger counter's rattle had done. There had been deadly dust here . . . and here . . . and here . . . and it had been removed by cutting things up and dumping them into large drums marked CAUTION: RADIOCTIVE MATERIAL! It had been there all the time Barney and she had been watching TV, eating, arguing, and making love according to schedule.

There was a hole they hadn't noticed near the top of one of the drapes. "How did it ever get that high?"

"When I fixed the cord on the Venetian blinds. Probably brushed against the drape when I climbed the ladder." He could see her on the verge of crying, and it made him angry. "What do you want me to do? I'm sorry. It was without my knowledge and beyond my control. I had nothing to do with that lousy accident. It could have happened to anyone, like a flood or a tornado or an earthquake. It's probably happening to thousands of other people right now—maybe not so bad all at once, but it doesn't make a hell of a difference because it adds up in your bones, in your lousy radioactivity bank account, and stays there for life. So just be glad there's no compound interest."

"And when those other things begin to happen to us, will the company still cover us, or is this four thousand dollars supposed to settle everything?"

He stared at her and then at the copy of the tally sheet Waycroft had left them. "I hadn't thought about that. You know, you're right. Considering what will probably happen to us, this four thousand dollars doesn't mean a thing. I guess we should talk to a lawyer."

"Too bad Dad isn't here. We could ask him—"

"Your father? He'd be in a hell of a position to give us advice about suing his firm's biggest client."

"Who said anything about suing?"

"I did. We should have thought about it sooner. No wonder they're being so generous with payments on our material possessions and current medical bills. But you notice no one is saying anything about the future. Sure, they'll pay for the obvious physical damage caused by the accident and the decontamination, but we have no assurance that they'll accept responsibility for what might happen to us in a year or five or ten years from now as a result of the accident. It occurs to me that unless we sue to establish responsibility now, we'll get nothing from them when we need it most. We're going to need a lawyer who has no connection with National Motors, and I think I know just the man."

He started for the telephone but was shocked to find it missing. In its place was a yellow tag indicating that the telephone company had been notified to replace the instrument and to bill National Motors for the cost.

"Son of a bitch," whispered Barney.

"I noticed the bedroom phone was still upstairs. You can probably call from there. This one was just an extension. Who are you going to call?"

"Someone I met at the university. Ed Marshack, a bright young lawyer I think I can trust; the kind of guy who wouldn't be afraid of taking on National Motors in a fight. The more I think about it, the more sure I am we'll have to sue now to protect ourselves for the future."

Two nights later, he stumbled out of bed and vomited in the bathroom. Her own symptoms hit more strongly in the middle of the week. Headaches, weakness, and nausea. Barney seemed to improve after the first four days, while she grew worse. There were other differences too. Unlike Barney, she had no further burn symptoms. While he had insomnia, she wanted to sleep all the time, couldn't stand the odor of coffee or cigarettes, and found herself nodding over a cup of tea or dozing off in front of the TV set. She had nightmares that she was pregnant and that those were the symptoms most expectant mothers went through (her recurrent adolescent fantasy, acted out with a small pillow under her nightgown, that her parents would come in shocked to discover her that way). She was torn between despising Barney and feeling sorry for him. But what else could she blame? Not science or progress. Not National Motors. (Although Barney had arranged with Ed Marshack about suing them, they were too impersonal to blame.) Whenever she remembered that Barney had brought this contamination into the house and onto her body, she hated him for it.

It put her on edge all the time now. Before the accident they had argued and bickered with the best of them, but now, without the energy to fight any more, it was mostly crying and throwing things and getting sick. Had she always been weak like this, a rag doll flopping with every shift of mood, sleeping all the time when she didn't want to face what was going on in and around her? She remembered vaguely that when she was a little girl they had taken her to a doctor because she slept so much.

Days floated by in murky sameness. Looking toward the night from morning, she saw an endless beach of white sand to the sea, each step toward night a breathless plodding, with sand clogging her eyes. But once night swirled in and she could look back, it was a short strip of white—a few feet, nothing more, and she could have reached back and touched the dawn. The day had been half a dozen steps, and there was nothing between daybreak and the sea.

Only once—had it been a dream?—the beach was laced with black seaweed, feathery between her toes, while up ahead the sands looked empty. But when she reached it there was the black seaweed, much of it, oddly, on her shoulders. She put her hands to her head and came away with kelp quickly charred by the sun. That night she tried to drown herself in sleep, only to be caught up and brought to morning in a net of her own black hair.

When she awoke it was on the pillow and the bed, and she screamed and fled from mirror to mirror before she finally came to her senses hard and sharp and forced herself to stand in front of the full-length mirror and boldly pull the remaining shreds of hair from her scalp. When she was completely bald, she let her nightgown slip from her shoulders and stood before the mirror like an undraped mannequin, arms out. (She was in a store window, people passing, women uncomfortable at the reflection of themselves, pink and hairless. Men looking at her legs, thighs, belly, breasts, face, and startled at the crown of sores on the blue-veined flesh of her scalp.) The sores had itched for a long time, but the fear of pulling out her hair had controlled her. Now she scratched the scabs, and the blood streaked down her face and neck.

Barney was terrified when he came into the bedroom and found her standing that way. "My God, what is it? What's happened? Why didn't you call me?"

"Sculpt me now, darling. Bleeding Venus rising, completely bald, from the radioactive sea."

"Get hold of yourself. You knew this was going to happen. They told us it would be temporary." He pulled a sheet from the bed and draped it over her shoulders.

"You're confused," she laughed. "I'm not your Venus of clay. Can't you tell the statue from the model? Here, see how it bleeds when I scratch these—"

"Don't!" He grabbed her arm to stop her. "Please don't . . ." He held her, pinning her arms, and pulled her close. "I can't bear to see you this way. I know you blame me for what's happened, and God knows I've cursed myself a thousand times for it. But we can survive it. If only we hang on and don't let these things overwhelm us."

She saw the tears brimming in his eyes and knew it pained him to see her this way. It was an odd feeling to have him hold her so firmly, but it was an embrace to keep her from hurting herself, she decided, like a strait jacket —not an embrace of love. She didn't resist when he picked her up gently and placed her on the bed. He took a clean towel out of the dresser and tried to wipe the blood from her face and shoulders.

"The sores will heal in a few weeks," he said, "and you know your hair will start to grow back in six months. You'll be as beautiful as ever. I know what your hair has always meant to you, but it'll come back. Meantime we can get you a wig."

"I won't wear a wig."

"Why not? Lots of women have trouble with their hair, and they wear wigs, and no one knows. I'll take care of the whole thing for you."

"You're trying to change me," she screamed. "I saw

what you did to me in your clay figure downstairs. I saw what you did to my eyes. You're making me over into someone else. What kind of a wig do you want me to wear? Blond? Redhead? What are you turning me into?"

"I'll take a sample of your own hair," he said. "I'm not trying to change you into anyone else."

"I don't want you to look at me any more."

"You won't pick at those sores?"

"No. I promise. But please get out and leave me alone."

He started out, but then picked up some of her hair from the bed. "They're pretty good at making wigs these days, but I don't think they'll be able to find hair as beautiful as yours."

He smiled weakly, but she turned away until she heard the door close behind him. She wanted him to know how she felt, but how could he understand? She wasn't sure what was happening to her, and nothing he or the others said could make a difference. Something stirring inside warned that her agony had just begun. Looking at herself in the mirror, she sensed what women must have felt who had their heads shaved for sleeping with the enemy. Her hair was gone; she didn't know why, but somehow it meant that Barney was her enemy.

He found a wigmaker, made a plaster cast from the Venus for size, and had a wig made. She refused to touch it at first, but one day, while he was out, she became curious enough to take it out of the box. Just to look at. Then she tried it on, but it felt like a dead animal against her flesh, and she tore it off. Several times she was drawn to it, and she finally put it on and tried brushing it. Well, he was trying to be helpful, doing what he could to make this nightmare easier, and he was going through his own hell too.

Finally, in the deadness of the days, she began to wear it. But she didn't go out of the house until she knew she had to see Dr. Leroy because, although she hadn't missed any, she noticed her periods were different—shorter and weaker. Last month it had lasted only half a day; this time there were only cramps. And though she realized it might be, as everyone insisted, only the violent upset, she began to think how different her symptoms were from Barney's, of her aversion to meat and coffee, her sleepiness, and the odd fullness of her breasts, and she began to suspect her body changes were more than just a reaction to the radiation.

Dr. Leroy was doubtful. He spoke at first, as Barney had, of cases in which overwrought women had psychosomatically induced all the symptoms of pregnancy. But when the report came in from the lab, he called and asked her to come to his office.

She didn't tell Barney where she was going. He was spending most of his days with Garson. The new car had been delivered the week before, and she took it and went. It was only a half hour's drive to Detroit, and she'd made it often enough before, but now it was like driving in a dream, as if the car were under its own control, and she had the feeling that even if she turned the wheel to pull off at one of the exits, before the one where she had to get off, the car would not obey.

These areas of the inner city were angry ghettos, and she had always driven past on the highway without thinking about them, reminded only when she saw children peering down at her through the wire fences of the overpasses. Now, oddly enough, she had the urge to drive through their streets, to get out of the car and walk among them. She would pull off her wig and show them her sores and tell them, "I'm suffering too. My life has been contaminated too. I'm in pain as you are." But the car wouldn't obey, and she stayed on the highway to where it came up from below to loop into the Lodge Expressway. Below, she saw automobile junkyards, freightyards, secondhand car lots, and parts dealers nestled in the armpits of Detroit's expressways, and she took the cloverleaf and headed north toward the Fisher Building, where the medical specialists had their offices.

She wondered why all the times she had come to Detroit she had never thought about the highway taking her past those slums and all the lost and lonely people—not until today. And even as she wondered, she knew it was because only now she had begun to suspect that her life was never again going to be easy.

She parked mechanically and passed, as if in a dream, through the ornate building, into the gold-figured elevators. She didn't recall giving the operator her floor, but suddenly the girl was staring at her, asking if she felt all right. She nodded and made her way into Dr. Leroy's office.

Dr. Leroy took her inside right away, although there were two other women waiting. They frowned and looked ruffled, and she wondered how he explained it to them. After the examination, he sat beside her instead of going behind his desk, and took her hand in his old, soft, dry hands and peered at her from behind his tinted glasses.

"You were right," he said. "I would never have believed it. I don't know what to say—where to begin—but you understand the problem. . . ."

"I've been wondering about it for some time now. I didn't know I was really pregnant. I didn't really have morning sickness or anything. And I thought the sleeping and aversion to things like meat and coffee were either psychosomatic or symptoms of the radiation sickness. But there was the premonition. What's going to happen?"

"We know so little about the effects of radiation on the human embryo. It's not an area where anyone has been able to do any experimentation, you understand. The literature is very sketchy."

"Will I be able to give birth? Will it live? Will it be normal?"

He was silent for a long time, then ran his fingers through his stone-grey hair. "You remember those mutations that resulted from the thalidomide drugs? Well, this is a similar situation, where even if the embryo survives, it may have had its genetic structure changed. Frankly, I'm astonished you're pregnant at all. Most cases where husband and wife have been exposed to radiation, there is usually

immediate natural abortion. This is so unusual. When do
you think it happened?"

"About two months before the accident, up at Torch
Lake, I would guess. It's hard to tell because I never really
missed my period. And you know how irregular I am anyway. But it happened, and now with the radiation—what
does it mean?"

He sighed, as if he had been afraid she would ask, and
gave a half-hearted shrug. "Possibly nothing. Or, possibly,
a child different from other children. A defect of some
kind. Mental, physical. The familiar mutations like harelip
. . . lobster claw . . . or something—"

"Don't. I've got the idea. Should I have an abortion?"

He took off his glasses, pale-blue eyes naked without them,
and his lined face looking very tired. "I'd like to be able
to advise you. It would be easier for both of you if I told
you there was no alternative. But I have no right to make
your decision for you."

She liked him for saying that. It had been, from the first,
one of the reasons she had confidence in him. He moved
humbly with his patients on the dark edge of knowledge,
honest when he didn't know.

"There is no right or wrong about this," he said, "no
best or worst course. Either way is a heartbreaking gamble.
At times like this, a woman's intuition may be better than
a busy specialist's decision."

Her hands in her lap were strangers meeting, hesitating,
touching, straining against each other. "What are my alter-
natives?"

"If you decide to have the baby, a strong chance of mis-
carriage at any time, which at this stage is very dangerous.
If it goes to full term, we may expect difficulty in blood
clotting; the delivery will be a marginal situation. I would
say you were justified in not risking your life, and there
would be no problem in arranging a legal abortion. Despite
your weakened condition, at this time I think there would
be little danger if you decided right away."

"And later?"

"The longer you wait, the more danger there will be."

"Would I . . . then . . . later on . . . be able to have children?"

He rubbed his pale, translucent hands together and stared at them, frowning, "I doubt it. For some time, as a result of this radiation, both of you will be sterile. How long, we can't tell. Maybe temporarily, maybe permanently. Considering everything, I would say it's unlikely. But, of course, with the new pills . . ." He shrugged.

She leaned back, feeling her lips trembling. "Not a very pretty picture."

He spread his hands to show her that was all there was. "You wanted to know the worst."

She swallowed to keep from crying. Any decision she made would be the wrong one. "Couldn't be much worse."

"Yes it could!" he said sharply. "You could both be dead." She couldn't answer that, and he put his hand on hers to soothe her. "If I thought you could bear children again, I'd be tempted to take the decision on myself and advise the abortion. But as things are, you'll have to choose for yourself. If you want to come back here with your husband and have me discuss this with him, I would be glad to—"

"No, I don't want him to know yet." The words choked out of her before she was sure what she was saying. "I want to think it through first and make my own decision." She was quiet for a moment, and then she added, "After what's happened, there wouldn't even be the chance of later adopting a child. So it's this one or none. Isn't it?"

"If I can do anything to help . . ."

"How much time do I have to decide?"

"Don't wait too long. Every week makes the situation more unstable. You're well into your fourth month. By next month at the latest."

3

From the first, he was overwhelmed at the thought of retracing his steps. How could he remember every place he'd
gone, and how could he face the people he had contaminated?

"Think of this as an epidemic we've caught early," suggested Garson. "The sooner we reach every contact, the
better our chances of preventing its spread. Start by list-
ing every place you recall visiting since the accident. Don't
worry about the sequence. We'll send out several teams
to work simultaneously. We don't expect you to remember
every place you went or everyone you talked to, but once
we get started you'll associate things—where you were just
before or after, what streets you took, who you spoke to.
Don't look so worried. People never think they'll remember
half the places they've been, but most of it comes back.
You'll find yourself almost reliving these experiences."

The first thing he recalled was his grandfather's funeral,
but he didn't want to go back to the cemetery. After all,
radioactive dust wouldn't hurt the dead (how close to dust
was Teofil Szutarek now?). Then he realized other people
would visit, and caretakers would work around the grave
where he had walked. He had to think of them. It was not
for him to decide what to omit. He told Garson about the
funeral.

Barney sat up front with Bendix in the white panel truck
while Garson rode in back with MacNight. They knew their
way through Hamtramck, and—remembering another plant
was located there—Barney wondered if Tracer Control had
worked the city before. When they arrived at the Holy Cross
Cemetery, Barney realized he would not be able to recall
where the grave was.

"We can check it in the office."

"His name wasn't Stark, by the way; it was Szutarek. Teofil Szutarek."

"Your mother's father?"

"No!" snapped Barney. "My father's father."

He saw Garson's eyebrows go up, and in spite of his determination to control himself, he knew his resentment showed through as he explained how he had changed his name from Bronislaw Szutarek to Barney Stark.

"I see," said Garson.

Why did he always feel called upon to explain and defend what he had done? "How can you see? Unless you changed your name too, to make your way in the world? How do you know what it's like to cut off your roots and wonder for the rest of your life if you did the right thing?"

"I meant I understood what you were telling me, not your emotional state. Verbal shorthand. Sorry if I've offended you."

"I'm on edge," said Barney. "After I changed my name, my father disowned me and warned me to set foot in his house again. He is a very emotional man. My cousin, Stefan, who lived with us from childhood, was there to take my place. My father calls Stefan his son now. The trouble is, when the funeral was over, he went off to get drunk somewhere, and I went home with my mother and my cousin."

"It's often embarrassing to retrace your steps," said Garson. "A man can do a lot in three weeks he doesn't want other people to know. Anything else we learn, I assure you, is in the strictest confidence."

Barney knew what he was driving at. "You mean, in case there was another woman."

"It happens sometimes. We're dealing with human beings."

"And radioactivity."

"Yes."

"Well, I'm sorry to disappoint you. But there's nothing like that."

"We have to ask. You understand."

Barney knew he was being reminded this was no game, no pleasure trip, and he respected Garson's impersonal efficiency. It made him feel better. Garson told him to wait while he went to check the grave site at the office.

He felt strange standing there among all those graves (one open nearby, waiting with the mound of earth beside it), knowing that his grandfather was among these thousands of dead, and that he had contaminated the old man's resting place. Garson came back with the identifying code: 7–N–423–15, which meant section seven, north field, block four, division two, row three, grave number fifteen. Barney wondered if this information was somewhere coded on an IBM card. The last number, superseding all others.

"You don't have to come to the grave with us if you'd rather not."

Barney wanted to go along. "No sense getting queasy at the start of the quest."

The truck rumbled slowly down the main paths between the graves until they found the spot. When they got out a few people stared curiously at the white panel truck with the purple propellers in the yellow circle. To Barney, it no longer looked like a propeller blade, but a purple flower— a three-petaled mutant violet. Did these onlookers think it was a white hearse with a new religious symbol—a three-bladed cross? Why not? Didn't people make gods of things that could affect birth, modify life, cause death? Why not worship Roentgen, the new god of radiation? Invisible and jealous god who eschewed noise and tumult and who, instead of hurling lightning from the heavens, silently spread his dust. Someday he would model a statue of the god Roentgen, scattering a handful of dust, sowing seeds of death and change. And at his feet men, in the stations of the three-bladed cross, would be suffering—Irradiation, Deterioration, and Death.

When Bendix and MacNight got out of the truck and moved in toward row three, grave fifteen, with their hoods closed and visors down, people who had come to pay respects and to put flowers on nearby graves drew back. Bendix had the counter, and MacNight had his decontaminating apparatus slung from his shoulder.

Teofil Szutarek's grave was marked with a small flat wood marker. It was too soon for a headstone; the earth would have to settle first. Barney remembered thinking during the funeral that he would like to carve the headstone for the old man. Grandpa Teo had always been proud of his grandson's work. The old man liked to tell the story of the woodcutter and the boar to the children, and once, after he told it, Barney (nine years old) made a clay figure of a boar. Grandpa Teo was amazed, showed it to everyone, boasting, "Bronislaw will be great artist when he grows up —great Polish sculptor." When Barney's father laughed, the old man shouted, "Don't make me out an old fool. My grandson will carve monuments of big stone, like statues in the square in Warsaw, and in museum at Cracow. Better than you with junker cars. He puts name of Szutarek in stone to last forever."

And he had thought that day he watched them lower the old man's coffin and stooped to throw a handful of dirt into the grave, even while the diggers were filling it in, that he would like to make the headstone—a bas-relief of figures from the stories the old man loved so well—and in the corner sign it as the old man would have liked it, with the name *Szutarek*. But his father would never permit it. As far as his father was concerned Barney was no longer a member of the family for having changed his name.

He had thought about that too, looking across the open grave at his father, who refused to meet his eyes, and seeing the enormous muscles under the too-tight jacket and the ripples against his white collar, unnaturally buttoned to his beefy throat. Barney would never have dared to come to the funeral if it hadn't been for his mother.

Afterward, his father handed Stefan the keys to the old Dodge and said, "Take her home. I don't come home for supper." And without acknowledging Barney, he lumbered off. Barney felt the old rage and resentment, but seeing the slowing in his father's walk, it occurred to him his father had just lost a father.

Stefan, holding the car keys, looked at Barney and then at his mother, and for a moment the three of them stood silently. Finally, his mother said, "Come home with us and eat." And knowing his father would not be there, Barney had gone with them. He had thought then that he would go ahead and make Grandpa Teo a beautiful sculptured monument, and sign it, because no matter what his father thought, it was something he wanted to do—something Grandpa Teo would have wanted, and someday his father would understand.

But now, watching Bendix and MacNight searching over the new grave with the Geiger counter, he wasn't sure any more. He heard the counter rattle and saw MacNight bend over with a small scoop and sift some earth from the edge of the grave. And he remembered how he had waited until the grave had been completely filled in, and how, before leaving to join the others in the parking lot, he had knelt and touched the earth—pressing it. And with his radioactive Midas touch he had contaminated his grandfather's resting place.

He had trouble fighting the thickening in his throat as he watched them. There was also contamination where he had stood when they lowered the coffin, back and to one side (across from his father), and again in the parking lot where he had stepped out of his car.

One of the bystanders, watching the decontamination work, finally came over to find out what was going on.

"Just some tests of the soil," Garson told him. Loud enough for the others to hear, assuring the man it was routine procedure. When Garson saw the disgusted look on Barney's face, he seemed annoyed and, off to one side, he said, "Well, in a way it's true. We *are* testing the soil, and for us it is routine procedure. Anything else would only upset them, and—"

"We can't have that," snickered Barney.

"What good would it do to start a panic?" growled Garson.

"You know what people are like when they're terrified of something they can't see and can't understand."

"They could take precautions. Check themselves."

Garson shook his head. "There's no way for them to get rid of the fear. They would panic, and, believe me, that would be worse than the little exposure to radiation they might pick up. Better let them not worry about it. Knowing or not knowing won't matter in the long run, so why stir them up?"

This, Barney told himself, is a man who has been through it before. He knows the best way to get things done. Who was Barney Stark to say Tracer Control was wrong?

"And now, if you're up to it," said Garson, "we ought to visit your parents' home, where you say you went straight from here. If you prefer, you can stay downstairs in the truck while the men take care of it. Or we could take you home first."

"I've got to face them," said Barney. "My father should be home for dinner now. At least with you and the boys along he won't throw me downstairs. . . ."

Garson didn't comment. He nodded and looked straight ahead, as if that way he could avoid involvement. Barney suspected he had been the kind of officer who was cordial and accessible, but who did not build personal ties with the men he had to lead. It would be a good head to sculpt: strong nose in single plane with the forehead, chin receding (but not weakly), eyes aloof, so that the effect would be much like an eagle. But it could not be left rough for the play of shattered light; it would have to be smooth and finished and hard.

When the truck pulled up in front of his parents' house, Barney couldn't move. His hands were clammy, and his chest was tight. Except for the day of the funeral, he hadn't been home for nearly ten years. After all the traveling around the country, all the nights and days of home-coming fantasies, this was the way he had to return—to tell them he had brought corruption into their lives.

Garson was making no attempt to hurry him, but he finally got out of the truck and led them to the entrance beside the dry-cleaning store. Above the bell was the name *Casimir Szutarek* in faded ink on the little slip of cardboard. Barney started to press the button, but hesitated. Only then did Garson assert his authority by leaning over and pressing it for him. Again, Barney knew the man's judgment was good; otherwise he might have turned and fled.

An answering buzz unlocked the door below, and Barney turned the doorknob quickly before the ringing stopped. Bendix and MacNight went ahead with the counter, and from what Barney could tell by the sound, the stairway seemed uncontaminated. It was dark in the narrow vestibule. His parents' apartment was up the long flight of stairs, and he waited for his mother to come to the banister and lean over to call out the challenge, "Who it is?" She always had the broom in her hands, as if to sweep away intruders. How she hated this apartment! From the time his father had gone into partnership with a distant cousin in the used-auto-parts business, buying wrecks and junkers for spare parts, she had begged him to move, to buy a small house outside Hamtramck. She was ashamed to live over a dry-cleaning store, and she pleaded for a house where people could come and visit, with a back yard, where grandchildren could play, a place for a small vegetable garden and an occasional cookout in summer. But his father refused to own a home. Though the auto-wreck business did well. (Whenever he saw one of the New Realists' crushed metal-scrap sculptures, he smiled and wondered what his father would say—amused that the old man's creations might make it to the museums before his did.)

"It's me, Mamma. Barney. I have some people with me."

She drew back for a moment, then leaned over the banister and whispered nervously, "Your father is here. You don't come now." She looked back, as if afraid her husband might be peering over her shoulder. Her voice trembled. "Why do you come? You know it makes him crazy."

"These men are here to do some checking, Mamma. It won't take very long." Barney was whispering too, as if to put off for as long as possible having his father know he was here. He smelled the distinctive odor of pot roast.

"Who it is, Stella?"

By this time, Barney had reached the head of the stairs, close enough to see the astonishment in his father's face. Catch him off guard, he told himself. Act as if it's the most natural thing in the world to be here. "Mr. Garson, I'd like you to meet my father, Casimir Szutarek, and my mother."

Stefan came to the door to see what was going on, and Barney greeted him. "And this is Stefan. My cousin teaches social studies in high school here in Hamtramck. He lives with my parents."

Garson moved in quickly, and nodded, bowing from the waist in a gesture just short of a heel click. "How do you do, Mr. Szutarek, Mrs. Szutarek. Stefan. May I introduce my assistants, Mr. Bendix and Mr. MacNight? I assure you our business won't take long, nor, I trust, will it inconvenience you too much. Your son was kind enough to assist us. Official business. May we step inside so that my men can get their equipment in? Thank you so much."

He took charge swiftly and smoothly, and in a few seconds the family was herded into the living room. Several times Barney's father—big, lumbering uncertainly, suspenders flapping like reins—started to ask what was going on, but Garson's tactic of assuming everything was going along smoothly, naturally, and would be explained in due time, kept them all off balance. Until, finally, the old man pulled up short and slammed his fist down on the table.

"What is going on here? Stop this stupid talk and tell me who are you and why you come into my house?" And pointing to Barney, he said, "I told you, you don't come into this house any more."

Garson pulled out his wallet and flashed a special investigator's badge. "Mr. Szutarek, if you'll allow me to explain. Your son is here as a service to us—to the public. You see, something serious has happened, and it involves not only him, but all of you here." He looked from one face to another, appealing for co-operation, and finally Barney's father sank down on a chair to listen. His mother stood, half hidden by the kitchen doorway, awed by Bendix and Mac-Night in their white coveralls.

"You see, there's been an unusual accident," said Garson, "at the Research and Development Center in Elgin City—in our radiation laboratory. And although your son works in a completely different department, he became involved—no fault of his own—because of his car pool. I know this is difficult to follow, but give me a few minutes and I'll try to make it clear."

Barney was impressed by the skill with which he explained the situation to people who knew nothing about radioactivity and radiation sources, without talking down to them. When the meaning of the words "radiation" and "radioactive dust" became clear, his father stood there thoughtfully, rubbing his finger against his greying moustache; Stefan looked startled; only his mother's frown suggested a lack of understanding.

"You mean like the fallout?" she asked.

"Like what happened to the Japs?" asked his father. "That stuff from the bomb that gave them the burns?"

"Not quite, Mr. Szutarek. If, indeed, any of the radioactive dust was spread here *accidentally*, it would be a very small quantity. Probably no one in the apartment has even come in contact with it . . . or there may be none here at all. Our job is to check for your safety, and to prevent its spread."

Barney's father avoided his eyes all the time Bendix and MacNight went over them and the apartment with the Geiger counter. When it first began its leisurely chatter, his father jumped up, terrified, until Garson calmed him and explained about normal background radiation. Suddenly, he turned to his wife and shook his fist in her face.

"See what comes when you don't do what I tell you? Letting him sneak around here behind my back—"

"Don't blame her," shouted Barney. "It was after the funeral. Just for a short visit, and—"

The look his father gave him was one of disgust, and his

mouth felt suddenly filled with sand. "You don't talk to me," his father sneered. "I told you before, you not welcome in a house of Szutarek. You don't like that name. Maybe I can't tell my son no more what to do or where to go or how to call himself, but in my house I say who comes, and I don't like people sneaking around behind my back. If not for this radio dust I don't even know about it—"

The sharp rattle of the Geiger counter made them all turn. The couch, where he had sat that day, was contaminated.

"Looks like just a few particles," said Bendix. He took out the shears and began to cut away a circle of fabric in the armrest.

Barney's mother screamed as if she had been stabbed.

"Do you have to do that?" asked Barney. "Can't you wipe it?"

He shook his head. "Can't take a chance. Some of it may have gone through the weave."

Barney remembered that this French-style couch with its sweeping curved back, in pink-and-gold brocade, was her pride and joy. They had always called it her "museum piece" because no one was allowed to sit on it. It was for guests and for special occasions, and on the day of the funeral she had insisted he sit there. Odd he should have forgotten, because he had been uncomfortable sitting on the couch forbidden to him as a child. Now she started forward to protest the cutting, but Stefan held her back.

"My couch! My lovely couch!"

"Maybe the hole can be repaired," said Stefan, but even as he spoke, MacNight found several spots where Barney had leaned back, and Bendix cut away patch after patch in the back, the seat, and the armrest, passing the contaminated fabric to MacNight, who dropped it into the container with the purple triple blade. When he was done, the pink-and-gold couch looked to Barney like some diseased creature, with gaps where skin had rotted away.

His mother was crying in Stefan's arms, and his father glared at him. "So you leave trail behind you. I tell you

now—I ever see you here again, I break you with these
hands."

"Mr. Szutarek, I assure you that it's not your son's fault.
The dust was carried into his car by—"

"I don't ask your opinion, Mr. What's-your-name. Finish
and get the hell out of my house." His father's face was
red, and from the way he was clenching and unclenching
his fists Barney knew that in a moment he would start
swinging at someone.

They found no other traces in the apartment.

Finally, they were done, gathered all their equipment,
ready to leave. Barney looked at his mother, but she turned
away and held Stefan's arm for support.

"I'm sorry," said Barney.

"Get out now," said his father.

"I'm talking to *her*." He stood there for a moment, hating
him. Seeing it, his father stepped toward him, his face red.
"I said get out of my house. First you dirty my name, and
then my house. Don't come here again."

Stefan came between them. "Don't answer him, Barney.
We're all upset about this. I'll call you."

In all the years Barney had been estranged from them,
he had dreamed of the day his sculpture would bring him
a reputation that would justify the life he had led, the de-
cisions he had made. He had even planned that when he
had his first child, he and Karen would invite them to the
christening, and it would break the hostility. But now . . .

Bendix and MacNight started out, and Garson took Barney's arm. "Come on. We've got other stops to make."

Barney nodded, turned, and ran quickly down the stairs,
knowing he could never come back.

That evening he lay awake in bed, remembering the boy-
hood fight between him and Stefan. Gentle Stefan, so
frightened ever since his own parents were killed in an
automobile accident. Cousin and friend. Barney had thought
he needed no one else—no brother. Stefan was as close

a comrade as Barney would ever know. But one day Barney's father had laughed at the "sissy sculpture" and sneered that Stefan did more manly things than play with clay all the time. A few days later Barney had let a quarrel over something trivial, unremembered now, blow up between them into a street fight. How old were they then? Twelve? Thirteen?

He found it hard to breathe, seeing it all again now in the dark. The pushing and name calling, getting more serious and out of hand. The neighborhood boys gathering, shouting "Fight! Fight!" . . . the jabbing and cursing and finally the unexpected surge as he threw a punch with all his strength, leaning into it, releasing all of himself in and behind it like an explosion that emptied him. Stefan going down, his head hitting the curb, the blood from his gash covering the sidewalk. Never had he seen anyone knocked unconscious before. Barney had stood there shaken, terrified, certain he had killed his cousin, caught between wanting to help and wanting to run, all his muscles suddenly tense and trembling as if someone had grabbed him from behind.

Why did he look up to the sky then? Who did he think had been watching?

He looked at his hands now, in the faint light through the blinds, feeling the same tenseness and trembling on the verge of muscle cramps. Something had happened to him that day. From that time he had never been able to release a blow completely. Something always held him back. There had been other fights with other boys after that, but whenever he tried to aim a blow something behind him or in him held him back and pulled his punch. He took beatings from boys he had dominated earlier. No matter how angry he got, no matter how rage building up made him want to let out his fury, he could never let fly with all his power, never release himself completely. Always at the last minute he would hold back, and, holding back, in panic lose everything. He suspected some deep fear of his own strength and violent temper—much like his father's—held

him back in other ways as well. In his sculpture, in his feelings and relationships with other people, possibly even in
sex.

Now, strangely, though Stefan had taken his place in
his home and with his parents, he didn't hate him for it.
Stefan had grown up into a decent man, but he had never
married or left the Szutarek home. Barney was sure Stefan
had never slept anywhere else for a single night. It was as
if, having found new parents to replace the ones he lost, he
was afraid to leave them. He had commuted to Hamtramck
Community College and then to Detroit University, and
when he got his teaching certificate, he took a job in a
Hamtramck junior high school. There was no sign of a
sweetheart or girl friend anywhere, and in all the years since
Barney had changed his name and clashed with his father,
and gone off on his own, he wondered what kind of fear
could keep a man in a state of childish dependence into
his thirties, wondered if it could have anything to do
with that fight. Perhaps when Barney had smashed him
that day, he had killed something inside him, leaving only
a frightened shell of a person. Oh, God, let it not be true!

He closed his eyes and tried to put that tableau out of
his mind—his mother and father in the apartment, and
Stefan there with them instead of himself. It was stupid to
dwell on it. He had brought it on himself with his temper
and stubbornness. Stefan was the only son they wanted now.
So why think about them? God, how it had hurt him to see
Stefan comforting his mother, coming between him and his
father when the old man got angry—as if he, Barney, had
been a stranger.

He wanted very much to cry now. He felt the pressure
inside him that demanded release. The sobbing would come,
if he could only let it, and overwhelm him and release the
tears waiting to break through. It would purge him, and
he would feel better. But he couldn't let go. Always something holding him back. "It's my own fault," he whispered,
first to the walls and then to the ceiling, and finally to his

pillow. But there was no comfort and no help, and he stared into the darkness knowing that he could never call or be called "Father," nor would he ever call or be called "Son."

4

The seemingly endless going back over the places he had visited during the three weeks between the accident and the decontamination was a recurring nightmare of having been through it all before, having seen the same people, said the same things, followed the same paths.

There was radioactivity at the gas stations where he had stopped for gas and used the toilet, at Alexi's Restaurant, where they had dinner the night Karen dragged him downtown to see the ballet at the Masonic Temple (center aisle, mezzanine, third row from the railing, they found a particle of radioactive dust embedded in the seat, and MacNight cut a four-inch swatch out of the leather padding).

Each time Tracer Control had to destroy or remove a part of something, they left a claim form with the owner, to be filled in and sent to the home office in Toledo, Ohio. Garson explained that when they were through, the claims would be sorted and compared with the work reports he would send in, and the computer would decide how much to pay. The bill would be paid by National Motors (covered by insurance, of course) and the complete decontamination would probably come to well over half a million dollars. When Barney looked surprised, Garson pointed out that Bendix and MacNight, as well as the men who had started to work with Karen, were highly paid technicians, and that three other teams were operating on secondary leads now in Elgin City. He figured it would take more than a month before they traced every one of Prager's primary and secondary contacts and the contacts of anyone who might have gone into Prager's office.

By the middle of the fourth day of retracing his steps, Barney became too sick to go on. Burns now appeared on his chest and his right side. The doctor at the hospital gave him salves and pain pills and sent him home to bed; he was told these primary symptoms would disappear in a couple of weeks.

Garson set up a tape recorder alongside his bed and told him to dictate into it. "Free associate. When you think of a place where you went to dinner, or someone you visited, see if you can recall where you were before or afterward. Whatever we miss on our own, we may be able to pick up later."

"You mean whatever you miss will still be there to give off radioactivity?"

Garson shrugged. "If you want to worry about it, you can go out of your mind. Look at it this way. There probably isn't much of it concentrated in any one spot, and in most public places there isn't much chance of a lethal or even a dangerous dose. We've got a pretty good check on the homes and places you've visited. Besides, when there's nothing else you can do, it's best to be philosophic."

The doctors, forewarning him of the cataracts soon to form, reassured him they would not be difficult to remove; it wasn't like losing your sight permanently. Yet he found himself staring out the window at trees, roots, clouds, and a large tortured rock he had fallen in love with out at the lake last year and hauled back to set on one side of his driveway; found himself memorizing lines and masses (the twist of the elm as its trunk split into a gentle V, the curious bulge where a broken limb had healed itself). A leaf fell, and, as he watched it, he felt empty. There was no time to absorb all the forms, spaces, movements, and he cursed himself for the years spent in scratching away at Nat Winters' designs, developing someone else's ideas when there were so many unfinished pieces and ideas for pieces, work he wanted to do—had to do before his time ran out.

All right, he told himself, you've got time now, and for a short while you'll have sight and it won't grow dark all at once. He could imagine how the cataracts would develop. First things would grow blurry, and then rainbow rings would form around lights, and then slowly the lights would dim in the haze until color would flow and the world would turn smoky. It would take many months, but it would happen.

Until then he could spend all his time sculpting. And when it was too dim to see, he could use touch. If Beethoven could compose after he became deaf, if Milton could write after he went blind, if Renoir could paint with the brushes strapped to his forearms, then he could shape his clay without sight.

The last week in July, when he was up and around and feeling much better, Garson brought him the news that Max Prager had asked to see him.

"How is he?"

"He got a big dose," said Garson. "I doubt he'll live very long."

"Why does he want to see me?"

"I guess there's nobody else. I've gone to visit him a couple of times, but he doesn't seem to have any friends."

"I don't know what to say to him."

Garson was silent for a while, and then he said, "You blame him for what's happened to you and your wife?"

"Who else is there to blame?"

"Do you blame yourself for passing it on to others?"

"That's different." He couldn't explain how or why it was different. All he knew was that Prager had stayed behind and played hero, and he and Karen were suffering for it.

"Did it occur to you that if he hadn't stayed behind to dispose of those pellets a lot of people would be dead now?"

He was annoyed at Garson for putting him on the defensive. "I've thought of that, but it doesn't help."

"In the Marine Corps we'd have decorated him," said

Garson, taking off his eyeglasses and methodically polishing the lenses with his pocket handkerchief. "Amazing how predictable people are. You're a sculptor, an artist, but your reaction is identical to people I've run across hundreds of times, all over the world, from chambermaids and laborers to politicians and scientists. When you're hurt by something you don't understand, you've got to find someone to take it out on. You're my first artist. I thought, somehow, you'd be different."

"Look, I'm sick myself. I got burned, remember? Besides, what good would it do for him to know how I feel?"

But he went two days later. Garson's words had set him thinking about his feelings, and he tried to convince himself that Prager had been as innocent as himself and Karen. Still, when Barney thought of him, muscles tightened in his arms and shoulders, and his blood quickened. All his life he had been appalled at his father's explosive temper, yet now he was responding in the same way: instinctive, muscular, mindless.

On the way up to Prager's private room on the fourth floor, he noticed people getting off on the third floor, men with flowers and boxes of candy and eager expressions. The sign opposite the elevator said "Maternity Ward," with an arrow pointing to the right. But below it, to one side, near the fire extinguisher, was the other sign that now always leaped out from building walls, entranceways, and corridors. He noticed it as the elevator door slid shut—the arrow below the three triangles, the orange-and-black sign directing the public to fallout shelters.

He wasn't prepared for the shock of Prager's face, swollen, red, hairless (even his eyebrows were gone); and the one arm exposed to receive the needle from the plastic tube looped from the upside-down bottle of colorless fluid was bubbled and blistered from severe burns. The other arm and the rest of his body was hidden under a sheet supported by a frame to keep it from touching his body.

"Barney . . . you came . . ." wheezed the voice through lips that barely moved, as if afraid to crack the mask of his face. "Siddown . . . tell me . . . what's been happening?"

"How are you, Max?"

"F-fine . . . Little too much sunburn. You look okay. I . . . was worried . . . about you . . . and the wife. But you look great."

"We did pretty well. Doctors don't tell us much, but I figure once the symptoms pass, we'll be in pretty good shape."

"Dammit . . . I'm glad . . ." he whispered. "You don't know how often I thought about you . . . wondering how bad . . . Figured you must hate my guts. . . ."

"Don't be foolish." But the words tightened in his throat.

Prager looked at him thoughtfully and trembled with a sigh. "I didn't know I was tracking it out." His voice raised, and Barney could tell he was in pain, trying to get it out quickly. "Didn't know. You've got to believe me. Forgive me . . . both of you . . . please. . . . Barney, don't hold it against me. . . ."

"Of course, we know it was an accident. Nothing to forgive. It was nobody's fault. Hell, Garson said in the Marine Corps they'd have given you a medal for what you did. And didn't I pass it on to other people myself? I've been going around with Garson and his men, back to people I didn't know I contaminated. Nobody's to blame. There's nothing to forgive."

Prager looked at him silently, and the warmth went out of his eyes. Without moving his head he turned his eyes away, looked up at the ceiling, as if he couldn't bear to see Barney's face any more. He was silent except for the rasp of breath, and then, "You're lying. . . ."

Barney didn't protest. Prager had seen in his face, heard somewhere behind his words, that he still blamed him. The old guy was too close to death to be taken in. "I'm sorry, Max. I want to. I don't know how." Barney wanted him to understand what he was going through. Crazy thing. He wanted Prager to forgive him for not being able to forgive. But Prager wasn't looking at him now.

"I'll come see you again," said Barney. "Anything you need?"

Prager didn't answer, just stared away as if Barney had already left. He sat there for another moment, then stood and waited for Prager to acknowledge him. "So long, Max. I'm all confused. Give me a little time, and maybe I'll be able to work it out."

No recognition.

Barney stumbled from the room, his face flushed with embarrassment and rage. What right did that bastard have to make him feel guilty? How come suddenly *he* was the culprit? The hell with him. Forgiveness couldn't be turned on like a lawn sprinkler. All well and good to talk about Christian charity, but words of forgiveness had a stench when they didn't come out of true feeling. And he couldn't force himself to feel good toward Prager just because he was dying. He wanted to, but, damn it, he had felt the muscles tighten, kept his hands from clenching by consciously forcing them open. If Prager had been his own father, he thought, he would have smashed his face as he lay there, because when you couldn't blame the cause you settled for the instrument, and, after all, Prager's pain didn't diminish his.

As the elevator went down, it stopped again at the third floor, and a beaming young man got on and offered Barney a cigar. "A boy," he crowed, "eight pounds, two ounces."

"You have my sympathy," said Barney ignoring the cigar, and punching the button to the lobby.

The young man stared, open-mouthed, still offering the cigar, and it was only when the door opened at the lobby that he reacted.

"What kind of a thing is that to say?"

But Barney was already into the revolving door.

When Karen was feeling better, they assigned her a three-man Tracer Control team. In charge was Josh Chamber-

lain, a stocky, middle-aged man who punctuated heavy
breathing with sighs, as if all this was too much for him.
She could never find his eyes behind his thick lenses, and
he was quiet and dignified as they began their scavenger
hunt.

His assistants were quite young. Stan, the tall one (hair
in his eyes and a shy smile), had played college basketball
before the war. He'd been trained in decontamination in
the army, he said, because he could reach high places. Marty
was a ruggedly handsome, blue-eyed flirt who seemed constantly to be appraising her, and in spite of herself she let
him catch her eye when he sought it, pleased that a young
man should still find her attractive.

Josh Chamberlain planned to visit the Food-Rite Supermarket at closing time. They entered the store as the last
customer left, and the manager and checkout girls, who
were going over their tallies, looked up and stared at the
men in white coveralls and hoods. Chamberlain explained
the situation, and the manager stared at them stupidly.

"What did you say? Radioactive what?"

"That's not important," said Chamberlain. "We've got
to check the place quickly and move on."

"I really don't have the authority to—"

"Look, if we can't check the place, we'll have to call the
sheriff and have him close it. Quarantine. Do you want
that?"

"No, of course not. I—I guess it's okay." He laughed nervously. "Until I saw Mrs. Stark, I thought you guys were
going to hold up the store. Those outfits . . ."

Chamberlain nodded. "Happens all the time. We
shouldn't take too long."

Stan and Marty started at opposite sides of the store
and met in the center. There was nothing until Stan's
Geiger counter sputtered at one of the checkout slots. Marty
took a cotton-tipped swab and wiped between the number
keys of the cash register. The checkout girls who had been
watching became excited.

"Relax, girls," Chamberlain said. "Little speck like that

don't amount to much. One of you must've picked it off a can or a box and when you rang up the purchase it rubbed off and fell between the register keys. Nothing to worry about. Anyone notice any burns on your fingers? Well, we don't know how long that speck was there, so if any of you do get burns or nausea in the next two weeks or so, get in touch with the Radiation Safety Officer at the Center. He'll know what to do."

She saw the resentment in their faces. She wanted to explain that she was an innocent bystander too, but the hard stares told her she had better keep silent.

There was nothing at the Elgin City Dry Cleaners, at Hecksher's Dress Shoppe or the nearby Coffee Corner, or at the other places they checked out during the next few days. But they found a trace had been left at Martino's Beauty Salon, in the chair where she'd had her hair set.

Mr. Martino and the girls who worked for him were panic-stricken until Josh explained as he had at the supermarket. The looks they gave her, blended of repulsion and anger, terrified her.

Mr. Martino mopped his face and blubbered, "My daughter—she's pregnant and she came here to have her hair done, and in that chair, after Mrs. Stark. What if she picked some of it up?"

"We'll send someone to her home if you'll give me her address," said Chamberlain. "But it's unlikely that—"

"My God! My God! What if she did? What if something happens to my grandchild?" He glared at Karen. "If anything happens to them, I'll—"

"Be careful what you say!" snorted Chamberlain. "You have no right to blame Mrs. Stark any more than you'd blame your daughter if she spread it to someone else. You ought to be grateful Mrs. Stark came along with us to check out these stores. A lot of people won't even help us that much."

But Mr. Martino wasn't listening, and there was hate in his face. "Don't ever come back here. Take your lousy contaminated business somewhere else from now on."

Karen knew she was going to cry. The tears were coming into her eyes, and she didn't want to break down in front of him. She turned and ran out of the store.

She was depressed on the way back, unable to respond to Chamberlain's assurances that there hadn't been much at the supermarket or at Martino's, and even if one or more people had come in contact with it for a short while, it would mean at most a burn that would eventually heal. But she was thinking of something else. Soon they would have to visit the people from the summer theater group. Of course, they were doing *Hedda Gabler* without her, but she'd been there during the first rehearsals, and there were many people who had touched her—especially Dale, when he tried to make a pass at her backstage.

He had been a little drunk that night, and he'd cornered her and taken her in his arms and forced a kiss. He had pawed her, slipped his hand into her dress to undo her bra before she was able to pull away from him. Now, remembering that they had found traces of dust on her breast, she wondered if he had picked it up, and if he had passed any of it on to his wife or other women he touched, and that thought made her disgusted with herself.

Chamberlain said he planned to check out each of the members of the group at home and then he would decontaminate the Elgin City Community College auditorium before the date scheduled for the next rehearsal. In his clumsy way, he tried to convince her not to withhold anything from him. "This is like the confidence between a doctor and his patient," he said. "So you don't have to worry about telling us who you were with. Sometimes people are afraid to tell us where they've been, or who they've been with, because they've got secrets to keep. I promise you one thing, me and Tracer Control will honor your confidence."

"What are you suggesting?"

"Nothing at all. But we've got to check out every contact."

"The way they do with people who've caught venereal diseases, you mean? Check out all of a whore's contacts to see how many she's contaminated?"

He was shocked and embarrassed. "Didn't mean nothing like that," he said. "It's my job to ask. I wasn't implying nothing."

"I guess you weren't. I'm sorry for talking like that. This kind of thing has a way of making me feel guilty and ashamed for just having touched someone. Well . . . there's a good chance one of the actors, Dale Wexler, picked up something one evening when he . . . made a few passes at me backstage."

Chamberlain nodded and made a note. "All right, and like I say, none of this will get out. Your husband won't be told none of this."

"Damn you! I don't care if he knows. I have nothing to hide. When you talk like that you make me feel guilty for something I haven't done. You can print it in the Sunday papers for all I care."

Nevertheless, when they let her off at the house, she knew her face was burning and she felt ashamed.

August

1

She had planned to tell him she was pregnant even before the quarrel with her parents. Although she knew they had returned from California a week ago, she pretended to be pleasantly surprised at her mother's phone call on Saturday,

and at the announcement that they were dropping by that
evening. Not for dinner, her mother insisted, just a short
visit. And by the way, she wanted to know, was there anything to those rumors about radioactivity? Any possibility—?

There was no danger, Karen assured her. The house had
been most carefully checked. The radioactive dust was gone.

When she told Barney they were coming, he slammed
his fist into his palm. "My God, they're sending Out-of-
Court Bradley to soften us up. They've decided to get to
us through your old man."

"He wouldn't do that."

"Oh, wouldn't he? Maybe I'm wrong. Maybe he wouldn't
sell us down the river if it meant strengthening his firm's
position with National Motors. If I'm wrong I'll beg his
forgiveness. I'll forgive him for all the widows and orphans
he's smooth-talked into trifling out-of-court settlements if
he hasn't let them use him against us. Fair enough?"

"You've always been against my family."

"That's not true. I always looked up to your father—a
man with roots, respected by the community. Ever since I
broke with my own family, I had the crazy hope he would
really accept me in a way my own father never did."

She was only half hearing him now, because for a moment she imagined a fluttering inside her, and she put her
hand to her stomach. Too early for movement, and still
she had been anticipating it. She hardly showed yet. And now
that her own radiation symptoms—so much milder than his
—had subsided, there was only the quiet waiting. Unreal. Warm. Like bubbles drifting to the surface. She
wanted him to know and wait quietly with her, but if
she told him now and there was an argument, he might
use it against her parents. She would tell him when they
were gone.

"Let's drop it until later," she whispered. "You don't
know why he's come or what he's going to say. Why upset
yourself. Lie down and rest until they get here."

Her calmness, her refusal to be baited, surprised him. It
was as if she had a secret assurance. As she sat back in her

chair he became aware suddenly how full and healthy she looked. Her face glowed young again, belying the rash on her neck, but more confusing was the placid warmth in her eyes.

"What did your mother say? Is something going on I don't know about?"

She pressed his hand gently. "Let's not quarrel tonight. I don't want them to see you weak and exhausted. Lie down and conserve your energy."

He wanted to be sarcastic, but her gentleness stopped him. "You're right. I'll save my voice for later."

Upstairs, light slanting through the bedroom windows hurt his eyes. He stumbled forward and pulled the blinds. Lying back on the bed, he reached for painful breath and tried to figure out what she was keeping from him.

The sound of a car pulling into the driveway woke him. He struggled to sit up, fighting off the giddiness and nausea. It had gotten so that, despite the relief it gave him, he dreaded sleep; the price of waking was terrible. He fumbled with his shoes in the dark and tucked his shirt into his trousers. He wanted to watch Jason P. Bradley cross the threshold, watch especially for signs of fear and repugnance. The Bradleys would be the first visitors in more than three weeks (ever since an unsuspecting salesman came in to make his pitch about how every American family needed an encyclopedia for the sake of the children, even those on the way, or off in the future, and Barney threw him out), and he wanted to see how they took it. His hand went to his hair, brushing it back, and he wished he'd taken the trouble to shave. He must look like a bum. Well, let them accept him as he was.

By the time he got downstairs, Karen was at the door, her parents framed in the entrance. Jason P. Bradley, tall and lean despite his fifty-eight years, with wavy white hair, was a substantial man who looked at the world from a peak of success. Barney had rarely seen him away from the background of books and oak-paneled walls and leather easy chairs in his colonial home. Here he looked the same, as if he had brought the aura of books and leather with him.

Laura Bradley carried herself well, but though neck and chin wrinkles had long ago been smoothed by plastic surgery, she wore too much face powder and lipstick, as if made up to be seen from a distance. She had put on weight, and when she dropped her wrap on the chair her dress bulged white flesh at the arms. Yet Barney could see where Karen got her features: same black hair and green eyes. What Karen might look like at fifty if she lived the leisurely life her mother had known.

Laura Bradley walked in gingerly, as if to keep her skirts clean. "Oh, my darling darling! Oh, my baby, how terrible all this must be for you. How dreadful. You have no idea—when Denis Engstrom called us in Los Angeles and told us what happened we were positively sick. Jason wanted to come right home, but he was in the middle of getting that horrible little lawyer to settle all those thousands of lawsuits against the company. Terrible man, dirty fingernails and shoes never polished, can you imagine? Well, never mind, we're here now. All this new furniture, and those new drapes—how lovely. I must tell you, we looked for your sister at the last address, but she was gone. No forwarding address. Just dropped out of sight—God knows where. She had been living in a dreadful neighborhood, and one of the neighbors told us she had been in the hospital. When she came back to get her things, apparently she was quite changed. Oh, that daughter of mine. The woman said she had converted to some new religion or something. Can you imagine that? Our Myra?"

Barney started to say he could, but she changed the subject quickly. She was so deft, his mother-in-law. "You've got to tell us everything—everything," she said. "Oh, dear, you look so tired. Are you in pain? Jason, look at her."

But Jason P. Bradley was looking at his son-in-law. He hesitated, then held out his hand. Barney sensed the effort it had cost, and it enraged him. "Better not," he said. "You never can tell about radioactive dust. Could be anywhere. You don't want to take chances."

"Barney, that's terrible!" Karen exclaimed. "Don't listen to him, Father. They've checked this house carefully. There's not a chance in the world of anything here."

"Unless they brought something in with them from the outside," said Barney. "It's all over Elgin City, you know, and I'm the one who spread it."

Her father stared at him calmly, surely aware from the bitterness in his tone that they were unwelcome. Laura Bradley tried to retain her composure, but she couldn't help looking around nervously.

"That's perfectly ridiculous, and you know it," said Karen, pulling her mother into the dining room. "Don't listen to him. He gets carried away with his artistic imagination. Dad, come have a drink."

Her father accepted the drink, but he was unwilling to let his son-in-law have the last word. "This has affected you more than you know, Barney. You always had a swagger and sneer to you, but you were never this vicious. You ought to see a psychiatrist."

"Well, I can't afford it just now." Barney laughed. "But if National Motors has sent you here with a decent settlement offer, maybe I'll do just—"

"Barney!"

"That's all right, dear," said Bradley. "You've both been through an ordeal."

"And we don't want your pity!"

"Understanding isn't pity."

"Oh, come on now, dear ol' dad, this isn't just a social call, is it? Be honest. You were sent by Engstrom to work on us, weren't you?"

The uncomfortable look on her father's face told Karen the story. "Daddy!"

"For your information, Engstrom did not send me. He was going to send someone else. I insisted on being the one to tell you because I assumed you would rather hear it from me than from a stranger. At any rate, it's to your advantage as well as theirs to get this thing settled quickly."

She looked away, and Barney could see she was hurt. Now she would realize there was no one left in this rotten town they could turn to. But he wanted her to see them in all their selfishness. "Of course," he mocked, "it's to our mutual advantage to have this thing settled quickly. Now, just what did Mr. Engstrom say the board of directors had in mind as a reasonable settlement? What have they finally decided it's worth when two people, through no fault of their own, have been exposed to their radiation? Let's see. . . . Well, on the physical level—the sickness, the nausea, the bloody diarrhea, the weakness. Now, the doctors tell us we—well, I at least—can look forward to weakening eyesight and, eventually, cataracts. I've developed a little spot on this eye. It's painful when there's too much light, so I keep the blinds drawn during the day, and that's why the lamps are dim, in case you were wondering. Of course, when the cataracts are completely formed, I can have them operated on, but in my weakened condition operations can be—"

"This is hardly necessary," said Bradley.

"On the contrary! It's quite necessary, I assure you. Because we've got to assess the damages before we can decide on a proper settlement. After that, possibility of leukemia, or bone cancer. If I take it easy, never work again, I may expect a reasonable life span. Karen too, of course. So there has to be enough to support us. Not mentioning the fact that we're undoubtedly sterile now, and we'll probably never be able to have a family. Not that it would make sense to bring a child into this world. But how much should we put down for being deprived of the right to have children?"

"All right, all right!" Bradley set his glass down on the table. "You're determined to be unpleasant about this—"

"You should have had children before this," said Laura Bradley to her daughter. "I warned you it was foolish to put off children. Remember when I pointed out—"

"Just a moment, dear," insisted Bradley. "I'm trying to make him see that this attitude is not going to get him anywhere."

"What attitude would you like me to take?"

"And it's making things worse instead of better. You ought to consider things—"

"Worse? What did you have in mind?"

"—realistically. You're not a child or a day laborer. You've had a career interrupted by a terrible tragedy, but you know what the business world is like. The average man has fantastic Hollywood notions about suing giant corporations for incredible sums of money. It's a commonplace daydream. But you know better."

"Do I?"

"You should know, for example, that they can hold off a liability suit for ten or even fifteen years, delay after delay, with no guarantee you'll win when it gets to trial."

"Yes, I know. After the witnesses are gone, and records and evidence have disappeared." He smiled triumphantly at Karen. "We're getting the Bradley treatment, dear. You're seeing your father at work."

Bradley appeared unruffled. "You've been with National Motors long enough to know that a man who co-operates with the company always comes out ahead in the long run."

But Barney was watching Karen. As her father spoke, she seemed to be shrinking away from him. As if she were seeing him for the first time, not at home or at a party, but in the arena, with blood on his sword. "Yes, tell us about the long run," he said. "That's the part we've been waiting to hear about. Isn't it, dear?"

She turned away. Her father saw what was happening. "I see we'd better put off this discussion. Perhaps it would be better to deal with your lawyer."

"Oh, no, *Dad*," said Barney. "Go on, please. You'll have to forgive the facetiousness. Pain and nausea sometimes make me unpleasant."

"We'd better leave," he said to his wife. "Coming here was obviously a mistake."

"Daddy, did they really send you here to make us settle out of court?"

Jason Bradley frowned at his daughter. "I'm not going to dignify that with an answer. Let's go, Laura."

Laura Bradley seemed relieved. She pulled her silk shawl around her and raised her penciled eyebrows. "I'm really shocked at the way you're both acting. As for you, young man, you seem to have very little respect for your wife's parents. After all my husband has done for you."

Barney was leaning against the wall now, toying with his drink. He found it difficult to hide his satisfaction at seeing the old man exposed this way. "No, I haven't forgotten that he got me my job through his connections. But then, I think I've paid for that in a thousand ways."

Bradley turned to walk out, but Barney stopped him. "Before you leave, don't you think you ought to tell us what the company's latest offer is? That way your visit won't have been for nothing. We'll have some idea of what they've decided, and you'll be able to take an answer back with you."

"Yes, Daddy, what are they offering now? It might be enough to permit us to rot away here quietly."

"My dear, you don't believe—"

"Tell us what they're offering," she whispered, "and stop playing *father*."

Halfway to the door—his wife was already on the threshold —Bradley turned. "They're being quite generous. I was thinking of your own well-being. Considering there is no proof of negligence—"

"So they've bought off the laboratory staff."

"—as can be proven by the independent testing experts—"

"Tracer Control's evidence won't be conclusive. They're the suppliers of the isotope."

"Are you going to risk everything to find out? Think of Karen."

"Get out!" said Karen, quivering. "And don't come back. Don't ever come back."

"Wait," said Barney, putting his hand on her shoulder. "Let's hear the offer. Maybe we're being hasty. After all, he might have convinced them to make a fair settlement."

"Barney, I don't want—"

"Shhhh! Go ahead, Dad."

Bradley hesitated, then shrugged. "The board of directors discussed the situation the day before yesterday at a special meeting. Their legal staff has gone over the case carefully, and they directed me to offer you—" the words came out hard—"ten thousand dollars."

"Ten?"

"Each. Each of you will get ten thousand."

"We're suing for two hundred and fifty thousand, and you offer us twenty! No wonder you came here instead of going to our lawyer. Tell your friends at National Motors that the radiation hasn't affected our minds yet. Tell them we won't be bought off with twenty thousand—"

"Wait, Barney. He said ten thousand each. That's not twenty thousand. It's thirty thousand. Ten for me and ten for you and then I'm sure the offer includes ten for the baby."

At first, Barney thought she was just topping his own nastiness, but her chin was trembling and there were tears in her eyes.

"I had hoped to tell you all in a happier way. But with a child coming and the future to plan for, we couldn't possibly accept that settlement. The child may be born deformed, you see. Possibly a custodial case all its life. Who will pay for it, if we accept such a small settlement? Oh no, they'll have to convince a jury. And I think you'll agree that our lawyer will be able to gain the sympathy of the courts."

Before her father could say anything, she fled up the stairs screaming, "Now leave us alone. We don't need your help. I don't ever want to see either of you again."

She slammed the door of the upstairs bedroom, and the sound echoed through the house.

"You should have told us," said Bradley. "I had no idea."

"Neither did I," said Barney.

"This changes things. You've got to make her see—"

"I think she's seen enough tonight." He held the door open and then watched them walk slowly down the path to their car. They had parked it at the curb across the street instead of bringing it up the double driveway as they usually did. It was a slow, tired walk, and Jason Bradley's shoulders were not as stiff and his head was not as high as when he had entered the house.

After they were gone, Barney went upstairs to talk about it.

"Not tonight," she sobbed. "There's been enough talk for one night. I don't want to think about it. Let's go to sleep. I just want to go to sleep."

But there was no sleep for either of them. She had drugged herself with sleeping pills, and her night was a carnival horror ride through a dark tunnel illuminated by creatures bursting into view, with claw hands or swollen heads or popping eyes or scaly skin, all of them blaming her for having given them life with deformed bodies.

Barney twisted until grey showed through the blinds. Finally, giving up all attempts at sleep, he went downstairs to put the coffee on. So she was serious about being pregnant. But why now, when the very idea was a mockery? How much did she know about the possible effects of radiation on the fetus? Then, remembering Dr. Leroy's candor, he decided she must know what to expect.

She obviously hadn't meant to spring the news this way. Still, it had been good to see the shocked looks on the Bradleys' faces.

When Karen came downstairs, her face was strained and pale. He studied her figure as she put a cup and saucer on the table for herself. She hardly showed. Yes, she had thickened out at the waist, and her breasts were fuller. How stupid not to have noticed it before. Preoccupied with his own physical changes, he had been blind to hers.

"So I'm finally to become a proud papa, after three years."

She put two slices of bread in the toaster without looking up at him.

"So all the time I thought your nausea was from the radiation, it was really because of this."

"No, Barney, not all the time. It was a little of both. My nausea was very mild. I think in some strange way the pregnancy has helped my body fight those symptoms."

"When is it to be? Or is that a secret too?"

"Late December," she said quietly, not wanting to provoke him or be provoked. She felt ashamed for having used it as a cheap way of shocking her parents.

"Who's the father?"

As soon as he said it, he was sorry. "Forgive me, that was a lousy thing to say."

"It was."

"Well, it was lousy to keep it from me. You must have known for a long time."

She sipped her coffee. "Only since last month for sure. Dr. Leroy thought I should tell you right away, but I wanted to think it out for myself first. I have to decide whether or not to have it."

"Don't I have anything to say about it?" Until a week ago, he would have put it on the line, but now, because of her fear and confusion, he wanted to be considerate. It would be too easy to hurt her now.

Her sigh fluttered in the muscles of her throat. "I don't want to be influenced yet. First I want to know what I want—I mean *really*. Not what I ought to want, or what I'm expected to want, or what it would be clever to want. I want to know what everything I've been and become— everything that's *me*—wants. If I find out, and follow that, no matter what happens it'll be all right."

"You're waiting for a sign."

"From inside. From me. I thought it might come in a dream, but all I've had are nightmares. When I was a little girl I used to sleep a lot. Whenever I had troubles or fears I would go to sleep and dream of elves and fairies, and they would give me ideas about what to do. You didn't know they took me to a psychiatrist because I slept so much, did you? Now there's no fairyland any more. Only frightening places." She looked at him shyly. "I haven't ever told these things to anyone before. We've never really opened up about ourselves."

"Never had much time."

"That's not why. There was always something in the way. We were never really close. I'd have been embarrassed. And—before the accident—you'd have laughed."

He took her hand, and she clung to it. "Barney, I'm frightened. I don't know what's right." Suddenly, her eyes opened wide with surprise.

"What's the matter?"

"I've got a funny feeling."

He came around to where she was sitting. "You're all tensed up."

"No. Like wings fluttering inside me. It's the baby."

"Are you sure? When are you supposed to feel it?"

"The fourth or fifth month. They call it quickening. Barney, I'm scared."

"It's probably nothing. Your imagination playing tricks. You didn't get much sleep, and after that session last night . . ."

The idea of life inside her frightened him. He should do something, but what? It startled him to realize that he was a mature adult and yet this was all strange to him. Why did he know so little about pregnancy and birth?

"In your condition it could be a lot of things, gas, or— What's the matter?"

She had her hand over her mouth. "I've got to decide," she gasped. "It's alive and growing inside me and I don't know what to do." She got up and headed toward the living room. When he started after her, she motioned him back. "I want to be by myself. Please, Barney, I've got to think."

He started to protest, but seeing the determination in her face, he backed off. "All right. If you want me, I'll be downstairs."

Down in the studio, he took the damp sheets off the Venus. Now he could see the difference. Of course, Karen had put on weight. Her breasts were fuller now than when he had first modeled her. He touched her shoulder. But was this Karen or Myra? Now he wasn't sure any more. If he succeeded in blending the two of them into one, it would be neither of them really, but a new woman. If the blend failed, it would be nothing. He didn't want her to have the child. There were problems enough now without babies around. He didn't have the energy to battle the world. He wanted to be left alone, to live in peace if he got better, or to deal with the suffering if the sickness got worse. All the medical advice came to the same thing. Take it easy, lots of rest, no stress. From the first he had desperately wanted a child, but now it was different.

From where she sat on the sofa, Karen watched the children playing on the lawn across the street and wondered what Barney was thinking now. It was obvious he no longer wanted a child, but how would he react when it was born? Now that she had told people, it seemed real for the first time. She should have decided before letting anyone know. How had her mother felt about giving birth? Laura Bradley was vain, and it must have been terrifying to have her figure swollen, first by Myra and then by her. But, anyway, Laura Bradley had managed to bear her husband two healthy daughters.

All her life, this tangible evidence of her family had been comforting. People might come and go from Elgin City to branches and plants all over the world, houses built or torn down, but this had been the Bradley home town for three generations. She belonged here, and this was where her child would be born and raised.

She got up and went to the doorway leading to the studio. "Barney."

"Come on down."

She went down and saw that he was working on the Venus, adding clay to her bosom and thickening her waistline.

"Does it show that much?"

"You've decided," he said.

"I want the baby."

He put down the modeling tool and wiped his hand on a towel. "Don't make a rash decision. Let's consider it."

"This is my only chance ever to have a baby of my own. It's here now, alive and being formed inside me."

"Or deformed."

She looked away, and he was sorry he'd said it. "That's a chance I'll have to take," she whispered. She sat on the edge of the stool, back stiff, trying to keep from trembling. "It exists here and now. I'll take whatever it is and I'll love it."

"Well, I can't promise to do the same."

"I don't expect that."

He was adding clay to the abdomen as he spoke, working the masses quickly to bulge even larger than she was.

"I haven't grown that much," she laughed.

"No," he agreed, unsmiling, "but that's how I'm beginning to see you. And I sculpt things as they appear to me."

"Then I don't want to see it," she said, turning away and starting upstairs. He was destroying his Venus, changing it into something else because of her.

"Of course not. You don't want to know the truth. You want to live in your little fairy world. You think it's going to transform your life—"

"Our lives. They say a baby brings a change of fortune."

"I don't want the world at that price."

"Are you going to spend the rest of your life down here, living in your world of unfinished creations?"

"That's not fair. You know damned well there was a time I could finish things. There was a time when the feel of the clay, the sight of it forming in front of me the way I visualized it, was the most important thing in the world. It used to feel great to finish things because I never worried about finishing them. It was always just working on it, feeling it change and develop in my hands, that was important. The finishing came naturally, without thinking or worrying about it. I still come down to work because I've got to use my hands; it's a compulsion, maybe, to work the material, to change it, even knowing it's never going to amount to anything because I've become too critical, too fussy about it."

"You always used to say you shouldn't be the judge of your own work, that it was your job to create and let others decide for themselves if it was good or bad."

He laughed. "That sounds like the preaching of a very young artist. When you're young you make up lots of rules and give yourself and others wise maxims to live by. But an artist can't cut off the judgment when he's reached the point of knowing the difference between good and bad, right and wrong. No, I still need the feel of the clay; I still have to work. Even though it's been a long time since there's been any joy in it, at least I can still work. A man could spend his life in worse pursuits."

"Well, I'm not a sculptor. I'm a woman, and I'm going to spend my life with people."

"That's up to you." He added a pellet of clay to the Venus' cheek, distorting her expression to one of determination—more like Karen now than her sister. "It's your life."

"Part of it. The rest is yours." She started upstairs. "I'll make lunch. You can come up whenever you're ready."

When she was gone, he felt drained. He sat for a few minutes staring at the form in front of him. Then he dampened the drape cloths at the sink and covered the figure and went slowly upstairs.

2

The Nuclear Energy Commission announced the investigation nearly three months after the accident. The item was buried among center-page advertisements in both the Elgin

City *News* and the *Daily Press*. Identical stories and headlines appeared in both papers:

NEC INVESTIGATES RADIATION INCIDENT

Elgin City, August 20 (ups). The Nuclear Energy Commission has completed its investigation of an accident at
National Motors involving the spread of radioactive dust
in Elgin City. Director of Radiation Safety, Dr. Edgar
McMahon, revealed at a press conference today that radioactive material was spread when a defective Iridium 192
pellet split.

Radioactive material passed unnoticed at the time of
the accident through ventilator ducts from the "hot lab"
to a small adjoining office, where senior technician Max
Prager picked up the dust on his shoes and spread it to
the automobile of Barney Stark, a clay-model sculptor in
the Styling Department.

Mr. Stark later spread the dust from his own car to
his home and to various places in the city.

For the past month, radiation health officers and technicians from Tracer Control of Ohio have been decontaminating various locations in Elgin City, Hamtramck,
and downtown Detroit. Although technicians are still
working in Elgin City, field chief Louis M. Garson assured the press that most of the radioactive material
has already been disposed of.

Mr. Engstrom of the Research and Development Center, and E. M. Jensell of the NEC, in a joint statement,
explained that news of the accident had been withheld
to permit Tracer Control to work without the confusion
that would have resulted if the news had been released
prematurely. Mayor Phinney assures the citizens of Elgin
City that there is no longer a danger to public safety.

Barney was unprepared for the city-wide hysteria that exploded when the news was released. The phone began
ringing early in the morning, and he and Karen took turns

referring people to the Tracer Control answering service. As the morning of an August day wore on—promising, according to the Michigan Chamber of Commerce, a good vacation weekend—local radio and TV announcers reported overloaded telephone circuits all over the city: newspapers, the city Health Department, the Mayor's office, the Chamber of Commerce, the Park Department—anyone who might have any knowledge of the accident, or advice to give—were deluged with calls.

"Can't you tell me where to go for treatment, or whatever they do? I was sitting in the bus next to a young man I'm certain works for National Motors. . . ."

"Look, I been trying to get through for more than an hour now. What I wanna know is, I drove past the Center late last week. Now, all of a sudden, my battery is overcharging and it never done that before. Where do I find out if I got any of that stuff in my car? I could of picked it up on the wheels or something."

"I'm sure of it. We were visiting with the Bob Hallecks whose cousin works for National Motors. And now I have these pains in my breasts. Both of them. Like radioactive needles sticking in me . . ."

"But this is urgent. I have top-secret information. This was done by the Communist agents who have been following me for over a year. . . ."

A housewife wanted to know if it was safe to touch the dust on her window sill. A vacationer wanted to know if the lakes were polluted. A lady's dog had been acting strangely; might it have picked up radiation from other dogs? Was it radiation, asked a farmer, that was causing this unseasonable weather?

Dozens of calls came from people in neighboring cities checking the possibility of "fallout." (One man, calling from the extension in his bomb shelter, where he had taken refuge with his wife, mother-in-law, and four children, was on guard with his rifle to keep everyone else away and wanted to know if an announcement would be made when it was safe to come out.)

Anyone who knew people who worked in Research and Styling, or who knew the Starks and had seen the comings and goings of the Tracer Control trucks, now made it a point to call the house and to say how sorry they were to hear what had happened. And how were you getting on? And what did you think was going to happen? And was there anything they could do to help? And—oh, yes—there was one other thing. Silly, of course, but they had been by your house two months ago—remember?—and was there any possibility . . . ? You see, they had children at home and they couldn't help worrying, about . . . well, you understood, of course. . . .

Yes, of course. And the only thing to do was get in touch with the Health Department, or with Tracer Control, and have an examination. Most of the radioactivity had been cleaned up, and the NEC had said it was unlikely any outsiders not already traced had been seriously exposed. And the Mayor had already issued a statement asking residents to set an example by remaining calm, ignoring unauthorized remarks by unauthorized people, and not allowing rumors to cause panic. So the best thing was an examination. Just a quick checkup. Yes, it was painless. No, it didn't cost anything.

Tracer Control had set up half a dozen examination stations in Elgin City and referred all callers to those points for checkups on the following day. Lines began to form the night before. By 6:00 A.M., these circled the block and snaked to several blocks beyond. There was a traffic jam along Main Street, and autos were rerouted along National Motors Square. Leaflets were passed out, quoting a resolution passed the previous day by the Detroit Common Council, voicing confidence in the Nuclear Energy Commission, Tracer Control, and National Motors.

Despite reassurances, or possibly because of them, the panic was on.

Summer people at lake-shore cottages stayed long enough to be checked, and then packed and fled. It was as if, after discovering they were "clean," people feared contact with anyone at all.

There was a rush on commercially available Geiger counters. (Although the Detroit Better Business Bureau warned that unscrupulous manufacturers were shipping in thousands of outmoded or unreliable Geiger counters at exorbitant rates, the feeling was that anything that clicked was better than nothing. It had become a talisman.) The wealthier residents of Elgin City were outraged by this kind of radioactivity that made their expensive fallout shelters and civil defense procedures useless: No warbling sirens could warn of someone carrying radioactive dust on his clothing.

A fight started on Wynn Street, downtown, when one man brushed against another. People stopped shaking hands, and a few hospital-type face masks appeared on the streets. The town's wrath was directed at first against National Motors, and each morning revealed vandalism at the Research and Development Center: broken windows, painted obscenities on the walls, garbage dumped on driveways and in the artificial lagoon in the center of the grounds. When the vandalism got too serious, National Motors announced the temporary closing of the Center. All research would be continued at the Hazel Park laboratories and at Eastern State University. So the people of Elgin City sought a new target. Max Prager was not available, but some of them remembered that the Starks had spread the contamination in the city, and the Starks were still around.

One evening, a rock shattered the living-room window, just missing Karen; a piece of flying glass cut Barney's forehead. He ran out the door, but all he could see was a car with the headlights out. As they passed under a street lamp, he saw men in the back as well as in front, but he couldn't make out the license number.

"Those weren't kids," he shouted, slamming the door. "They were adults." The anger was choking. He wanted to grab someone. He was furious enough to kill—not cleanly, with a gun or knife, but to beat someone to painful death. He slammed his fist into the doorjamb, pounding one hand and then the other until he had to drop back on the couch.

She found a note tied to the rock. "Get out of Elgin City," she read, "or we'll burn you out."

"I was afraid of this," he whispered. "They'll hound us until we get out of here."

' A week later there was another rock and two attempts to set the house on fire. After the second attempt, Mayor "Sleepy" Phinney came to the house and explained that he had authorized the Chief of Police to station a uniformed man out front. It could only be temporary protection, he apologized, until things died down. He had thought they'd be selling out and leaving the city, like some of the others from the Research Center.

"We can't," said Barney, "not until the case is settled."

Mayor Phinney nodded with his best campaign smile, lids half closed, as if nodding happily in sleep. "Heard the company offered you a nice settlement. Thought you'd be glad to get shut of this mess."

"I don't know what you've heard," said Barney, "but they've offered us next to nothing. We'd like nothing better than to sell this house and get out of here today, but our lawyer has advised us not to do anything yet."

Barney thought the Mayor was going to fall asleep smiling on the couch, but he snorted and pursed his fleshy lips. "I heard from Mr. Engstrom's brother-in-law that you people are trying to make a big profit out of this and don't care that if there's a court case they might keep the Center closed for a long time and throw a lot of people around here out of work."

"What kind of nonsense is that?"

"That's the rumors going around. Even talk that they might move the Center down South, where a lot of other companies have been relocating."

"Oh, come on now, you know as well as I do that's absurd. The Center will be open as soon as the panic dies down."

"May be, but there's a lot of people around here who are worried about their paychecks, and they figure you're the one who's partly responsible. I think you're making a great mistake not selling out and moving elsewhere."

"We talked to a real-estate agent last week."

Phinney nodded. He'd heard about it. Obviously, the Mayor's office had a direct line to every real-estate agent in town. (Elgin City was well known as a town that could control the kind of people who could purchase property, much the way Grosse Pointe had done with its famous "Pointe System," and any arrangement would be carefully scrutinized by the most popular mayor Elgin City had ever had.)

"Then you also know," Barney sputtered, "that he told us people wouldn't buy because they'd be afraid there was still radioactivity here."

"Well, that's not exactly what I heard. Lester Parkson tells me he suggested a fair sale price for this place—considering the circumstances." He looked around as if he approved of the house they had lavished so much care on.

"Fair price?" Barney knew he had to control himself with the most powerful man in the city. But it was boiling up inside him to smash that sleepy smile, see it register surprise, anger, pain, anything but that bloated, heavy-lidded mask. "Twelve thousand dollars is fair? This place has a thirty-thousand-dollar mortgage. We'd be in debt for the rest of our lives."

"Well, like you said, you've got to take a loss on account of the radioactivity. And you'd be making a nice profit settling right away with the company."

"We're not settling under pressure, damn it. I don't care if it takes us years to get it into court. We'll fight them."

For the first time, the eyebrows went up and the smile threatened to die out, but then Phinney shrugged. "Well, it's your . . . decision" (Barney knew he had started to say "funeral") "but I don't think you're doing smart. Chief Bonnard will have a man on duty round the clock—for a few days anyway—and maybe things'll simmer down. But you got to understand after that he can't keep a guard all the time. Elgin City don't have a very large police force."

"I'll ask him for a gun permit," said Barney. It was a foolish idea, because he'd never dare to use it, but he said it out of bravado.

"No. Don't imagine the Chief will okay a permit," said Phinney. "One thing we don't need is someone with a grudge against the whole town, wandering around with a loaded pistol. I guess not. We had a bellyful of that kind of thing during the riots."

When Phinney left, Barney called the Chief of Police and found out, as Mayor Phinney had predicted, that it would be against the welfare of the community to give him a permit to carry a handgun.

Over Karen's protests, he went to a sporting-goods store in downtown Detroit, where no one knew him, and bought a double-barreled shotgun and two boxes of cartridges. He had never hunted in his life, but for the next few days he took several trips out into the woods and practiced shooting at trees and tin cans, as he had seen them do so often in Westerns, until he felt he could handle the shotgun in an emergency.

"Things will get better once the scare dies down," she insisted, "and when the Center opens again. In a few weeks, everyone will have forgotten about it."

But the owner of Verne's Service Station, where they always bought their gas and oil, asked them to take their business elsewhere because the station had been losing regular customers who were afraid the gasoline pump might become contaminated from the Starks' new car. Barney argued with him, and the man agreed there was nothing to it, but his customers weren't always logical, he said. As long as people were afraid of being contaminated, they wouldn't do business at his station, and, after all, he had four kids and another on the way. Barney threw the money in his face. As he started the car he gripped the wheel so tight she was sure he was fighting the urge to run the man down. She touched his arm, and he stared at her wildly, and then drove back slowly to the house.

It was the same when Mr. Harkness of the Food-Rite Supermarket asked them to take their trade elsewhere, and when Norton's Dairies stopped milk deliveries to the house. The paper boy phoned apologetically and said his other customers insisted that he might pick up radioactive dust from the Starks' porch if he went to the door to get paid each week. He would throw the paper onto the steps from his bicycle as he had always done, but would they mind mailing a check once a week for the newspaper service? More and more it was necessary to do their shopping outside Elgin City, and they went twice a week to downtown Detroit to buy food and supplies.

A few people sent notes of sympathy. One of Karen's distant cousins from Grosse Pointe sent a basket of fruit. Nat Winters phoned to find out if there was anything he could do. Watching Barney talk to him over the phone, she could see, at first, he was guarded, as if waiting to discover the underlying motive for the call, but when it became clear to him that it was just a thoughtful act, Barney was moved.

The only ones who came to the house were an elderly couple from the next block: Mr. and Mrs. Lausch, a retired accountant and his little wife, in their seventies, who often waved from their front porch when she or Barney went by. They came one hot afternoon, very formally, she in a blue-and-white print dress, with a flower-laden straw hat and white gloves, and he in a seersucker suit and tie, bringing homemade cookies and a jar of currant jelly. They had been meaning to visit sooner, Mr. Lausch said, to see if they could do anything to help.

Karen invited them in and asked them to stay for tea. At first she was afraid Barney would be annoyed and sarcastic, but he talked with Mr. Lausch about the weather, the crab grass, the school-bond issue to be voted on that fall, while she talked with Mrs. Lausch about the recipe for

the cookies and got some pointers about how to put up
currant jelly. When they left after about an hour, Karen
cried and Barney held her.

"I want to be like them when I get old, Barney. I want to
be good and kind." She looked into his face, but he seemed
far away and the expression in his eyes was sad.

He had passed the first stages of nausea and bloody diarrhea,
and he fought the increasing weakness and depression by
working furiously to exhaustion. He started a series of
new projects, the most important of which was a figure he
had thought of doing many years ago—the corrugated features of the Ancient Mariner, with his long finger and ex-
pressive face that could hold the wedding guest while he
told his harrowing story. He had long ago decided the alba-
tross around the old guy's neck would be too obvious. He
needed no symbolism. He wanted the figure emaciated—
not the bone-wasted limpness of refugees, but with great
tension in the arc of his neck, the face illuminated with
pain-rubbed sensitivity that hurls him fanatically into life
—wanted it nervously alive, telling his story and holding
the wedding guest with his "glittering eye."

The image and the challenge to do it came back to him
as it was when he'd first thought of the idea in high school.
His English teacher, in love with Coleridge, had read por-
tions of the poem aloud, and Barney still recalled the re-
strained emotion in the teacher's voice. That was forgotten
until years later, when on a cold night in Cadillac Square
a drunkard wearing a sailor's pea jacket and a black knit
cap stopped him and asked for the price of a drink in a
rasping voice, and said how long he'd been without a ship.
Barney gave him a dollar and that evening made the first
sketches for his Mariner.

But they didn't satisfy him; the tortured lines of face and
hand wouldn't come to life. After all, what did he know of
suffering, of thirst and heat and despair? He put the sketches
aside and forgot about them, concentrating on subjects he

understood (he had won the Detroit Institute Student Award for his "Fallen Acrobat," and the "Exhausted Runner" had earned him the fellowship at Eastern State University). Now it came back to him as a challenge again, as if he knew the old guy's thirst, felt his flesh burning, shared his timeless world where yesterday and tomorrow crumbled in his hands like dried clay.

But it didn't come easily—nothing came as he visualized it; there was something stubborn about the figure as there had been with the Venus; heads and legs became strange objects—and finally, in desperation, he put aside all sketches and models and worked to recapture the memory of the lonely man who had stopped him on that street, and to blend it into the mood he had felt when he had first heard the poem.

As usual in the beginning, he soon felt himself lost in the work—forgetting time, pain, and the world. He always felt, at the start of a new piece of sculpture, this excitement that promised absorption and completeness and direction to his life. Of course it was wonderful to finish something and know it was good, but it was more important to begin something that had possessed you for a long time, and to feel the work go well. So it was for nearly two weeks with the Mariner. But then a terrifying thing began to happen. The realistic shape was a lie. The figure became twisted and knotted, and each time he tried the Mariner it pleased him only when the body was snaked out. And yet the strange shapes were grotesque in their torment. At times they were so distorted there was no point in going on. Even though he knew the face and body were true, there was something struggling to come out of him that he couldn't understand or control.

One afternoon it seemed he had the anguish of the face right, but involuntarily his hand reshaped the mouth into an expression of overwhelming hatred. Wrong. This wasn't the tormented Mariner now. Just a dirty old man hating the world. Frightened, he grabbed a cutting tool and slashed the face. It made him sick, rubbery-legged, and if he

hadn't grabbed the back of the chair he would have collapsed. Holding onto the wall, he made his way upstairs,
and when he came into the living room Karen was frightened.

"My God, what is it?"

He lowered himself into the chair, trembling. He felt a
sudden loss of strength. The stopper had been pulled, and
all the energy was gone.

"Do you want me to call the doctor?"

"I'll be all right." He'd had these feelings before, but
always if he rested the weakness passed and he was able
to go on. It had never been this bad. Was this what old
people felt when they were close to dying? So it was getting
worse. "It'll pass," he insisted. "Don't worry about it."
But the doctors had explained about the accumulation of
radiation in his bones, and told him he could expect attacks like this with increasing frequency.

In the beginning he had tried to learn about the effects
of radiation, spending hours at the Detroit Public Library
and calling professors at Michigan universities. What was
available in books he could understand was inadequate,
and the rest was too technical: studies of radiation biology
based on people who had suffered high radiation exposure
—victims of major explosions like those in Japan, and others
who had died as a result of accidents in testing centers and
runaway reactors—and the study of the Marshall Islanders
based on the testing fallout in 1954, or the people involved
with the reactor that exploded at Idaho Falls. None of
these provided a comparable situation. What had happened
to him and Karen was closer to the small industrial accidents—about which there was very little information,
strangely enough—like the case of the girls who worked
in watch factories painting dials with radium paint and
came down with symptoms of radiation poisoning.

He began to wonder how many people who worked
close to companies that used radioactive isotopes were
building up enough exposure to give them cancer in later
years. And how much of what passed for ordinary blood

and bone diseases was unknowingly caused by radioactive traces? There was so little being published about the effects of accidents in industry that he began to have the strange feeling of an unspoken conspiracy between government and industry to hush it all up.

3

One evening late in August, Karen heard a car pull into the driveway. She drew the bedroom curtain aside and saw a woman with a suitcase get out of a taxi. A moment later the doorbell rang. Quickly, she slipped into her robe and went downstairs, calling Barney to tell him someone was at the door.

"Probably kids," he shouted back from the basement. "Don't answer it."

"It's a woman with a suitcase."

He came to the foot of the stairs and looked up at her. "Who is it?"

"I don't know."

The bell chimed again. "Well, answer it, and send her away," he shouted. "I'm trying to work."

"I'm frightened."

"Oh, Christ." He climbed the stairs and shouldered past her to turn on the porch light. "Who is it?"

"Can you put up a weary traveler? It's me, Myra."

"Myra!" he shouted. "Karen, it's Myra!" He fumbled at the door latch, dimly aware that the blood was pounding in his head and chest. But when she came inside he stared in dismay. Except for the voice, he never would have recognized her. "Karen!" he called, unnecessarily now, because the sisters were rushing to each other.

He knew he was gaping, but he couldn't help it. She had

cut her hair close, and without make-up her face, incredibly aged, was lined and weary. Her tweed suit was far too heavy for August, and the chalky stockings and flat heels denied shape to her legs. Only her throaty voice and the blue-eyed gaze were the same—but those eyes bulged now, stared too harshly.

"Not much change in you, Barney," she said in response to his obvious surprise. "A little older, tired-looking, but I'd have known you anywhere. I read about the accident in the back pages of the Los Angeles *Times*. I bet it made the front pages in Detroit. You people must be famous here."

Barney had picked up her suitcase, noting it was cheap fibreboard with straps, and was setting it down in the living room. "Infamous, you mean. The dangerous, radioactive Starks. Contaminators of the fair city of—"

"Barney, please, give her a chance to sit down. Don't get started."

"But there is a difference between famous and infamous. I just wanted to keep the record clear."

Myra touched Karen's cheek and smiled. "You look lovely. Pregnancy agrees with you."

"How did you know?"

"I called Mother from the airport to get your address. You look simply wonderful. I can't get over it."

"She's blossoming," agreed Barney, "while I—"

"Pregnancy has curative effects on the female body," said Myra, looking at her sister thoughtfully. "The miracle of creation."

Karen jumped up and said, "How about something to eat? You must be famished after such a long—"

"I have my own food with me. Just some fruit and nuts, but I'll have a glass of cold water."

Barney studied her smiling, calm face and the intense blue eyes that hadn't changed. "You're different," he said, finally.

"Yes, a great deal has happened to me since college days. I've passed through a kind of purifying fire. I know the meaning of suffering. When I read what happened, I felt you and Karen needed me. I want to help, if you'll let me."

Barney said nothing, but Karen got up quickly and took her hand. "Of course. I need someone around, and who else but my sister? You'll stay with us."

"Are you sure? Because otherwise I could stay with people in Detroit, at the Mission—"

"Don't be silly," said Karen. "We want you here."

Myra looked for his response, and he saw her cheeks hollowed and gaze so intense it was painful to look into her eyes. He was confused now. He wanted to know what had happened to her; yet something warned him that if she had become some kind of fanatic it would be dangerous to let her get involved in their lives.

"I don't know," he said. "We're in a state of siege here."

"All the more reason to have someone here to help you," she said.

"They'll label you radioactive too."

"I've passed beyond worrying about the judgments of men. I won't get in your way. I'll merely do what I can to help you and Karen. If after a few days you find I'm a burden, I'll leave. If having me here serves a purpose, I'll stay as long as you need me."

"Now, it's silly to talk about being a burden. You won't interfere with his work, and I'll have someone to talk to when he goes off wandering. Come upstairs, I'll show you the guest room."

Barney looked at both of them silently and then shrugged and went downstairs without saying anything further.

Myra stared after him as they headed upstairs. "Where is he going?"

"His basement studio. Sculpture is the only thing he cares about now. He should go to the hospital twice a week for checkups. The doctors say if he takes care of himself and does what they tell him to, his body can cope with the attacks on it. They say a great deal has been learned about radiation sickness. But he refuses to go. All he does is work downstairs."

"He may be doing better for himself than you imagine, if he has the sense to keep away from doctors. Perhaps his instinct for self-preservation has taken over."

Karen stopped to get sheets out of the linen closet. "We have the best Michigan doctors available."

"Perhaps both of you need the kind of doctors who minister to the suffering spirit rather than the body."

Karen studied her for a while. "You've changed. It's hard to believe you're Myra."

Her sister laughed, reaching out to help Karen make up the guest bed. "In a way I'm not the person I was. You might say I've been reborn. Oh, not that I want to talk about it yet. It would be only words to you, and I want it to mean a great deal more. I want to guide you when the time comes—"

"I hate to say this," said Karen, "but I've been through a great deal myself these past few months. I'm not Baby Sister any more."

"I know," said Myra, "and my own ordeal allows me to understand what you and Barney are suffering. Not the same thing, of course, not radiation, but there are other kinds of contamination. A guide helps when you pass through purgatory. I've been there. I know."

Myra followed Karen into the other bedroom, talking all the while persuasively about the need to communicate and share the suffering they were going through. "That's the only thing that can overcome pain and give meaning to it. Only man, of all the earthly creatures, communicates his anguish to his fellow man, and in sharing human suffering we are all touched with immortality."

It came too unexpectedly, and Myra was too strong to argue with right now. The throaty voice, the dry touch of her hand, the strength in her eyes were reassuring. Karen sat down on the bed. Perhaps Myra could help. It didn't have to be a religious thing. Just having her there to talk to would be enough.

"I'm glad you came. I've been so alone."

"You haven't been alone, dear. You mustn't say that."

"Oh, Barney's drawing farther and farther away. He's all wrapped up in his work."

"I wasn't talking about Barney." Myra smiled and patted her arm. "I didn't mean it in the physical sense. . . ." But seeing the frown on Karen's face she let it drop. "Never mind. We don't have to label it. The important thing is to remember you have your own creative act to complete —a trust—a new consciousness to bring into this suffering world. And I'll be here to guide you. Now rest and let me get you a cup of warm milk."

"You don't have to do that. I can—"

"Listen to your big sister," said Myra, pressing her gently but firmly to lie down. "I came here to help. And that means you're to leave all these details to me, and just relax and prepare for the weeks to come. You've been ill, you need rest. A time to meditate and let your spirit restore you."

In a way it was a relief to have her here. She lay back in bed and nodded. Myra smiled and turned out the light.

"Rest, think, dream. At crucial times in our lives we are open to spiritual communion with the universe. Things happen if we let them. I'll bring you a little snack on a tray."

"That's not necessary—"

"Shhh! You must have rest and quiet."

Barney saw Myra become part of the household. Her Spartan frugality intrigued him, and made him aware of his and Karen's dependence upon possessions. (Was it *things* that kept them in the world? Like hundreds of handrails for clinging to the slippery side of reality?) Myra cooked their meals according to dietetic principles that he was willing enough to go along with until he discovered after the first two vegetarian dinners that there was to be no meat. When he rebelled against being converted to gluten and soya patties, and demanded meat at least once a day, she yielded and cooked for herself separately.

Time and again she asked to see his work, but he put her off. He had no desire to share it with anyone yet. He had stopped working on the "Rising Venus," experimenting now with the Mariner, who had become one of several smaller figures in a strange, violent tableau. He wasn't sure where he was going with it—just following his inner promptings, delighted in starting new figures for it, vaguely aware that each new start was a way of setting up obligations to commit him, at least to the world of his work, if not the world of people.

But he was curious about what had happened to Myra. The harshness of her prematurely aged face and ragged hair, set off against her still penetrating blue eyes, fascinated him. He hinted that he wanted to know what had happened to her, but she always changed the subject. It was as if she wanted to avoid being misunderstood, as if she were waiting until the time was right.

Completely unafraid, she often left the house late at night for long walks, to see the old neighborhood she had grown up in, she explained, ignoring Barney's warnings that it was dangerous.

"Who would bother an unattractive female? I no longer have to worry about men making indecent advances toward me. They take one good look and leave me alone."

One night, two weeks after she had arrived, the police brought her home.

Her face was bruised and her right eye nearly closed. The buttons were off her jacket and her blouse had been torn open; she held the top closed with one hand, and there was blood on her collar. She had been followed and beaten by two men as she passed through one of the rougher neighborhoods of Elgin City.

Karen had come down while Myra was talking, and blurted out, "You ought to know better. Don't you know how dangerous it is for a woman to walk into that neighborhood at night—alone?"

Myra took the wet towel Barney handed her and shook her head. "I didn't think they would bother me." Her voice was quavering. "I'm not pretty any more. I was sure they—"

"It's not that simple," said Barney. "They know you're here with us. The whole town knows it by now. And besides, some disturbed character looking for a woman on a dark street doesn't worry about what she looks like or how old she is. Some poor bastards get their kicks out of terrorizing solitary females. They probably didn't even intend to rape you. Frightening you would be enough for some. But for others it might have been necessary to kill you." He realized his explanation was upsetting her, but he couldn't bring himself to stop. "If you thought becoming plain and unglamorous would put you out of reach of men, you've been kidding yourself. You've been going out as a test, haven't you? You thought no one would see through that disguise that you were a woman. Well, I've got bad news for you. You're still a damned desirable female. Not as glamorous as before, but your basic attractiveness hasn't been destroyed."

Myra reddened and quickly looked at her sister.

Karen laughed it off. "Look out for him."

"Oh, don't get me wrong. I have no intention of making a pass at you. But whatever happened to change you hasn't affected that core of vitality. When you walk into the room, the current is on, and you can't shield that with short hair and mannish clothes."

She was trembling now, on the verge of tears, and he let up and stalked out of the room.

"I have changed," said Myra softly to Karen, who sat beside her to hold the wet towel to her swelling eye. "He's wrong. I'm not the same as I was. He doesn't understand. Oh, God, there were two of them. One grabbed me from behind, tore my jacket and blouse and held my breasts, while the other one put his hand under my skirt. Filthy animals. Why do they do it? It's not as if I were pretty any more. When I was pretty and young, I knew what they were thinking all the time. Oh, God, won't they ever leave me alone?"

She began to cry, and Karen tried to soothe her. "Now, now, it's all over. It doesn't look too bad. Only a bruise."

"It's never over. They always want to grab at your body and maul you. They're all alike. It makes me sick, Karen. I tell you, if I'd had a knife I'd have killed them both for touching me. I wanted them to die. All my life I've had to fight off that kind of thing. I was sure I was free at last to come and go as a human being, so sure I wouldn't have to fight that battle any more. And now this. You can't understand. I've dedicated my life, now, to the suffering. It sickens me to have stumbled back into this corruption of men who make everything they touch filthy."

"You're distorting things now, Myra. Yes, there are lots of men like that. I've been through it too. Not as much as you have—in a sense I was luckier, not being as beautiful as you were—but I had my share of dates, necking in cars, and fighting them off when it came too close. But that was part of growing up. A lot of men grow up too; they're not all that way."

"Oh, Karen, I didn't mean to include Barney. He's not like the others. You're lucky. He's one of the few men who doesn't give me the shakes when he looks at me. He's honest. That's because he's creative. He has his mind on a higher plane."

Karen smiled. "Now wait a minute. Let's not go too far in the other direction. I don't think it's wise to make generalizations about any man. Sure he's honest, but as a sculptor he's a very sensuous and physical person. Perhaps you didn't notice how he was looking at you. What I mean is, don't make another mistake like the one you made tonight. You ought to be able to see that he's still in love with you."

September

1

Myra went with her to Dr. Leroy when Barney refused to leave his studio. She was in good enough hands with her sister, he said, and as much as Karen wanted him to come with her, she knew better than to pressure him now. She tried to imagine what it would be like for someone whose whole life had been a search for form and light to be confronted with not only pain, but also darkness. He was trying to make sculpture his world, now, trying to find with his hands some shape and meaning to an existence that had suddenly crumbled. Her decision to have the baby had been right. Something to look forward to, a reason and a way of living for her—what Barney was struggling to shape for himself out of his work.

She and Myra took the expressway downtown to the Fisher Building more often now that she was in her sixth month, and Dr. Leroy checked her pressure, weight, urine—giving her a new awareness of her body. Because she could see change from week to week, her fear gave way to fascination as she massaged herself to prepare for breast feeding. Dr. Leroy noticed the stains on her bra, though she had put on a clean one before leaving the house, and she was embarrassed. She had begun secreting soon after last month's visit, she told him, and it was one of the few things about her pregnancy that had made her sad, a sign that she had in some final way become a woman.

He smiled. "Oh, come now. It's quite normal. And don't worry about your breasts. You'll regain your shape. Nursing does wonderful things. I understand the way you feel, or, rather, I accept without understanding. Hundreds of women have come through this office, but I never expect to fathom the emotions connected with childbearing."

As she was dressing after the examination, he asked her how Barney was coming along.

"Not as well as he might be. He has attacks of nausea and weakness, and he seems to be drawing more and more into himself."

"Is he under medical care?"

"Doctors from the company health center insist we haven't suffered permanent damage, but he calls them medical prostitutes and he won't take their advice. The other doctor, the one our lawyer got us, takes the opposite view, very pessimistic, as you would expect. So he doesn't believe any of them. He's become so suspicious of doctors and medicine I don't think he really believes I'm pregnant. The strange thing is that my sister doesn't believe in doctors, either. She insists the only way to have a baby is with pain, what she calls an involvement with the suffering of the world."

He looked at her hard. "I hope you're not going to let her talk you into anything foolish."

"I used to be influenced by her a lot when we were girls. I think she came here expecting me to take her advice without questioning. But, somehow, I think now I have the strength to resist her."

"Good. Follow your intuition. I have great respect for a woman's knowledge of what to do when she's having a baby. Especially," he added, "when she's under the care of a good obstetrician."

His lightheartedness, his confidence that things were going well, elated her, and she refused to be drawn into Myra's gloomy mood on the way home.

"I never expected you to have such a closed mind," said Myra. "I always thought of you as being open to new ideas."

"Oh, no. You were the one always hungry for new ideas, new sensations, new causes," said Karen. "I just wanted dates. I was perfectly willing to watch you go off in all directions followed by worshipping males."

"Lusting males, you mean," said Myra, staring ahead. "I know now that's all any of them wanted, to get their hands on me, in the bushes or on the back seat of a car. They only pretended to be interested in the things I was involved in."

"What did you think they were, eunuchs? Those were natural desires."

"I never believed that. I wanted them to see I had a mind. I wanted them to share my ideas and dreams. Oh, what a fool I was. I nearly died, but that was nothing to the death I knew when I realized they were only pretending to believe in those things, while all the time they only wanted to use my body. But some great teachers have shown me the way. If only you would let me pass on that knowledge to you."

"Why are you so interested in me after all these years?"

"Both you *and* Barney. Because you're suffering. And that's the first step. My mission is to reach the suffering. As soon as I read about the contamination, I knew both of you would be going through the kind of experience that would prepare you to receive this knowledge. And I thought, how blessed to bring my own sister and her husband into the Brotherhood."

Karen sensed that Myra was probing to see how she would respond to this kind of talk. Myra had come to convert them to some new religious sect and knew enough (or had been trained) to do it slowly, surreptitiously, lest she frighten them away. Karen smiled and shook her head. Whatever religious cult Myra had become involved with, for whatever reason, was no longer of interest to her.

"Don't you feel the need for some deeper commitment?"

"I've got my baby to think about. That's commitment enough for the time being."

"But that's only the beginning of things. You must—"

"Then let me have the beginning. I was never a person who could take more than one step at a time. Don't confuse me. I have enough to think about."

Myra was silent, and Karen was sorry she had made her angry. Once back in the house, Myra went off to her room to read, and Karen had an inexplicable urge to do house cleaning. She did the tasks violently, as if in the physical acts of scrubbing and polishing and sweeping she could find the answers.

Later that evening, in the middle of helping Karen prepare dinner, Myra suddenly said: "What about Barney? Perhaps I can help him through his suffering."

"Barney? You're not serious."

"But I can help him. There are many artists and composers and writers—all creative people—who know what he's going through. He doesn't have to bear this alone. Unless you're opposed to it. . . ."

"Of course I'm not. But—"

"Then I can still accomplish something while I'm here."

"Barney has strong ideas about religion and mysticism. He's always been strongly opposed to the kind of thing you're talking about."

"Ah, that doesn't worry me," said Myra. "My ideas flow from a universal source. This goes deeper than ordinary religion or mysticism. It touches on something in the creative spirit that an artist will understand."

Karen was silent for a moment, appraising the look in her sister's eyes. "I told you before that he was in love with you once. Do you think it's fair to—"

"That has nothing to do with it," Myra said sharply, and then, carefully lowering her voice, "You're much more beautiful now than I am."

Which was Myra's way of saying, she realized, that their marriage was merely physical. She suddenly wondered if she was making a mistake, if it wouldn't be better to ask Myra to leave him alone and save her missionary work for others. It was as if Myra were testing her ability to win converts, as if she were saying: Ugly as I am now, I can still take him away from you spiritually.

"If you prefer, I'll leave," said Myra.

"Not at all. You're my sister. Think of this as your own home. He's an intelligent grown man. I have no claim on his soul. His world is the work he's doing; mine is planning for the baby. If you can help him, I have no right to interfere."

There was no mistaking the excitement in Myra's face. It seemed to her that all through dinner Myra couldn't take her eyes off him. Just how much influence could she exert over him? In his present condition there was no telling what might happen. Well, let's leave the field clear, she thought, and give her a fair chance. "I'm going to bed early," she said. "I've had a tiring day."

Something was going on. The way Karen watched Myra all through dinner, the way Myra looked at him. At first he suspected they had hatched some scheme to involve him with the baby, but when nothing was mentioned during dinner, he guessed Karen had delegated Myra to get him to do something. But what? The tip-off was Karen's having gone to bed early to leave them alone. He would find out soon enough.

Myra came into the living room and sat on the couch with her legs drawn up under her. "Barney, when are you going to let me see some of your work?"

"Not yet," he said. "I don't have anything finished. I haven't finished anything for a long time."

"Why is that?"

"I go from one thing to another. Experimenting. Nothing seems to come alive. Nothing satisfies me any more—not the way it used to."

"But what's wrong with my seeing your work in progress?"

"No—I know it sounds foolish, but I can't stand to have people see my work until it's complete. One smile of approval freezes something I might otherwise have changed; one frown could send me into a depression for days."

She looked disappointed, and for a moment he was tempted to take her down to the studio. She was silent for a while, and then suddenly her blue eyes turned on him.

"Barney, we haven't had much chance to talk since I've come back. How much do you know about what happened to me since I left here?"

"Not much. I knew you didn't marry him. Your mother told us you were in a hospital for a while, and that later you became involved in some religion."

"Do I seem changed to you?"

"Yes, in some ways."

"I came here for a reason, Barney. Didn't that ever occur to you?"

"You said you came to help."

"But not just this way. There's more," she said, hugging her knees as if to coil herself completely. "Barney, I nearly died in San Francisco."

"I didn't know. All these years I thought of you caught

up in one of your causes: organizing the migrant workers or doing antiwar work—something like that."

"It was that way in the beginning. But things went downhill very quickly. After about a year, Floyd left me and went back to his wife. I was a drug addict, pregnant, and alone in a cheap hotel room. That was the night I died."

He hadn't expected her suddenly to reveal herself. He felt awkward, but she was talking, and her voice, persuasive as ever, caught and held him.

"I'll never forget that night, Barney. It was raining, and I was alone. I thought of suicide then, as I'm sure you have since the accident, but I was terrified of killing an unborn baby. And in that room, stinking of dirt, I woke from a nightmare, wondering what was going to happen to me. Where would I go? And then I heard it. At first, I felt only a presence nearby, something enveloping me, and when I heard the voice I thought it was someone calling me through the door. But there was no one there. Then I heard it again, clear, deep, as if echoing through empty corridors. 'Find the Church,' and again, 'Find the Church.' Now you know the kind of person I was, Barney. I knew it was impossible. But it happened again that night and the next. Five times. Five blessed times. Until I said to myself, well, if there is no other way, maybe I ought to listen. Even if it's from inside my own head, maybe it's trying to save me."

She paused, breathless, flushed, transformed as she spoke, but there was the same intense glow in her eyes, and the hand outstretched, grasping the thought to hold it for words. "And the voice showed me what a fool I had been. Let me tell you, I wandered through the streets of downtown San Francisco that night in the rain looking for the church my voice had spoken of. Most of them were closed, and in the one I did find open, the priest kept asking me if I wanted to make my confession. I knew that wasn't what the voice had meant. Then I realized it had said to find '*the* Church'—some special church where they would understand what I was suffering, and would care about me here and now. I collapsed in an all-night diner where I stopped for a cup of coffee. I recall a sailor slipping into the booth beside me and putting his hand on my thigh, and nothing after that. When I came to myself three months later I was in a mental hospital. I had lost the baby during those months and never knew it."

"Why didn't you write to us, or call? We could have done something." For some reason, he felt responsible.

"What could you have done? That was my Night of the Soul. Despair I hadn't thought possible this side of hell. What I didn't know then was that I didn't have to suffer alone. Sure, they healed me after I lost the baby, and brought me out of my confusion with other drugs, but when I got out I remembered the voice commanding me to find The Church. And I started my search again."

She was dramatizing as she spoke, using her hands and the movements of her head, her voice cracking into emotional hoarseness, drawing him to her intensity. She put her hand on his arm and looked into his eyes, and a strength seemed to flow from her into him. He didn't understand it, and he felt guilty at the thought of Karen upstairs while something she could never understand was passing between her husband and her sister.

"After I got out of the hospital, I wandered all over California, speaking to hundreds of ministers and priests and rabbis and yogas and Zen masters. And followers of the Sufi and the Arcanists. All of them believed they had the true answer; all of them pretended to know a God-without-suffering. But finally one day I found it. I was lost in a strange part of Los Angeles one morning, and a small, ugly brick building in the center of the block attracted my attention. When I got close to it, I saw the small stained-glass windows above the door and the small bronze plaque with the words *Crucifist Mission*, and I knew I had found it. I summoned up the strength to ring the bell, saying to myself over and over, let this be it, let this be it, and by the time a white-haired old man opened the door to me, I was crying."

It hurt him to think of Myra, standing in the doorway of

a strange house in a strange city, before a strange man—
weeping. Why hadn't she come home? Why hadn't she
come to him?

"His name was Brother Wallace," she continued, "and
he took me inside. When I told him what had happened
to me, and about my voices, he said I could stay at the
Mission for a few days to see if it was what I had been
searching for. And it was, Barney. It was. It's like no other
church in the world. They call themselves the 'Crucifists,'
not just here in the United States, but in a Brotherhood
all over the world, part of each other in one great web of
suffering. We have brothers who were at Hiroshima, a former
astronaut who was irradiated in space, survivors of Nazi
concentration camps, and hundreds of others dying of cancer and other incurable diseases—all creative or socially-
minded people who have proclaimed themselves sharers in
their torment. Barney, if you open your heart before it's too
late, you can become one of us."

This wasn't what he had expected at all. It repelled him,
as he realized the vitality in her voice and eyes had turned
into fanaticism. "It's too late for me," he said weakly. "I've
always faced things alone. It's too late to change."

"That's where you're wrong, Barney. I was the same way.
And at the moment of my greatest aloneness I found that
pain and fear had to be borne, yes, but not without meaning. Sharing and discovering with others gives strength and
inspiration beyond belief. I know, Barney. I lived through
it and died through it, and I was reborn in the Crucifists."

As she described how she had been instructed in the
Crucifist Mysteries, Barney felt himself being drawn into
her mood. She was a missionary seeking converts, and part
of him was responding. She must have sensed his desire
to cut it off because she spoke more quickly, as if to clasp
him by the hysteria in her voice.

"There are secrets, Barney, ways to make the mind use
the suffering, to focus the pain, concentrate the experience instead of wasting it, and through it become part of
the Crucified Spirit of our time. Don't you see, Barney,

our pain is cosmic pain? One man's agony—yours, mine, Christ's—every suffering mind, like a throbbing nerve, sets up a resonance in other nerves and communicates suffering to the whole network. And it's through this sharing that the darkness is illuminated and we enter something deeper and more wonderful than appears to one pair of eyes alone."

He stood up and tried to clear his head. "It's late. I've got to get to sleep."

"Doesn't this mean anything to you?"

"Yes, and I want to hear more about it," he lied, "but not all at once. I've got to think about some of the things you've told me."

"There's so much to tell."

"Another time." He didn't want to reject her there and then. Was it because he didn't want to hurt her? Or because he didn't want to lose her again?

She hesitated, not wanting to stop her outpouring, yet fearful of alienating him. "Just one thing, Barney. In case you ever get the chance, even if you don't believe. There's a Mission of the Crucifist Brotherhood in downtown Detroit. And a wonderful brother there, an artist—Brother Luke. I'm sure if you went to see him he could make this much clearer than I have been able to. I'm just a novice, Barney, but I know what your despair is like; I've been through it myself. I swear to you, this is the answer you've been seeking."

She stopped then, at least her voice stopped, but he could see her trembling as if she clutched something with an effort that set every muscle vibrating. She searched his eyes to read there the effects of what she had said, but he looked away, shaken inwardly and, for the first time, frightened by her power.

2

When the board of directors called a meeting for the purpose of making a new settlement offer, Barney's lawyer, Ed Marshack, wanted him to come along. His first reaction was one of terror; he hadn't the energy to face a room full of hostile strangers. But Marshack convinced him that he needn't say anything, and his presence might help to influence some of the board members.

Riding with Marshack through the company grounds, Barney thought how he had driven here every day of the past three years without really seeing any of it. Now in his blurring vision it took on the intensity of a Van Gogh painting: the clean sweeping curves of the streets, the overgreen plush of lawns bordered with sculptured hedges and cooling ponds, the white fountain sprays looping high against the sky to frame glass- and metal-textured buildings. But a moment later it was more like a plywood-and-plastic architect's model of some future city—none of it real or permanent. Slight trees with shallow roots, and buildings behind green cellophane shrubbery.

Fortunes were made and lost here, people worked and created and made their impact on the economy and the world, but he saw now they were merely markers and toys in a gigantic game of Big Business and Careers and Monopoly, and a huge hand might come along at any time and sweep all the pieces back into the box.

In the conference room he thought he saw Karen's father (or was it someone who looked like him?) at the far end of the table near Vice-President Engstrom and a battery of other lawyers. At the start of the meeting, someone handed out a mimeographed report from Tracer Control describing the progress of the decontamination. Page four had a section on "The Estimated Effects on Non-Research Personnel." It was too blurred for him to read, but Ed Marshack said it was obvious they were still trying to minimize the effects.

"I thought we had reached the point," he said, raising his voice to address the meeting, "where National Motors was willing to engage in realistic discussion. This report talks about property damage and estimated physical effects *as of now*. But you know our basic difference lies in the fact that my clients haven't begun to realize the full effects of this accident, caused by the company's negligence."

"That's exactly the problem, Mr. Marshack," said an unfamiliar voice. (It wasn't his father-in-law, and he couldn't make out the blurred faces at that distance.) "There is just no way to assess future effects, and no basis for damages. And besides, there is no clear evidence—"

"Oh, the evidence is there," said Marshack, "and I'm sure when we subpoena the records of Tracer Control we'll be able to demonstrate the extent to which the radioactive dust was spread to Mr. Stark's home."

Barney found it difficult to concentrate on what they were saying. The light streaming in through the window hurt his eyes, and he had to shield them with his hands. They probably all imagined he was deep in thought. Ed Marshack was a fine young lawyer. Down-to-earth, bright, energetic. He seemed like a fighter, and Barney admired him for that. Barney looked up when someone presented the company's most recent offer for a settlement. They were doubling the amount—twenty thousand each for him and Karen, and if the baby lived there would be another twenty thousand. If it died, ten thousand. He laughed, and they all looked at him, but he covered his eyes again.

They also agreed to buy the house at fair market value, but Marshack pointed out that fifty or sixty thousand dollars was hardly a settlement, considering that they were suing for two hundred and fifty thousand.

"This cannot be thought of only in terms of today, gentlemen. After all, considering medical and hospital costs, and the fact that my clients are now uninsurable, your offer would hardly cover hospitalization and specialists' fees in the event that either or both of them should be stricken with leukemia or bone cancer. You're asking my clients to sign a waiver of all future claims in the one situation where the future looks bleak. Each day Mr. Stark shows increasing evidence of physical and . . . well, physical deterioration. Right now his eyesight is undergoing changes, and—as you know—the doctors say there will be cataracts and complete blindness in a few months. And what of the shortening of life expectancy?"

One of the other lawyers (still not Jason Bradley, if that was Bradley sitting at the other end) pointed out that it was not the practice of most juries to award damages for possible future effects that could not be proved to be a direct result of the accident.

Marshack fished around in his briefcase and came up with a sheaf of documents. "This has recently been released by the United States Nuclear Energy Commission. An unclassified document that I expect to introduce into evidence at the trial. It is the two-year summary report on 'Radioactive Fallout and Industrial Contamination' prepared for presentation at the congressional hearings on that subject before the Joint Committee on Nuclear Energy. Under the subheading 'Research Activity: Studies in Man' the following conclusions have been drawn from a study of data on approximately fifty thousand Japanese and a comparable number of unexposed people to determine the effects on life-shortening of direct exposure to radiation; in this case, of course, they're talking about detonation of weapons, but we can bring in experts to show that the results are comparable in the case of other forms of radiation exposure.

"The report points out that leukemia has been observed in the survivors at a two- to threefold greater frequency, on the average, than in unexposed Japanese, although the increase is statistically significant only at doses of fifty roentgens or more. And then there's the report on American radiologists who practiced before nineteen-forty-five, which shows that leukemia deaths are consistently higher among these men than among other medical specialists and general practitioners. And this one, which tells us that when mice are exposed to radiation in a prompt or acute manner the per cent reduction of life has been shown to be an accelerating function of the dose. The report goes on to say . . . here, let me read the exact language: 'In other words, as dose increases, the effect increases at a rate greater than would be calculated on a simple direct proportionality of linear hypothesis.' "

Barney hadn't the slightest idea what Marshack was talking about, but it was obvious that the young lawyer had done his homework. It was all impressive and depressing. It seemed that Marshack had assembled convincing evidence that whether or not they developed leukemia, their lives would be shortened by a measurable amount, and that was their basic argument—the heart of their case. It would all boil down to how much a day was worth, or a week or a month or a year. But weren't there different kinds of days— days you wasted, and days in which you accomplished a great deal? Could you say that they were of equal value? Was all time worth the same amount, no matter what you did with it? Or did you just average it out? Was the day in which Picasso completed a masterpiece worth the same as a day on which a laborer did nothing but rake dead leaves? Days when you were seventeen didn't seem worth as much as days in your old age just before dying. A man might give away the fortune he'd spent years accumulating to gain an extra few weeks of life at the end.

Marshack was citing evidence in the studies of the watch-dial painters who had built up what one report called "a burden of radium," and how the data on radium retention in man was now used as a standard to which other isotopes could be related, and through this it might be possible to project the effects on his clients.

Suddenly Barney became annoyed and said, "The hell with all this crap. I want the company to issue a statement to the newspapers to the effect that they accept full responsibility for what has happened."

Marshack tried to quiet him, but Barney shook him off. "I'm serious," he insisted. "Just because National Motors is a large corporation it has no right to escape its share of the blame. I want it to admit to the world that it is guilty. If it does, I'll accept the latest offer. If not—"

"Barney, sit down," Marshack choked out, "before you blow the whole thing."

Barney could hear the expressions of outrage from around the huge conference table, the shuffling of papers and feet, and finally one of the blurred faces spoke out.

"It was a mistake to bring my son-in-law here, Mr. Marshack. He's an artist and lets himself get carried away by his fantastic imagination."

"Imagination?" shouted Barney. "Why is it my imagination? Isn't someone besides me to blame for what happened? Who's responsible, my dear father-in-law? I'll tell you who. You are, and all the rest of you."

"Barney, please let it go."

"I can't let it go, Ed, because there's a question of guilt to be shared. *Measurable guilt!*" he boomed, to silence their protests. "And the burden of guilt is like the burden of radium you were talking about. It accumulates in your brain cells as self-hatred and leads to cancer of the mind and leukemia of the soul."

"My son-in-law has obviously become mentally ill."

"Why am I any more mentally ill than you and the rest of the people in this city who blame me for being contaminated by the radiation brought here by the company? Do you know why we are blamed? I'll tell you why. Because the presence of a victim makes people feel guilty, and that leads to self-hate, which is unbearable. So the guilty mind turns its hate upon the victim to keep from hating itself."

"But we didn't come here to discuss your theories of guilt," said his father-in-law. "We came here to discuss a settlement."

"Ah, yes, your specialty," said Barney, "but the issue is pertinent, because the burden of guilt must now be included in that settlement. You see, you've already started the cancer in my mind, but instead of hating myself for what I've done, I've had to turn it outward, so that right now I hate all of you."

There was a murmur of outrage and it spurred him on to speak more quickly, for fear they would stop him.

"Why does that shock you so? Why shouldn't I hate you? All I'm talking about is releasing natural destructive feelings, instead of turning them on myself. You'll all admit that the person who pretends to love everyone and hate no one is denying a natural feeling that goes back to Cain's hatred of Abel."

"Barney, this is doing your case no good."

"Exactly, my dear father-in-law. Your do-gooders start out loving the whole world and end up hating themselves—the strong ones, that is; the weak ones end up in mental hospitals. Our psychologists don't like to talk about the basic human need to hate. You know who have learned the truth? I've been thinking about this for a piece I'm working on— called 'The Victims.' I'll tell you who. The ones who have found the outlet that insures against cancerous guilt feelings, who can get it out of their systems—the haters. They will inherit the earth."

Someone stood up as if to face him down, and there was a sudden quiet in the room. It was Engstrom. "Young man," he said, "you're sick. This gospel of hate is what has torn our nation apart—a nation built on the principles of charity and love—"

"My God, have you forgotten?" shouted Barney. "How this nation was founded on hating the British and the red man? Or perhaps you've forgotten how close we were to the Russians and Chinese who helped us hate the Japanese and Germans during the Second World War. And how it was so good to get that hate out of our systems that we made our enemies our friends and started hating our allies. And after that, of course, we had the Cubans and the Viet-

cong and the North Vietnamese to hate. Charity and love
—shit!

"Haven't you ever wondered at this fantastic switching
of friend to enemy and enemy to friend, that strange ambi-
guity of love and hate? Well, don't you see? We don't hate
people or nations because they're evil. We call them evil,
make them evil, because we *need* someone to hate. That's
exactly what you were doing there when you called me
evil. You were giving yourself the right to hate *me*—the man
who was the victim of your company's carelessness. You
industrialists have a natural sense for those things, like the
politicians who know that masses of people aren't held together and moved by love or sex or power or fear, but by
a common enemy. 'Groups that hate together stay together.' It doesn't rhyme, but it's closer to the truth. So
you've brought it out in the open now. I am your natural
enemy."

He stood there, rocking back and forth, looking at the
audience that had grown silent in shock at the attack on
their leader, but he couldn't make out their faces. Then a
desperate feeling of weakness swept over him and he dropped
back into his chair and covered his eyes.

"I must apologize for my client," said Marshack finally.
"He's not feeling well."

"Don't apologize for me," said Barney, barely able to
get the whisper out of his throat. "To hell with them."

But by that time the meeting was over, and they filed
out quietly.

3

Karen had never seen Elgin City so beautiful as it was now, moving toward crisp weather and turning leaves. She loved to look out the windows in the early morning and watch the children pass on the way to school, fresh faced and neatly dressed, and then in the afternoon to see them on their way home, clutching papers to bring to their mothers. She could not recall being so happy before, and time and again she would catch herself up short when she remembered what Barney was going through. But the wonder of what was happening inside her displaced the momentary pangs of guilt.

One evening in mid-September, playing gin rummy with Myra, she was hardly concentrating on the game as various name combinations kept coming to mind. Just as she was trying out *Justin* and *Justine* with *Stark*, she felt a sharp movement and gave a screech of surprise.

"What is it?" shouted Myra.

"I just felt—oh! There again!"

Barney, who had been in the kitchen, came running in with a bread knife in his hand, as if expecting to confront an intruder. "What's wrong? Are you all right?"

"It moved. I was thinking of the names Justin and Justine, and it moved."

She saw disbelief in his eyes. "What moved?"

"The baby. I was going over names, and—"

"Well, damn it!" He threw the knife on the floor. "You scared me, screaming like that. You've felt movement before."

"Not like this. If you put your hand—"

"No thanks." He threw himself down on the couch, his arm across his face.

She was annoyed with herself that she had asked him to share it with her. She had to remember he didn't want to know about it, as if by denying its growing, squirming presence he could will it out of existence. "I keep forgetting you don't like me to mention . . . I mean, it's hard not to have it on my mind most of the time. . . ." She didn't want to cry, but tears began to form.

"I'm sorry," he said. "I have one of those lousy headaches. I didn't mean to upset you. Things have been happening in my work that I don't understand, and it confuses me. I think something is finished, and then I don't know. For nearly a week, now, I've just gone down and stared at it, and I just don't know."

"Why don't you let us see it?" asked Myra, obviously trying to get them off the subject of the baby.

"Not until it's finished," said Barney.

Karen tried to warn her with a glance, but Myra ignored it. "You just said you thought it might be finished."

"Maybe it is and maybe it's not. But you're not going to like it, either of you, and I'd rather not be influenced by your reaction until I've decided for myself."

"He's right," said Karen. "I don't think we should intrude. When he's ready—"

"I disagree. We wouldn't have to tell him what we think of it," Myra insisted. "Just if we thought it was finished. We could keep our judgments to ourselves."

He laughed and got up to pace back and forth. "Now that's absurd. Can you hide your feelings? My wife can't. It shows in her face, in the things she doesn't say. The problem is, she never really liked the things I've done. She doesn't care about my work."

"Now you're being unfair. I care very much, but you shut me out of your studio and out of your life. So what do you expect me to do? I haven't seen anything of yours except the Venus in a long time. I can't respond to something I'm not permitted to see."

"All right. Come on down now and look."

"Never mind. Not like this. No matter what I'd say, you'd get upset."

"I really want you to see it," he said, grabbing her wrist and pulling her toward the basement. "You too, Myra. Let's have a showing. Come on."

"Barney, not like this," Karen begged. "Not when you're angry with me and with God knows what. I want to see it when you feel it's finished and when you're in a good mood."

"There are no more good moods. And it'll never be finished. So come and tell me what you think of it, both of you. Now what's the matter?"

She felt it again and pressed her free hand to her abdomen. "Nothing, just a cramp," and seeing the darkening look on his face she controlled herself and moved with him toward the basement. "I'm all right—and I really do want to see your work."

He quickly opened the door to the basement. She knew he really wanted both of them to see it now. Why not? How could anyone create for long without anybody knowing what you were doing, what you were going through? Even though she knew he had long ago outgrown the amateurish need to show unfinished work to gain approval and direction—to be certain others liked it before going on—still, he used to like to talk about the stages of the work, explaining what he was doing, testing it against people and not really caring whether they understood or not, liked it or not, as long as he could see his work in terms of some reaction.

These days he kept it all inside, and that was frightening. Now she had to be very careful how she reacted. This was no time for honest critical opinion. He could get criticism later from others; what he needed now was encouragement.

"Not too close," he said, unlocking the studio door and turning on the lights. "This is a cluster of figures, a tableau, and you've got to get the whole before the parts."

She waited as he arranged two lamps, one on each side

of the sculpture, still covered with damp cloths, on the turntable in the center of the room. He was unusually excited. Though the air was cool and dry, he was perspiring. She wished it hadn't come up tonight. It would be difficult enough for her to hide a negative reaction; it would probably be impossible for Myra. One sign of dislike would send him into a depression, the last thing she wanted.

"Now remember, when I remove the cloths, it's the over-all impression first. What I mean is, you've got to get the whole before you respond to the parts or to the relationship of the figures to each other. As if you were seeing it from a distance at first. Now, even if you don't like the subject matter, I mean the people and what they're doing, try to keep an open mind and see the rhythms of the structure and the way I'm trying to define empty space as well as form—"

"Oh, Barney," laughed Myra, "stop stalling and let us see it."

Myra was never one to hide her feelings. Of course he was stalling, because he was afraid. She would have waited him out, but Myra had always been impatient with other people's weaknesses.

"All right. Here it is. I call it 'The Victims.'" As he pulled off the sheet, she tried to do as he asked, to see the whole, look for rhythm of line and mass, but there was no time for that. The torn and hating faces exploded at her. It was a riot scene of people attacking a terrified woman as they pulled her down from her pedestal. Those in the mob who could not get at her were attacking each other.

As she walked around it, other figures came into view. Smaller figures than Barney usually worked with—about one fourth life-size—a one-armed beggar battered by a man with a hammer; a child being trampled underfoot. But in the center of it all, the terrified woman being pulled down into the mob, her dress torn away by clutching hands, throwing her head back to scream as a clawlike hand digs into one of her breasts. Each person doing something violent and brutal to another.

The tableau reminded her of a pornographic photograph someone had shown her once, with several men and women entangled in a sexual pose, each doing something to someone involved with someone else, no one paying attention to the person using him or her as a sexual object, from above or below or behind, with hands and mouths and sexual organs, each merely a link in an orgiastic chain. She had mentioned her revulsion to Barney, but he had laughed at her disgust and said, well, at least they were people involved with each other, and it was better than being alienated. But when she had argued that each was using and being used without caring what was being done, and therefore each, thinking of his pleasure alone, was still alone, he had no answer for her.

Now he had carried out the form and movement of that photograph, replacing sex with an orgy of brutality. She tried not to show how it revolted her, but she felt the squeezing inside her, and found it difficult to breathe.

"Beautiful," said Myra, walking around it for the second time. "You've captured the essence of human degradation and violence. All the hatred focused on the woman in pain, who has tried to stand above the human condition, fearing to be involved in mankind. But they're not going to leave her alone. They're going to pull her into the mob and . . . and . . . destroy her."

Then Barney turned for Karen's reaction, but he must have seen how it sickened her. She couldn't control the disgust and horror that made her want to gag. There was no need to put it into words. He must see how she was fighting to control herself.

"You don't like it, do you?"

Why was he making her put it into words?

"The rhythm of the forms is . . . exciting. . . . So much going on—"

"You think I can't see in your face how it repels you? I'm not blind yet. What I can't understand is how, after all that's happened to us, the way our lives have been torn apart, the way the people of this town have treated us, you can still deny the inhumanity of man. Can't you accept the truth?"

"Truth?"

"Don't you think it's true?"

"It's not what I expected."

"You're both getting too excited," said Myra. "It's not good for either of you."

"What did you expect? A smooth-faced Madonna and Child near a fountain, with little cupids playing around them? Is that your truth? All you care about is what's in your belly. So what if it turns out defective? You'll give birth to your selfish desire in the guise of motherly love."

"I'm sorry, Barney. I didn't know there was so much hate in you. All this anger and sickness boiling to the surface."

"Well, thank you. At least I know what you think of my work. The product of a sick mind in a sick body. No, I'll tell you something. I don't accept your judgment. Your mind is so filled with stereotypes of life and love that you've forgotten the radioactive hell we've been consigned to—to say nothing of the killing and evil and hatred that makes a hell of the whole world. Your vision is clouded, and all you can see are diapers and bottles and formulas and all the pretty round faces in those nauseating baby magazines they've been sending you. I may be sick, but through my sickness I've learned about life. It's not the horn of goodness and plenty waiting for someone to come along and blow it out at us, as the do-gooders and bleeding hearts would have us believe. And I'll tell you something else. Myra is right. It's the best thing I've done. It's got more power and truth in it than most of the junk in the museums."

"I'm sorry, Barney." She turned away from his shouting, and started to leave. "I'm sorry."

"Go to hell! I don't want you to be sorry. And don't come down here any more. I'll destroy my work before I'll ever let you look at it again. Keep away from my studio."

She ran upstairs, sick because instead of helping him and bringing him closer she had driven a wedge between them. Now, when she needed him more than ever. Perhaps her

foolish memories of the happy faces and serene forms like
the Greek and Roman models he used to copy in art school
and the Venus he'd been working on were all wrong in
these days, but his violent swing in the other direction was
wrong too.

She needed someone to talk to. Not Myra. Someone who
would understand her side of things. Some time soon—
maybe next week—she would call her mother. Barney might
not approve, but she had other things to consider now.

She turned on the light and, looking into the mirror,
pressed her fluttering stomach. Quiet now, Baby, it will be
all right. Strange to be swelling like this, with growing flesh
and bone. Even if she had never written a story or painted
or sculptured, now she was creating. She tried to visualize
the shape inside her, recalling the repulsive fishlike forms
in the books on prenatal care that so upset him. She remembered a curled body with stringy arms and legs, belly
swollen, oversized head, like a blind sea creature at the
end of a line snaked upward and attached to her own in-
sides. The more human the form looked, the more frightening it was.

"You'll be normal," she whispered. She closed her eyes
and turned away from the mirror. "You'll be all right. If I
don't think of it, you'll be all right. Only please, dear
God, don't let this destroy him. Let him work out this
hatred and sickness before it's too late."

But it was terrifying to realize that the woman in the
tableau, the one being clawed and torn, was herself.

He was pleased that Myra liked it, pleased that she seemed
to understand. He had wanted her to share it with him.
Now he studied the tableau, turning it slowly to see all
the sides and dimensions—annoyed by the limitation of
being able to see only one angle at a time when time
was so short—squinting as the mass blurred, to bring the
lines and forms into focus. First, the woman screaming as
a hand coming out of the mass clawed at her breast (the

hand of the Mariner, whose eye was being gouged out by the beggar), and he realized something was missing. There was another hand brushing near her face, the free hand of the man with the hammer, and he knew what he had to do. He forgot Myra and began to work with the moist clay, rolling the pellets and kneading them in, until the hand was closer to the woman's mouth. While screaming, she would be about to bite him. Better to give and receive pain at the same time. It completed the cycle.

"Do you know why I call it 'The Victims'?" he asked suddenly.

Myra came closer to where he was working. "I think so. And what you're doing with his hand is right. Each of us is a victim at the same moment he is victimizing someone else. Each of us is an instrument for receiving and giving pain."

Why could she see it and not Karen? She was standing so close he smelled her cleanness, and for an odd moment he saw her as he remembered her four years ago. She hadn't changed all that much: exciting as when all his fantasies had lain in her embrace. He wanted to hold her, to put his hand under her blouse and feel her body as he had imagined it all these years.

"I'd better go up," she said.

"Not yet."

But she turned to go. "It's beautiful, Barney. Something conceived and created out of deep feeling. I wanted to see what you were working on, and now I think more than ever you should continue to seek the meaning and purpose of that suffering. I know if you joined us you would find the way."

"I've always been a loner," he said, moving closer to her.

"Exactly, and so was I. That's the point. Pain that is meaningless alone becomes purposeful when we join each other."

"Then why are you backing away from me?"

"That's not what I mean. You know that's not what I mean."

She went up and left him alone to work on the tableau further, but even as he began to reshape the face to bare the teeth in the act of biting the hand, he lost interest in what he was doing. All he could think about was the Myra of his college days, and how desperately he wanted her. Then he felt a pain in his eyes, and it seemed as if the lights had dimmed. He covered "The Victims" and dampened the cloth. There would be other days to work on it.

4

The following Saturday he had a good day. The fatigue that had gripped him for the previous week seemed to be gone, and he became restless to get out of the house, to drive off somewhere and be with people who didn't know what had happened to him. He could still see well enough to drive—a little blurred, but all right. He said nothing to either of them, and after dinner he took the new car and went off alone.

He hadn't planned it or thought about where he was going; he would just move around, visit some of the old bars in Detroit where he used to hang out when he was single. There were a few near the university, and a couple downtown where he used to be able to relax with a drink and find someone pleasant to talk to. Perhaps he would get himself a woman. Once he would have felt guilty for Karen's sake, even just thinking about it, but now there seemed no reason not to. Since the decontamination, there had been—for both of them—a physical aversion to the point where even touching became unpleasant. As if each feared the other might still be contaminated.

He started off the freeway at the Woodward Interchange to hit some of the bars near the university, but suddenly he realized there wasn't much point to that. He would be out of place there. He wasn't a college student any longer, and he wasn't interested in college girls. He swung south instead, and headed for downtown Detroit. There was Tony's Hideaway, and Lou Martin's and the Purple Palace. At least some of the bartenders and waiters might remember him from the old days. The thought of the women that frequented those places excited him; one of them might be able to get his mind off Myra for a while. Last week he had tried to work, but Myra kept coming to his mind in fantasies of love-making. Perhaps an evening with another woman—a stranger—would calm the bubbling under his flesh.

Tony Grisko recognized him when he came into the club. The crowded place brought back memories of good talk and interesting women during his college days. So often during the last few years he had wondered about the old places, if his friends were still there, the girls he used to know. But he never dropped in. Even when he believed the marriage was breaking up he had always felt it would be wrong. He knew how loathsome it would be to her if she ever learned he had been with another woman. Now they felt nothing for each other—they were dependent, bound by what had happened to them, but that was all—and he was free to find affection elsewhere. Simple sensuality would be good for him, uncomplicated sex with a stranger. The outward forms and body contact—nothing more.

He sat down at the bar gingerly, away from a noisy group, as if unsure how his body would hold up under the strain. He avoided the spot Tony offered because of the bright light that hurt his eyes, and he took a seat at the dark end. The red and green lights, and the mirror-reflected bottles behind the bar had rainbows surrounding, crossing, intersecting in a fuzzy haze (rainbows seen only by him from the pressure in his eyes that forecast oncoming clouds), so pretty the way they floated and circled every spot of light—sculpture with space and light. Maybe he would try to recapture these lights and rainbows and call it "Tony's Hideaway: Construction Number One."

"What'll it be, Barney?"

When he squinted and made out the familiar shapes of the schooner on the yellow label it comforted him to be able to identify it in the blur. "Cutty and water."

Tony served him, and he explored the shape of the glass with his fingertips, feeling the slippery roundness and the wet trace on the polished mahogany bar. He played that game often these days, trying to find his way by touch and recognizing things only by shape and texture.

He sipped, holding the liquor in his burning mouth before swallowing. He took another. And then a third. It had been a long time since he'd dared to drink so much. Soon he became aware of a woman alone at the table to his left against the wall. If he lowered his head and glanced just over his left shoulder, he could see her. She wasn't looking at him, so he squinted to bring her into focus. Attractive: thin, parchment pale with black hair, lipstick that shocked against the dead-white skin. Starkly attractive, with a jaded B-girl quality, she had a black lace stole across her white shoulders. She turned to look at him, and he smiled and nodded and motioned to the bottles behind the bar, "Tony, give the lady another of whatever she's having."

Tony shook his head and frowned. "Ixnay," he whispered, "this lush ain't for you. Don't waste your time and money."

Barney nodded and smiled. Tony was basing his judgment on the old days, not realizing that a man who had been away, and who was as lonely and lost as he was, couldn't be choosy.

"Go ahead," he said, and Tony shrugged and poured something from a bottle on the ledge and took it around to her table. On the way back he said, "She wants you to come over and drink with her. But don't say I didn't warn you. This one can guzzle it all night. It'll cost you a bundle."

Barney picked up his drink and made his way toward her through the press of bodies. Closer, he could see she had not long ago been beautiful. She was sexy in a lacy, smooth-skinned way that appealed to him, and that might be enough to get his mind off Myra. Her black hair against the pale skin reminded him with a shock of an older Karen (lines in her neck and around her eyes and mouth showing where flesh had yielded to time), but he found her attractive, and the idea amused him.

"Not often these days a man sends a drink to a lady's table," she said. "Very lovely gesture. Don't see many lovely gestures these days." She touched her hand to her hair, and then with clawlike fingernails took out a cigarette from her pack and leaned forward for him to light it. She steadied his hand in hers while she drew the light to the cigarette and said, "Such beautiful long fingers. Do you play the piano?"

"I'm a sculptor."

"An artist! You don't look like one. One expects to see artists with shaggy beards and dirty clothes and sandals and smelling like they never had a bath. Not dressed so nicely in a dark suit and tie." And then she put her fingers close to his face. "And your face looks so smooth. Not like those hippies and beatniks, you know, taking drugs and having free love and all that kind of thing." She went on about how hippies and subversive college students who demonstrated should be thrown out of the country because they were undermining democracy and free enterprise.

"Let's go someplace," he said.

"So early? You just got here." She looked around, regally, and took the room in one sweep of her arm. "Night's young. People haven't started leaving."

"But I want to leave," he said, stroking her arm.

"Imp-pestuous young man. So headstrong. Just come in and sweep a woman off her—feet. I like that. I haven't been swept off my feet in a long time. Just one more, for the road."

She had another double Scotch, teasing with her eyes and pressing her knee against his to allay his doubts, and then finally permitted him to slip her black lace stole across her shoulders. He felt how bony her back was, shoulder blades sharp and angular. And when she stood up, he noticed regretfully that she was very thin.

"Okay, you impulsive Romeo," she giggled. "Lead on, Macduff."

At the doorway she stumbled, and as he grabbed her quickly by the waist, the boniness of her ribs, distinct under the slipping silkiness of her dress, repelled him. He thought for a moment of ditching her somewhere, but he wasn't sure he really wanted to. He used to be attracted to slender women, and the sharp contrast to Karen's swelling body made her even more interesting. It would be dark, and quick, and her sexuality would compensate for her thinness. As long as he didn't think about her boniness, which kept reminding him of Giacometti's elongated figures, all would go well.

But it was impossible not to think about it, because every place he touched he found elbows, knees, ribs, and when she nestled against him, his hands on her back felt the spinal-column bones protruding to be counted like the beads of a giant rosary.

Her place was a short walk away in a rundown apartment house. As they went toward the elevator he saw their reflection in a mirror, and he looked away quickly, thinking she had been young and beautiful once and it was the blurred image of her past he would make love to.

Upstairs, her room was neat (done in what he called "Mail-Order Modern") and the odor of fresh cut flowers surprised and pleased him. On the couch, among the throw pillows, lay half a dozen expensive-looking dolls. He could see the bedroom through the open door, and the pink chenille bedspread was covered with stuffed dogs, cats, tigers, and teddy bears.

"Do you have children?" he asked.

"Don't be silly," she giggled. "Those are mine."

He thought again of leaving, but she tickled him under

the chin and said, "Make yourself a drink," pointing to a bottle and some glasses on the side table, "I'll change into something comfortable."

The place, her every word (even down to the "something comfortable"), chipped away at his anticipation with the sense of living through a burlesque skit. Her clothing, the black lace that showed occasionally from under her dress, gave him the feeling of having lived this moment before, and of knowing what would come next. (Was he damned to retrace his steps forever—to pass through every experience with the feeling of *déjà vu* that blurred reality with a thick coating of dream?) He knew she would come out in a filmy black negligee, and she would stretch out on the pink chenille spread, among her stuffed toys, and invite him with open arms. But as he started to make love to her, something would happen. But he couldn't remember what it would be. He warned himself to cut it out or there would be nothing left of the evening. He poured himself another drink to wait with, bothered by the vague feeling that he had forgotten something, and a few minutes later she came out in a black negligee.

She turned most of the lights out, and although he usually preferred the light, he was grateful because the glare was hurting his eyes.

"You're so different," she cooed as he nuzzled her neck. "You know how to treat a lady."

He remembered the old buddy who had told him once when he had gone along for the first time to pick up a girl, "Treat a lady like a whore and a whore like a lady." The lesson had stood him in good stead in his youth, he had to admit, more with ladies than with whores.

But kissing her, he discovered, was unpleasant. Her lips were thin and papery, and her skin was clammy. He contented himself with stroking her cheek and neck. She helped him remove her negligee, and as he unhooked her brassière and stroked her body, his hands discovered that her skin was not as smooth as her face and throat had led him to expect. She was covered with sores. He pulled his hands away quickly, and as she lay there motionless, eyes closed, lips parted with waiting, he had the terrifying thought that she was dead.

He had no idea what the sores were, but they were all over her back, down to her hips, and on her thighs, and suddenly he felt weak again, and nauseated. He had to get out of there as quickly as possible.

He moved away from her, and when she looked up to see what was wrong, he pointed to the bathroom. Once inside, he turned the water on full and flushed the toilet to mask the sound of his gagging. When he came out, he went directly to where his clothes were hung over the chair.

"What's the matter?" she demanded as she saw him getting dressed.

"Sorry," he said, "but I think you'd better see a doctor about your skin."

She sat up and glared at him. "There's nothing wrong with me. I had a little skin trouble a few months ago. It's all healed up. Just a vitamin deficiency. What the hell do you think it is?"

"I don't know, but I still think you ought to see a doctor."

"You think I've got some disease?"

He said nothing but finished dressing.

"You think I go around infecting people? You think I'm dirty? Get out of here, you bastard. Get out!"

"I didn't mean to hurt your feelings," he insisted. Pulling out his wallet, he took two twenty-dollar bills and laid them on the table near the kewpie doll. "This is for your time."

She started after him, in a rage, and clawed at him with her nails. He managed to pull away in time, but he knew that if those claws had caught his face, he would have been badly hurt. He pulled the door closed behind him and walked quickly down the hall, his heart pounding and his temples pulsing. She pulled the door open, standing there naked, and screamed after him, "Don't come back to Tony's. I've got friends who'll mash your ugly face for you. Don't you forget it, you cheap bastard."

He bypassed the elevator and stumbled down four flights

of steps. His head was bursting, and the fluorescent lights were painful to his eyes. He half walked, half ran through the nearly deserted streets that merged like spokes into the hub of the park in Cadillac Square. He was sick to his stomach, and the thought kept coming: Everyone infects . . . everyone corrupts . . . everyone contaminates. . . .

He walked past scraggly lit-up trees and clipped bushes and paths lined with benches, ignoring the blurring and unblurring colored lights playing on the fountain, down through the entrance to the triple-level underground garage over which the phony park had been built.

That was when he heard it. A blurred whisper in the darkness of the third level. He turned, but there was no one, and then, as he fumbled with his car keys to open the locked door, he heard it again, this time a resonant echo in the cavernous chamber.

Find the Church!

Myra's voice, of course. And he sat at the steering wheel, trying to squeeze out the throbbing by pressing his fists into both sides of his head. Again and again. *Find the Church! . . . Find the Church! . . . Find the Church! . . .*

It finally subsided, and he drove out quickly up one ramp and then the second and the third, and roared up the street ramp and crosstown to the highway and then all the way home with the radio turned to screaming music so that if the voice came again he wouldn't hear it.

5

Several days later, Karen went with her mother to an evening Red Cross class in Detroit, for prospective parents. Dr. Leroy had suggested it. She had tried to get Barney to sign up with her, but he had refused. What could he say to her now that she had made up with her parents? She had become so happy and outgoing in these past weeks it was hard to believe she was the same person. It irritated him that she really believed she was going to have the baby and live a normal life, but he had stopped arguing about it. Let her enjoy her illusions.

He had an early dinner with Myra, and afterward they sat and looked at each other in the living room. Somehow her sureness, her religious aloofness, angered him now. He resented her self-satisfied air of having found all the answers. He wanted to strip this certainty from her and see her as vulnerable as he was.

"I have to go out this evening," she said, "but I hate to leave you alone."

"I'm alone even when there are people around me. Go ahead. I'm all right."

"I was hoping you'd come with me. There's someone I've wanted you to meet."

"You know I don't like to meet new people."

"This isn't 'people.' Ever since I saw your sculpture I knew you should meet Brother Luke. You two would have so much in common. He's a painter, and there are things in your work so close to him I know it would be good for you to meet him."

"What kind of painting?"

"It's difficult to describe his work. But the feeling I got from seeing your tableau was like the feeling I had when I saw his figures of tormented souls in his 'Cycle of Suffering.' Two of his paintings are in the Detroit Artists' Co-operative Show. Why don't you come with me to the gallery and see his work? Then, if you want to meet him, we can go to the Mission; if not, I'll go on alone. But I know it would be good for you."

He hadn't expected to go with her, but his curiosity was aroused. "You seem very sure of what is good for people and what isn't."

"I've found some of the answers," she said.

"You thought you knew the answers four years ago."

She looked at him as if he'd slapped her face.

"I didn't mean that," he said.

"I think you did."

"All right. I'm not very patient these days with people who think they know the answers and explain what has happened to Karen and me with oversimplified religious concepts. It's like seeing an overinflated balloon figure in a Thanksgiving parade. I itch to puncture it and see what it has inside besides hot air."

She laughed, and it irritated him that nothing he said could get a rise out of her. She was so damned sure of herself, so much in control that she could ignore his nastiness. So different from Karen, who had always been oversensitive to the slightest anger or sarcasm in his voice. Myra could adjust the volume or filter out the hostility. He longed to hit her, but she would probably only smile and take his hand.

"Come on with me and see Brother Luke's work."

"All right," he said. "I'll go."

At the gallery, he stood before two paintings signed "Luke P." The first, a shattered sunset whose orange reds split off into planes of landscape below, as if seen through several layers of water and air, the sun itself stripped and pasted back together with jagged edges as if by a child, denied a whole and coherent vision of nature. He knew what the artist meant, and Myra must have seen that he was trying to do something like it with "The Victims."

The other was a self-portrait.

"Brother Luke as he saw himself before he joined us."

"Do you know how he sees himself now?"

She pressed her lips together for a moment to control herself. "What I meant was, he no longer paints himself like that. His more recent work shows change."

"Do you attribute that to the Brotherhood?"

"Yes."

Nevertheless, the portrait was of a man who would have easily fitted into his tableau. The same technique of stripped surfaces and shattered planes when applied to the human face was terrifying. The mouth was closed, but even so, split in three places with lines that should have met, it gave the effect of a man screaming with his mouth closed. The same with the eyes and a lifeless hand—all screaming.

"Yes, I'd like to meet him," he said.

She drove. The Mission was not far from the gallery, in one of the Detroit neighborhoods where nineteenth-century mansions had become slum boardinghouses, crowding dozens of families together. Boarded-up windows reminded him there had been a riot here not long ago. All Barney could think of as they got out of the car in front of one of these buildings and saw the garbage and refuse in the streets, and the people on the porches and leaning out of windows on this too warm and muggy September evening, was how poor they were; and somehow he was partly to blame. He knew they hated him for his good clothes and his new car, and he could understand that they had to hate him to keep from hating themselves. It was necessary for them to hate. He was just learning that lesson for himself. He was only a beginner at hating, and it was still difficult, but he had already learned that it eased the pain, the way when a person smashes his finger it helps to curse the hammer and throw it to the ground. A child knows it when he stubs his toe and kicks the chair or screams at the ground that has scraped his knee. Why add to the burden of guilt and self-reproach by blaming ourselves when we can curse the sky? And there flashed into his memory words his father always quoted in Polish from Job when things went wrong: *. . . I abhor myself, and repent in dust and ashes.*

But his father was wrong. The answer was not to abhor himself, but to turn it outward. Find someone to hate. Did it matter if God or man brought down this affliction that cursed his flesh? One still had to find a way to live.

The Mission was in an old mansion, red brick scored and crumbling, defaced with chalked slogans and signs in white and red paint saying, JESUS SAVES, and someone's answer, AT 5% INTEREST. The heavy oak doors had been scarred with a thousand knife cuts and holes that might have been made by a sniper or the National Guard. Someone had carved the words: GOD HURTS! and he felt a kinship with the people who faced all their lives an anguish he had just discovered.

She reminded him that he'd better close the windows and lock the car. She rang the bell, and a few seconds later someone opened the door. It was a huge man in shirt sleeves, his skin covered with white scaly scabs.

"Sister Myra, come in, come in. Welcome to the Mission, Mr. Stark."

He was startled to be addressed by name and hung back as the man held the door wide for them.

"Please come in," he insisted in a soft, thick voice. "We've heard so much about you from Sister Myra. We've been looking forward to meeting you."

"I should have prepared him," she said, "but I was afraid if I told him too much he wouldn't come. Barney, this is Brother Luke."

Brother Luke held out his scabby hand. He saw Barney hesitate and smiled, but insistently waited for him to take it. Myra waited too, and Barney choked back the same fear he knew his neighbors must have felt when he and Karen passed close to them, the fear his father-in-law had felt that evening at taking his hand, and forced himself to grip Brother Luke's hand firmly.

"Leprosy isn't really very contagious," he said, sharing Barney's thoughts. He ushered them into a room whose sole furnishing was a huge crucifix, not hung but on the floor, leaning against the wall, with a figure of Christ, side pierced, blood dripping from the crown of thorns and from the spikes in his palms.

"That's Brother Abraham's work," Myra exclaimed. "I didn't know he was here in Detroit."

"He came in last week. That's his latest. Just finished it two days ago."

He had seen Christ with many expressions—in serene sleep, looking up in prayer, looking down to bless, in silent suffering—but never had he seen one like this: eyes rolling upward, hands clenched upon the spikes, the whole body contorted in agony. It was painful to look at, even through his blurred vision.

"Touch it," said Brother Luke.

For a moment he thought Brother Luke was going to guide his hand to the lifelike body, and he drew back. Instead, Brother Luke reached out to demonstrate. The figure quivered away from the hand and began to writhe as if it were alive. Myra let out a scream.

"It's a new idea of his. Made of a synthetic rubber that gives it a gelatinous quality even though it looks quite firm. It's built up over armatures of coils that vibrate. Touch it and you'll see."

His interest as a sculptor overcame his revulsion. He touched the body and felt how perfect the material was for the subject. The clamminess gave a sense of dead flesh, while the movement gave the effect of torment, as if the body were trying to pull itself free of the spikes. It was horrible and it was beautiful.

At that moment someone passed by and, seeing them, came in. He was a small spare man, also in shirt sleeves, with a very drawn face and a startling double chin that seemed about to choke him and made him tilt his head to one side. Except for that, the face was obviously the model for the figure on the cross.

"I see you're examining my molded-rubber sculpture. I can't tell you how pleased I am to meet another sculptor." He took his hand out of his pocket and held out a thin stump of a wrist where a hand should have been. Barney forced himself to grasp the butt of his wrist and noted, when Brother Abraham pressed the other one over it, that both hands were missing. Just below his right forearm was a number tattooed in blue. "We have several painters here, but no other sculptor. I would be so pleased if you would look at some of my other, more conventional pieces, when you get the chance. As you can see, I believe in having science and technology serve art. I told Sister Myra, when she was in Los Angeles, I first began to think of you for our Brotherhood when I read about what had happened and that you were a sculptor. I had no idea then that she knew you. At any rate, Sister Myra has been keeping Brother Luke informed about what you're going through, and I'm sure I speak for the rest when I tell you we're all anxious to share it with you. I know your suffering will make a contribution to our small family."

Barney started to protest, but Brother Abraham lifted the smooth stump and silenced him. "I see I'm premature. Out of eagerness, I assure you. But I'll leave you now in better hands than these." He started away and then turned back. "One of these days I should really like to talk shop with you. About the kind of work you're doing. Sister Myra was describing your tableau—'The Victims'?—to Brother Luke. I should like so much to see it. We have much in common, I think."

Only after he left, with a wave of his bony stump, did Barney look back and notice that there was a number tattooed in blue on Christ's forearm.

"Yes," said Brother Luke, once again guessing his thoughts. "Brother Abraham was a sculptor in Germany during the Nazi holocaust. In the concentration camp one of the officers had him do a bust, promising that if he liked it he would spare his life. He did, but then he decided that no Jew had a right to such talent, so he crucified him. The little sculptor refused to die, and the officer decided to allow him to live, and had him cut down by chopping off his hands. As you see, Brother Abraham has found a way with new materials and new themes. He straps his cutting and modeling tools to his forearms."

"Every month, Brother Abraham sends photographs of his work to the Nazi officer," said Myra. "He's now an assistant principal in a school in a suburb of Hamburg, and he is terrified that Brother Abraham will denounce him."

"Why doesn't he?"

Brother Luke and Myra both smiled. "If I know Brother Abraham," said Brother Luke, "he will never do any such thing. As for why, I think that's something you'll have to discover for yourself." He put his arm on Barney's shoulder. "You have a lot to think about, my friend."

"It makes me feel rather stupid," said Barney, "to find out about all of you, right here in the middle of Detroit. You knew about me, and I never even suspected the existence of this place."

"We don't advertise," said Brother Luke. "It takes a particular combination of personality and historical events to bring people into the Brotherhood. No one joins us unless he needs us as much as we need him. From what we've heard, you are right for us. The question is, are we right for you?"

As they passed a room with a closed door, Barney heard a piano. Someone was going over the same haunting, discordant bars, so unmelodic it made his flesh tingle.

"That is Brother Gregory working on his new concerto. He was in the space program before he came to us; composing was his hobby. He was on the capsule that passed unexpectedly through a radiation belt on the way back to earth. You and he will have much in common. You will meet him another time, when he is not working."

They followed Brother Luke into the library, and on the walls Barney saw other paintings in the same style as those at the gallery; commonplace objects and simple figures transformed by the tension of broken lines and shattered planes into works of great power. Brother Luke offered him a glass of sherry, but after he accepted it, he saw that they were going to drink only water.

Brother Luke insisted, "Please don't feel you have to do as we do, unless you decide to become one of us. I have nothing against other people drinking spirits or eating flesh. One of our basic tenets is never to impose our beliefs on others. I am told it is very good sherry. Please drink."

They sat and talked for more than an hour, about Brother Luke's painting, and how difficult it was for him to sustain long periods of work because of the fatigue. And Barney felt very close to him. He knew what it was like when the weakness closed in.

"For some," Brother Luke was saying, "pain is the key to creative achievement. Who can deny the creative power of suffering? Think of the great names—Milton, Beethoven,

Van Gogh, and hundreds of others. Creating out of pain is not the end, however, but the entrance to the Crucifist Brotherhood. Just as an infant born into its own and its mother's pain is a beginning, an entrance into the world, so it may be for the man bearing pain—laboring in the right direction, as a woman labors in childbirth. We can focus our suffering with the mind, use it as a pathway to vision, and through that to spiritual oneness with the universe. Timeless . . . matterless . . ."

"What I don't understand," said Barney, "is why I need the Brotherhood for that. I've always worked at my sculpture alone. What's the point of joining a group?"

"One reason," said Myra, "is that through the Brotherhood you can learn not only to focus the energy of your pain, but also to narcotize it without drugs during those periods when you are not creating. It can be controlled with your mind. Yogas have long known the secret of that, but we have found the pathway to vision and contact with the inner mind—the kind of thing young people are trying pathetically to achieve with mind-expanding drugs, but much greater and much more meaningful."

"There is another reason," said Brother Luke. "We have discovered that the group provides a ground—a base of common experience—against which the creative or humanitarian mind can clarify the meaning of his experience. At different times in history, in many places, there have sprung up Crucifist Brotherhoods: among the untouchables of India; among the Christian martyrs; in the Nazi concentration camp, where Brother Abraham found meaning for his life with others. We like to think of the Brotherhood as a lifeline of the creative spirit thrown to those drowning in despair. Help—not hereafter, but now—not through supernatural intervention, but through the combined mental energies of certain selected individuals."

"But why selected individuals? Why not all people in pain and despair?"

"Ah, the humanitarian in you asks the same questions I did at first. The answer is simply that it requires a certain

kind of mind to accept our faith. If we reached out to all
the suffering souls on earth, we would be inundated. Besides, there are those who *want* to suffer, people who find
pain a means to the end of wallowing in self-pity. We
use pain for an end too, but for a spiritual break-through to
something deeper, higher, more significant than one man
can achieve alone."

He sighed and shook his head. "Who can label it? Some
touch the hem of it with drugs or psychotic vision; mystics
have sought it through fasting, meditation, self-punishment.
Why else do you think St. Simeon Stylites sat on that
pillar all those years? But self-inflicted pain is not our way.
We are not a gathering of masochists. There is too much
self-interest in that, which prevents the break-through to the
Other. The pain we share is used for a way out of meaningless suffering to an understanding of pain as a special kind
of grace.

"You see, Mr. Stark," he said, rising to indicate that the
meeting was coming to an end, "anyone can stand suffering
that has a purpose: a woman having a baby; a man fighting
for something he believes in, being imprisoned, starved,
beaten for a cause. Pain has many guises, but if you learn
to see the meaning and purpose in it, you will reach levels
where anything is possible."

On the way out, they passed a Negro woman, startling in
her tallness. She moved across their path slowly, almost glid-
ing, and her eyes, half closed, showed only slits of white.

"That's Sister Vivian X," whispered Myra. "She came to
us after the riots of 'sixty-seven."

"She looks as if she's in a trance."

Brother Luke smiled and shook his head. "She's working.
Sister Vivian X used to be a poet. Now, ever since the
fires, she has been a creator of daydreams. She puts nothing
down on paper, commits nothing to destructible materials.
Hers is an unshared art, perfected for herself in her own
mind. One might say hers is the purest art form of all."

"But how do you know she's doing anything? Perhaps
there's nothing there at all."

Brother Luke shrugged. "Couldn't the same be said for many of today's artists whose work you think you can see and hear? And does it matter? Our concern is not with what materials, forms, degrees of communication are involved. She is a creative person who has suffered. She shares her pain with us, not her product. That is enough for us."

Suddenly, Brother Luke held out his hand, and this time Barney took it without hesitation and thought he saw the trace of a smile on the leper's face.

All the way home, he couldn't get that smile out of his mind. He suspected Brother Luke was very sure he had made another convert. He wondered if he had been a revival preacher before his affliction had made him seek out the Brotherhood. Myra had been awed through most of Brother Luke's conversation. He could understand why. And although he had come prepared to mock them, he had to admit it was tempting to give up isolation and solitary suffering for a cause such as this—the ultimate cause of fraternity in suffering that Myra, after all she had been through, had discovered for herself. It was a very strong feeling.

Karen was home when they returned.

"Practiced bathing the baby," she said, "with a rubber doll. There were quite a few husbands there tonight. This is for practice." She pulled a large rubber doll out of her shopping bag. "They let us take them home. Doesn't it look like a real baby? What they do with rubber these days. Touch it. It feels like real skin. You have no idea how frightening it is to bathe a doll when you're pretending it's a real baby. Mother told me she dropped Myra in the bath once when she was a baby. Now she says maybe that's what made you so unmanageable."

She chatted on for a while, not once asking where he and Myra had been, and not giving either of them a chance to tell her. It occurred to him that she knew something was going on between them, but she didn't want to interfere, and she didn't want to know about it. And then he saw that she was holding the rubber doll very tightly, as if she were afraid someone was going to take it away from her. She had it tipped backward, and only one of the eyes was closed. The other one stared.

6

He was in the garage, hunting through lengths of pipe to make an armature for the new figure he was planning, when a car pulled into the driveway. Two men got out, and thinking it was Tracer Control he raised the garage door. But as they came closer, he saw one of them had a camera.

"Hi. You're Mr. Stark, aren't you?" said the one without the camera. "I'm Ty Westlake—with *Newslife*—and this is Ben Potter. We've been sent over to do a story on you folks, a four-page spread with color pictures."

He was stunned for a moment, but then he glared at them. "No thanks. I'm not interested."

"Normally, our editor would have written and arranged things in advance, but I've just come from the hospital. Things are breaking fast, and our people will be getting in touch with you some time today. We've been sent over to get some pictures and some of the details. We'll top any other offer for an exclusive."

"What do you mean, 'breaking fast'?"

"Didn't you know? Max Prager died this morning. We got the word that you were still around."

The news hit him hard. He recalled Max's face, eyes looking away in frustration and sadness. What right did he have to let a man die that way? What right did he have to withhold forgiveness?

Suddenly, he realized the man with the camera was taking pictures. "What are you doing? I don't want any story."

"Well now, Mr. Stark. It's up to us to decide that. The public has a right to all the facts concerning this accident. My editor feels there's a human-interest story behind the cold facts of the Nuclear Energy Commission's releases. We'd like your angle on it. What it felt like to be contaminated. How your wife reacted. What it's done to your life. How the neighbors behaved when they discovered you'd spread the dust all over the—"

"Get out of here."

"What?"

"I said get out of here before I let you have it with this piece of lead pipe. And if you don't tell your partner to stop taking pictures, I'll smash his camera."

"You don't understand, Mr. Stark. This is *Newslife*. There's a lot of money involved."

"You vultures. As long as you can open wounds and draw blood to raise your circulation, you don't give a damn what it does to people."

"But the world has a right to know the truth—"

"The world has a right to go to hell. What do you know about truth? Take your truth and your money and your cameras and get the hell out of here. There isn't going to be a story."

"That's what you think," said the man, dropping his cordial tone as he backed away from Barney's menacing weapon. "I've spoken to some of your neighbors. We've got enough to do a story, and we don't need your permission, either. You're news, and you can't stop the public from knowing. We just wanted to give you a chance to tell your side of—"

Barney swung the pipe at the photographer, trying to knock the camera out of his hand, but he missed and hit the side window of the car. It cracked. Both men got in the other side of the car as Barney swung again, making a dent in the door. The car gunned in reverse, and when he was out in the street, the reporter rolled down his window and shouted, "You crazy bastard, I'll get the police after you. You have no right—"

Barney flung the pipe. It bounced off the hood, and the men sped away.

He felt elated. Letting go like that without caring about the consequences was good for him. He felt lightheaded and springy, and for the first time in a long time he found himself whistling.

She watched through the window, and seeing him like that frightened her. It wasn't that she expected him to be a model husband or a good citizen, but why did he have to antagonize everyone? He spewed hatred everywhere. In a way, perhaps, it was better than having him take it out on her (he was gentler with her now, even though he still resisted the idea of the baby), but there were times when the look in his eyes terrified her, when she saw in them that he wanted her and the baby dead. He wanted to be cut off from the world completely. He had intentionally embarked on a campaign to insult everyone, because he wanted to be left alone.

But she couldn't let him isolate her. Not now. When you have a family you need friends, relatives, the neighborhood. She wanted people to forget the nightmare and begin to think of them as normal human beings again. There was the future to consider.

He was spending more and more time down in the studio, living in the dark like some blind creature in a cave. What was he creating now? It was strange to know he was still working with his hands although he was in pain. Once she had thought he had the most beautiful hands for a man, thin, sensitive, loving hands, with long fingers to bring to life the yielding clay. Now they were strained and tired-looking, with cords tight beneath his wrists and the fingers and backs still peeling from the burns.

What frightened her most was the shotgun. She could appreciate how he felt, surrounded by hostile neighbors. It was hard for him to be forced to live where people wanted him out (no question that they would be better off living where people didn't know about the accident), but, as the lawyer said, they would have a better chance to recover damages if they were still in Elgin City when the case came to trial.

Suddenly, she felt a cramp in her leg, knotted up, pulling as if the muscle wanted to tear itself out of her body. She screamed. Myra was out at the Mission. She screamed again, unable to stand or sit, falling onto the bed and trying to grab it with both hands.

She heard him coming, heard him crash against the coffee table in the living room. Then she saw him standing there in the doorway with the shotgun in his hand.

"No, Barney! No! It's my leg! Cramps! Oh, do something."

He put the shotgun down and sat beside her on the bed, furious that she had frightened him with her screams. But he didn't seem angry at her as much as at himself for panicking. Running his hand along her leg, he pressed the swelling muscle of her calf. "All right, take it easy now and try to relax."

"It hurts."

He worked the calf muscle with both hands, rubbing, stretching, kneading the flesh until it went soft under his strong fingers.

"I'm afraid to move it. God, I thought it would never stop. It kept pulling and pulling. . . ."

"It'll be all right. Relax."

"I know it's nothing to worry about. The book mentions leg cramps. But I didn't think it would be so unbearable."

"How is it?"

"Okay, I guess. But I'm afraid if I move it'll start again."

"Get off the bed. Walk around."

She got up, gingerly at first, but then walked about, re-lieved that the muscle showed no signs of contracting again. "What's that for?" she asked, pointing to the shotgun.

"I thought those guys came back. I just grabbed it and came."

He picked it up and held it under his arm, the barrel pointing downward.

"You wouldn't ever use it, would you?"

"Why not?"

"You might shoot someone by mistake."

"I can see well enough yet. When I can't make out details, I'll let you or Myra guide me."

"No."

"Oh, yes. As long as there are people in this lousy town who have to take out their frustrations on us with stones through the window, or trying to burn the house, I'm going to have something on my side. And I think you'll guide me when the time comes, because you don't want to take the chance of losing the baby."

But after that, she told herself, no matter how bad it was when she had a cramp in her leg, she would be careful not to scream. She would control herself and call him, and he would come up to work out the knotted muscles and soothe her fears. It occurred to her that she was no longer repelled by his touch. In fact, she was happy to have him hold her.

October

1

As a sculptor, he was fascinated by the changes taking place in her body—the stretch marks in the skin, the dark line down the center of her swelling abdomen, her backward leaning to overcome the earth-pulling pressure—and he went

on with his new Venus, a pregnant one. At first he concentrated on the problems of masses—bulging, expanding,
bursting (the occasional distortions of a leg kicking from
within against encasing flesh)—but never could he please
himself with the result. Just as he had moved away from
the violent forms (not only because he had grown sick and
tired of them, but also because they seemed false once he
had given them substance), so he found himself obsessed
by the idea of sculpting embryos in various stages, coiled
intrauterine shapes—part human, part fish—expressing, in
all their ugliness, the whole of evolution. He was grateful
that he could still see well enough when he worked up close.

In place of hatred, he thought in terms of the waiting
unaliveness of the floating fetus, curled up, waiting to burst
into shoulders and thighs and arms and legs, to be squeezed
into the world like a lump of wet clay, slippery between his
squeezing fingers. He was curious and awed by the forms he
was making.

He became so absorbed in these that when she called he
went unwillingly, and sometimes he ignored her call if he
knew Myra was around to help her. The preparations for
the baby bothered him. Baby booties, receiving blankets,
diapers, bassinets and bathinettes (he confused these two
constantly), crib, scale, and glass jars filled with hundreds
of cotton balls, all the paraphernalia connected with the
child he knew was never going to live in that room. He
resented the way she and Myra looked at each other from
time to time, as if to say, what does a man know about
these things?

Of course, he could understand why she insisted on going
ahead as if everything were normal. She had a purpose now.
Having a child would be a culmination, a creation to
give meaning to her existence, something like the satisfaction and fulfillment he was seeking in his work. In this
time of quiet waiting, it seemed as though the world had
forgotten them.

So it was incredible when the threatening calls began

again. The first one came just after breakfast. He was close enough to take it, but Karen, who had gone upstairs, must have picked up the extension, because he heard a click.

Then a woman's voice screeched, "You bastards, get out of Elgin City or we'll burn you out!"

"Who is this?" he shouted.

"You and your pregnant bitch have contaminated our city. You ought to turn over all that money to the people you spread your filthy dust to. Get out with your whore and her radioactive baby in her belly."

He heard the sharp intake of breath and realized Karen had been listening. He shouted at her, "Hang up! Don't listen to this foul-mouthed slob—this pervert." And he slammed down the receiver.

In the next hour there were two more calls, a man threatening to bomb them if they didn't leave him a box with twenty-five thousand dollars in a car that would be parked two blocks away from their house, and a woman offering to share with him, for five thousand dollars, a cure against radioactivity. He told them both to go to hell. When the phone rang for the fourth time that morning, he let it go unanswered for a long time, and then he finally picked it up and shouted, "What the hell do you want, you crazy bastards?"

"Barney, it's me, Stefan. Are you all right?"

For a moment he couldn't answer, and then he choked out, "Stefan, I'm sorry. I've been getting crank phone calls. This town has gone crazy suddenly, without any reason."

"Haven't you seen your article?"

"My article? What are you talking about?"

"In *Newslife*. It came in this morning's mail. Don't you subscribe to it?"

"No. What kind of an article?"

"How could you let them publish a story like that? You don't know the hell we've been going through here all morning. The phone hasn't stopped ringing. Curses. Threats against our lives unless we get you to turn part of the money over to the city of Hamtramck. Your mother is on the edge of a nervous breakdown. Whatever possessed you, Barney?"

"I had nothing to do with it, Stefan. I told them I didn't want them to write about me. But they don't need my permission. What does the article say?"

Stefan described the pictures of Barney ("the man with the radioactive touch!") on his front lawn brandishing a lead pipe, and from another angle a picture of the house ("The Radioactive Hothouse!"). There were also pictures of his parents coming out of the apartment in Hamtramck, and one of his father standing near the second-floor window in an undershirt, apparently taken with a telephoto lens ("Son contaminates parents in Hamtramck!").

The story described the accident in full, much as Max had told it to him (Max wouldn't have told them; they probably bought the story from someone else at the Research Center), as well as the step-by-step decontamination of Elgin City.

"The big thing in the story," said Stefan, "seems to be the idea that you're suing for a quarter of a million dollars. It says here: 'The Stark touch: Sculptor turns hot dust into gold dust!' And there's another shot of Karen taken in some maternity shop, and underneath it says: 'Boy, girl, or mutant?' "

"Those bloodsuckers!"

"Why didn't you stop them from publishing it, Barney? This'll whip people up to a frenzy."

"I told you, I had nothing to do with it." He tried to explain what had happened with the reporter and the photographer, but he didn't really expect his cousin to understand.

After Stefan hung up, the phone rang again, and he didn't answer it. He just let it ring. He knew it was only the beginning. They were in for a wave of anonymous calls, threats, filth. And he shuddered at the memory of the last time; the rocks through the windows and the garbage on the lawn. But this time, he decided, it would be different because he had the shotgun, and if they started something he would use it.

Two days later, Barney got a telegram from Dr. Leroy, asking him to call his office.

"Your phone is out of order," said Dr. Leroy. "I've been trying to reach you."

"We haven't been answering." Barney explained about the crank calls, and Dr. Leroy said he'd seen the article.

"I got a call from the director of the Elgin City Memorial Hospital. They tell me that there has been a mistake and there won't be room for Karen to have the baby there." Barney began to rage, but Dr. Leroy calmed him. "As far as I'm concerned, the only thing that matters is not to let her get upset about the change. She doesn't have to be told why we're transferring. I have lots of my patients admitted to Downtown Central in Detroit. We'll tell her just what he told me, that there's no room at the hospital."

"But you know damned well that's not true. That damned article scared them, or someone saw it and put the pressure on."

"What good will it do to get angry? People are frightened by what they don't understand."

"So we're to take this the rest of our lives?"

"I don't know about the rest of your lives. I know only that I've got to put this baby above convenience, justice, morality. You certainly have the right to feel outraged, but I don't have the right to let your feelings interfere with a safe delivery."

"You know how she feels about the Elgin City Hospital. It's where she was born, where she had her broken leg cared for. She knows lots of people there, and it's only ten minutes away. Dragging her off downtown is a forty-minute drive. What if the baby comes during the middle of the night? What if we can't get there in time?"

"I don't see any alternative. We're better off there than in a hostile situation. Look, Barney. Frankly, I argued like hell with the director. I've known him for years. But he has a point. People who work there and those who live nearby, and other couples who are going to have their babies there, are all frightened at the thought of Karen being on the same floor, or even in the same building. The minute any of them got the news she was there, it would be a very dangerous situation. Frankly, if this were anywhere near a normal case I'd deliver it in your home, but there might be complications that would require other specialists or hospital equipment. Oh, I know how upset you are about it, but what good is it to take all the precautions for a delivery that's going to be difficult enough as it is, and still have to put up with a hostile mob? Who knows what someone might do if he imagined his own wife and child were in danger? No, I think it's best not to fight them."

Barney finally agreed that when the time came they would go to the Downtown Central. At least there, as Dr. Leroy said, people wouldn't know who they were. He let Dr. Leroy tell her the necessary reasons, and she never questioned them. Arrangements were made for the room to be available in late December. Almost two and a half months away.

There were more calls, and they seemed to her designed only to terrify them. She no longer dared to answer the phone, but let Barney do it. He would pick up the receiver and after a few seconds his face would grow tense, as if he were waiting for something, and she knew that the person at the other end was being silent. But other times when his face flushed and he looked as if he wanted to crush the instrument, she knew the caller was being obscene.

The sheriff refused to do anything, hinting that they had co-operated with the magazine reporter to publish the article; there were stories all over town, he said, about the fantastic sums they had been paid for it. The public disclosure that they were suing National Motors for a quarter of a million dollars seemed to catch the people's fancy.

Many of them made the mental leap, assuming the Starks had the money already, and most of the calls were extortion threats, warning that their lives were in danger unless they were willing to share some of the loot. After all, the reasoning went, the whole town had suffered. Some of them had been laid off when the Center was closed; business was hurt in the shopping centers and small shops near the Center. And so some of the money rightfully belonged to them.

Her fear was compounded because of the shotgun. She knew if someone got bold enough to come to the front door, or if Barney ever caught the ones who were painting obscene words and threats on the walls or on the front walk, he would certainly use it. And he wouldn't distinguish between child and adult. His temper had become so unpredictable that with this accumulated rage, she was sure, he would shoot first and not bother to ask questions.

These were nightmare days and nights, a time that should have been, according to the books on prenatal care, the most wonderful months of her life. Most women, she came to understand, were happy during these final months, when the upsetting symptoms were past and the baby was settling down to wait, but she was close to hysteria most of the time. Dr. Leroy was worried about giving her too many sedatives. He was also concerned with her tension, and he made her promise to relax, but even as he said it, running his hand wearily through his stone-grey hair, and shaking his sad lined face, she knew he didn't expect her to be able to. Although he had other maternity cases to worry about, he had somehow made her problem his own.

"It should be a happy time for you," he protested. "Having a child is one of the most important times in a couple's life. It shouldn't have to take place in a state of tension."

Before the article came out, she had tried to convince herself that the worst was over, that people had forgotten and were prepared to let them live as they had before. But it was as if the hate had been there, just waiting to consume them. She was angry at first that Barney and Dr. Leroy should

think she believed their story of why they had to change
hospitals. As if a child wouldn't have seen through it. Then
she decided to pretend she believed the lie.

She had thought she would be upset about showing, but
now when she looked in the mirror at the fullness of the
swelling, she was awed at the life she and Barney had created with their bodies. Soon it would be outside her, filling its lungs with air and crying. Oh, God, she begged,
please let it be normal. She knew she had sworn to love
it even if it was deformed, but it didn't *have* to be that way.
What she was trying to say was that she'd accept anything,
but if it was all the same to Him please let it be all right—
half wish, half prayer. She was ashamed of the bargaining
sorry-for-herself thoughts, and, after all, what was she praying at, looking in the mirror as if God were herself or the
new life inside her? Perhaps that was God, new and pure
and sharing some greater spirit that all women carried within,
and with each child born a bit of God called "soul." The
way the Hindus believed. Was it Atman or Brahma? She
always confused which was the inner god, but maybe she
was praying to that one because she was afraid to face
the outer one. Or was it wrong to pray with her massive
belly reflecting in the mirror? Weren't there primitive tribes
in which pregnant women were taboo and had to hide? Or
was that when they were menstruating? Why could she
never get these things straight? She should look it up and
try to remember it. She should be reading more, preparing
herself, improving her mind, so that her child would not
grow up ashamed of her.

It seemed to her that Barney looked at her strangely
these days. Once, when he was rubbing her leg to work out
a cramp, the top of her full blouse had lifted and under
the scooped-out top of her maternity skirt the slip had worked
down, and he saw her navel forced out flat, and it upset
him. She could understand his being so disturbed these
days, but his behavior was frightening. He didn't recall
things that had passed. He confused last week with yesterday,
and sometimes talked about what happened this morning

as if it had happened a long time ago. As if the past and present were mixed up in his head. And he wouldn't look at a clock. If she asked him the time, he became angry and told her to look for herself, because he didn't want to know. Part of him was someplace else, and she was lonely.

Frightening to have to bring a child here and try to give it a normal life when he was so far out of this time and place. Did all women feel so frightened, so awed?

She didn't talk about these things to Barney, only to Myra and to herself. Especially in the night. Was that healthy? Possibly she was dwelling on these things too much. She should become more outgoing, visit places, look at pretty things—not that she believed that old wives' tale, but what if it did affect the unborn child if the mother was exposed to good music and art? Why should she take the chance? What if in some strange way the things she saw and heard were transmitted to it? She must get some good books to read. All these years she'd been planning to read *War and Peace* and *Ulysses*, and go to more art galleries and concerts. She should do it now.

As the delivery date grew closer, she became frightened of little things—noises, shadows in the dark, strange feelings in her body. Frightened by the overwhelming idea of caring for an infant. She told herself over and over again that having children and raising them was something most women do as a matter of course—the uneducated, the confused, the handicapped, all have children and manage to raise them—and why shouldn't she be able to do the same?

It didn't help much. She was still afraid of the thought of a tiny creature, howling and screeching for her to keep it safe and alive. What if she did something wrong? What if she accidentally let it die? Or worse, what if, in some fit of depression or uncontrollable mood, she killed it?

Blind, unreasoning fear, she told herself. She had been through a great deal, but she would be able to take care of her own child. She would give it more love, more attention, more affection than if none of this had happened. But when she tried to visualize what the baby would look like, her mind conjured up physical defects—from harelip and cleft palate to lobster claws and armless or legless masses of flesh. But no matter what the body looked like, the face was always pretty, with blue eyes and damp brown curls.

And sometimes her daytime fantasies took the form of her being lost in the desert, and all around her were sand and enemies, ghostly shapes that loomed up and tore at her clothes and her body and screamed that she was radioactive. And where they touched her, sores blossomed and blood ran.

She was upstairs with Myra, ironing some things, when they heard shouting. She opened the window and saw shadows moving on the lawn. Then she heard shouts of "Give it to the son of a bitch good! Kick him in the balls! Teach him a lesson!"

She recognized Barney's voice screaming, "Kill me, you bastards! Go ahead, you better kill me now because I'll get you. God help me, I'll get you."

"It's Barney," she said. "They're beating him up."

"Call the police," screamed Myra.

Someone yelled, "There's his whore at the window." She moved aside as a rock came through the open window, just missing her and breaking a lamp by the bed. Terrified, she went for the phone and heard the voices from outside again.

"C'mon, let's get out of here."

"He's crawling away. You're letting him get away."

"C'mon, stupid. You don't want to kill him. They're calling the cops."

They ran, and seconds later the street echoed to the roar of cars being started up and engines gunned, and two cars without lights sped away.

"Damn you," she whispered, "I hope you crash and die a horrible death." And then she caught herself and choked the words back. "No, I don't, dear God. I didn't mean it. They don't know what they're doing. Forgive me."

Someone answered at the other end, and she screamed

into the phone, "Please hurry. This is Mrs. Stark. Some men were here beating up my husband. He's badly hurt. Come quickly."

There was a silence, and then the voice at the other end, quiet, unperturbed, said, "All right. We'll see if we can send someone down there in a little while."

"Hurry!" she begged. "Please hurry!"

She slammed the receiver down and ran downstairs to join Myra. Barney had dragged himself up the front steps and was sitting there, rocking back and forth, sobbing.

"I couldn't fight back. I couldn't cut loose at them. I wanted to smash them with my fists but I couldn't do it." He clenched his fingers and stared at them. "I could have gotten one or two of them. I've got strength in these. I wanted to break their heads, but my hands wouldn't do what I wanted. They won't ever do what I want. They're tied . . . tied. My goddamned hands are tied. . . ."

She wanted to soothe him, but he turned away. "I called the police," she said.

"What good'll that do? You know that bastard sheriff won't do anything. For all we know, they were some of his men."

"Are you all right?" Myra insisted. "Is there anything we can do for you?"

"I'll live, unfortunately."

"Don't say that," said Myra. "You mustn't think like that."

But he wouldn't speak any more. He let them guide him upstairs to the bedroom.

"You want some ice?" Karen asked. She could see him trembling, and she longed to touch him, hold him, help him find some way of releasing his rage. He didn't answer, and she realized he was glaring at the Fertility Clock on her night table. "What's the matter, Barney?"

"There's no time."

"For what?" asked Myra.

"It's too late."

Karen touched his arm. "Barney, pull yourself together."

He flinched from her touch and pointed to the clock. "Look! Red!" he shouted. "The fertility zone. Too bad you're pregnant."

"Barney, please . . ."

"How about you?" he asked Myra. "Care to try your luck? You just bet on the red."

Myra shook her head and looked into his eyes. "Don't torture yourself. You've gone through a lot—"

"Hell!" He grabbed the clock and yanked the cord from the outlet. "We don't need this any more."

"Barney, don't!"

"I can still throw things." Her shout was too late to stop him. He flung the Fertility Clock across the room. It bounced off the wall onto Karen's dressing table, knocking over her cosmetics and shattering to the floor. "Look, my hands don't hesitate to throw things." Then he grew quiet, looking at his moist palms and then at the clock on the floor. "I'm sorry. I shouldn't have done that. I couldn't stand to look at it any more. There's no time for anything any more."

He sank onto the bed and lay back. "Leave me alone. Just go away and leave me alone—both of you. I'll be all right." He was quiet for a moment and then he said, "If the police come, tell them not to bother." He turned his face to the wall. "Tell them it's too late, and there's nothing anyone can do."

Lying there, Barney remembered his father's violent temper, remembered that once, just after a heavy snow (beautiful white drifts piled up to play with), his father would have killed that red-haired boy if he had caught him. Running after him like a madman, swinging a shovel because the boy had knocked down Barney's snow fort and punched him. It occurred to him now that his father must have been watching through the window, because he came bursting out of the house in his shirt sleeves and slippers, grabbing the shovel and chasing the boy (and then slipping on the snow because the boy, about ten years old, like Barney, was too fast for him) and coming back red-faced, blowing puffs of breath in the cold air and patting him on the shoulder because he knew his son had not been to blame. Barney had been the innocent victim, and his father had seen it all and understood.

And the other time, a few years earlier—in summertime— right in front of the house, an older, bigger boy started a fight, had him down on the sidewalk punching him. And then Barney heard the crash of glass and saw the boy look up to where Barney's father was leaning out the window. "I kill you if you hit my boy again!" In his hand was a bowl. He threw this one too, and it missed again, but a piece of glass cut Barney's arm. The boy, terrified, jumped for his bike and pedaled away furiously, screaming back, "You old Polak bastard! You crazy old fart!"

Barney had never heard his father called those things before, and he was shocked again when he went upstairs— handkerchief wrapped around his bleeding arm—to hear his mother screaming that his father might have killed the boy, or even his own son.

"But that bully was picking on him. I saw it."

"You could have killed him, and then where would we be? You've got to control that crazy temper."

"Aw . . ." With a wave of his hand, his father showed his disgust. It was never possible to convince his father he had been wrong. Once he made up his mind to something, that was that. Barney had been close to tears, but he knew it would infuriate the old man even more than the fight. A man doesn't cry. A man can get angry, but he doesn't cry. "That's all right, boy," he said, ruffling his hair with a big calloused hand, "I seen the whole thing. It wasn't your fault."

Where was his father now? Why wasn't he here to break their heads with his massive fists, to beat and bloody them as he had done then?

The beating Barney had taken seemed to have a strange effect on Myra. When he refused to let Karen help him or comfort him, Myra became increasingly disturbed. Several times in the next few days he saw her studying him, as if to figure out something she couldn't understand.

One afternoon when Karen was out at a Red Cross class, he went downstairs to be alone, but Myra followed. "Barney, you're a human being," she said. "You shouldn't try to bear this all by yourself."

"I have to," he told her. "I can't cry on anyone's shoulder. When something like this happens, you feel ashamed and guilty. Maybe I'm to blame in a way. If I hadn't been so worried about the future, if I hadn't taken the job at the Center, I would never have contaminated everything and everyone around me. If I hadn't denied the past, if I hadn't denied my father, if I hadn't—"

"Don't blame yourself, Barney. You mustn't turn the guilt inward. Haven't you seen yet that we all share in what has happened to you? We claim your suffering as our own and gain strength from it. Barney, we need you as much as you need us."

"There is only one thing I really need now," he said, "my work. And it has to be done alone. When you're an only child, you learn from the beginning to face things by yourself. Even friends are outside and temporary. I'm alone when I sculpt, when I think, even when I . . . Well, never mind. I'm not a part of anything or anyone. I was born into aloneness; I'm alone as long as I live; I'll die alone. I can't share my guilt and suffering. I can't lose myself in your beautiful Brotherhood. . . ."

There were tears in her eyes as she pleaded with him not to isolate himself. What had happened to him had happened to countless others in different ways, and with others it could be given meaning, not wasted.

In her fervor, he heard the Myra of four years ago, who could have swept him into any cause, any involvement, any dream. He suspected that in her new-found religion she could move men in suffering as she had earlier moved them in love.

"You've got to want something besides yourself," she

insisted. "The way Karen wants the baby. Don't you see? Alone we're nothing."

"I want something," he said finally. "I've always wanted you."

"I don't want to hear that."

"How can I believe anything you say, if you deny me?"

"What I'm talking about is spiritual, not physical."

"First I am physical, then I am spiritual." He took her hands and held her from backing away. "You can't ask me to follow blindly while you elude me again. How can I accept a brotherhood of suffering when you're afraid of me?"

She pulled free. "It's not the same at all. You're perverting my meaning."

"You want to feed off my suffering and give nothing in return."

"I have nothing to give you that way."

"I wanted you that way when we were in college. You swept me along with words then too, and when I reached for you, you handed me mimeographed manifestoes. You should have married me instead of running away with that professor. Well, now I need more than words. If you have no feeling for me then go away and leave me alone."

She was looking at him desperately, unwilling to give up. "Barney, you're twisting everything, turning our whole relationship upside down. This desire for sexual conquest—"

"Conquest?"

"—is a false illusion. It isn't real."

"God Almighty! What do you think I've been doing down here these past weeks but trying to make some sense of reality. And who said anything about conquest? All I'm trying to discover is whether there's a way to survive without looking at the world through Brother Luke's shattered vision and saying, 'That's what the world is all about, broken, impotent, without hope of ever mending or reviving life.'"

"But there is hope of those things. An artist creates out of his suffering. . . ."

"Yes, I know, 'and a woman creates out of her pain and

labor,' but first there must be physical, sexual, orgasmic love. And you're a liar if you offer me a creative world without it. That's sterile spirituality. Oh, no. Love me with your flesh, and then I'll listen to your words."

He took her hands into his again, but this time she didn't pull away. She whispered protests as he kissed and caressed her.

"Barney, no . . . please. I'm not beautiful any more. You have no right to make love to me."

"You're still beautiful to me," he whispered back, pushing her down onto the cot, unbuttoning her blouse. "I'm not put off by disguises."

"Oh, God, Barney . . . no. I don't want you to. It's wrong."

"This is something I dreamed of from the time I first met you."

"I'm not the same as I was then. You mustn't."

He undressed her as her protests weakened, and finally she sat there as naked as the Venus he had caressed so often, trying to cover herself with her hands, as he had seen her a thousand times in his imagination.

"You're still you," he said, "with the body of my original Venus. Did you know I started it from my memories of you at the beach?"

"You don't want to understand—"

He touched her lips with his fingers. "Words won't make me understand. Only this . . ." He cupped her breast in his hand and kissed the soft skin where it met her shoulder. He felt her breast grow firm, and finally she slipped her arms around his neck and clung to him.

"But it's not fair to Karen. She'll know."

"It doesn't matter," he said, "There's been nothing between her and me for a long time now. Not since the accident."

"That's what it is," she said, facing him defiantly. "You want to use me because you need a woman to prove your maleness. That's all you care about, your momentary gratification."

"Damn you," he said, pointing to the draped figure in the corner. "Is that why I first created the Venus in your image? Is that why I couldn't change it to Karen's face, no matter how many times I tried to destroy it, wipe out your memory, start over with her? Is that why you've been in my visions and dreams all these years—because I wanted momentary gratification?"

"It's—it's not . . . fair to her . . ." she said weakly. "You belong to Karen."

He pushed her back gently but firmly, kissing her lips and whispering into them. "I never stopped belonging to you."

She pressed her thighs together, still refusing him—"It's wrong—" pushing at his chest as if afraid he would overwhelm her. Then her thighs relaxed, and magically, as if the cold clay of his sculpture had come alive to his touch, the "Rising Venus" of his imagination came to life beneath him. Not passively and yielding, but as he had imagined she would in his earliest fantasies: demanding, with hunger that matched his own. Her movements were aggressive, arching up to meet him, seeking equality. She tried to take control, and he was frightened for a time of having released some uncontrollable, dammed-up energy, of having brought to life a Venus rising violently beyond his capabilities. It was a struggle, as if she felt challenged to prove that no man could dominate her even here. She was strong, and in his weakened condition he thought for a moment she would roll him over and ride him from above. Something in him wanted to yield, to let her take over, but he found the energy to fight her down until finally they were both done and slack and he tried to pull away.

Even then she demanded her rights, holding him prisoner between strong arms and legs, keeping him inside until she should decide it was time. Then she quivered and sighed; released him, rejected him, and looked at his nakedness.

"Does it make you feel like a god? Do you feel like a god now?"

"What are you talking about?" He touched her shoulder, but she drew away. "Stop this craziness. You wanted me as

much as I wanted you. You were holding all that back just
as I was. It was as if suddenly both of us came back to life.
Hell, with you there would be no reason to be alone."

"Don't talk about it."

"If I could stay with you I'd join the Crucifists. I'd join
the goddamned army."

She glared at him. "Don't make jokes about it."

"Why so grim? Where's your sense of humor? That was
exciting. Talk about the battle of the sexes—"

"You're dirty."

"What are you saying?"

"And you've dirtied me. Filth, that's all you men are.
And now you've poured your filth into me. That's all you
really wanted, didn't you. To get me down and to contaminate me with your slime. Oh, why did I come down into
this hellhole of filth and corruption?"

The sudden change frightened him, and he tried to calm
her, but she tore away from him, picking up one of his
sharp chisels from the worktable and holding it like a knife.

"Myra, put that down."

"If you come near me again, I'll kill you."

He knew enough to back away. "All right, I won't touch
you if you don't want me to. But, damn it, you're taking
something beautiful and twisting it into—"

"Beautiful?" She spat the word. "I always thought you
were different, but you're like all the rest, pretending to
believe and care about the things I believe in, when all
you really wanted was to get me into bed, to use and degrade me."

"That's not true," he said, angered at the turn this had
taken. "But don't try to kid me. You wanted it as much
as I did. Maybe you don't want to admit it to yourself, but,
boy, you were trying to dominate and degrade me. All these
weeks, you've been testing your spiritual strength against
me—against both Karen and me."

"That's not true."

"You came to us thinking that because of the accident
we'd be weak enough to manipulate."

"Damn you."

"But Karen's pregnancy has made her stronger than you believed your weak, romantic sister could be."

"I warn you, Barney, stop it."

"And you're angry now because I was physically stronger than you bargained for—strong enough to take you and make you like it. Hasn't anyone else ever made love to you like this? Wasn't your professor man enough to satisfy you? Or were you always on top, riding him too, until he had to get you pregnant and hooked on drugs to get out from under."

She flung the chisel, and it nicked his cheek.

"Now I know where I made my mistake," he said, looking at the chisel on the floor and the blood dripping down onto his arm from his face. "I tried to capture you in clay. You would have had to be done in stone."

She dressed quickly and slipped past him up the stairs.

He sat there quietly, trying to stanch the blood, listening to her footsteps above. It should have been done in marble, material to resist his force, something to struggle against and overcome. It was a shame he had discovered the answer too late.

A short time later he heard the front door open and close, and through the basement window he saw Myra walk down the path carrying her cardboard suitcase, watched her go down the street until she was out of sight.

He wondered what Karen would say about Myra's leaving. Would she know that something had happened between them? He started upstairs. Then he realized he was still naked, and remembering she had asked him if he felt like a god, he laughed. "If I were a god," he thought, as he dressed, "would I still have to put on my trousers one leg at a time?"

Karen, peculiarly, made no reference to Myra's sudden departure. But when they heard nothing from her in the next two days, Barney became worried. She had reacted strangely, and she might do something to harm herself. On

the second day after she'd left, he went to the Mission to find
her and ask her forgiveness.

Brother Luke seemed impassive. Myra had left the Mission, he said, and was on her way to Africa.

"Rather sudden," said Barney.

"Yes," said Brother Luke, eying the bandage on his
cheek, "but she was supposed to have gone several months
ago. She decided to stay in Detroit to help you and your
wife first. She felt she could be of service here before she
followed her call."

"When will she come back?"

"I don't think she will."

"I see. Did she leave a message for me?"

"She said she still believed you should join us, but she
doubted you would. Is there a chance of winning you over?"

The caution in his voice was unmistakable, and though
Barney was sure Myra hadn't told him what happened, he
must have guessed something from her change of plans.
And looking at him, Barney was thrown back four years
to the suspicions and jealousies that tormented all of those
who followed her. None of them trusted the others, each
harboring the thought that she had favored one above the
rest. There was always the fear you were making a fool of
yourself. Well, that part of it was no longer true.

She must have been a moving force in this group, but not
the same way, and though Brother Luke surely suspected
something had happened between them, he was still interested in having Barney become a Brother. Barney was impressed with such selflessness. The Brotherhood was one way
out of the world of Elgin City. It would cut off all responsibility to Karen and the baby. But even as he yearned for that
Gaugin-like release, he knew he was incapable of leaving
Karen now.

"I don't think so," he said finally. "I'm a loner. I'd only
disturb your community, and while I believe in what you're
doing, I don't think I'd fit here."

When Barney left, Brother Luke seemed genuinely
troubled, and in fact saying good-bye was painful. Well, no

matter. The Crucifists had found one path. He, through his sculpture, had found another, lonelier, less satisfying, without the sharing of fellow artists, but, for better or worse, the way he had chosen; and as long as he could work things out with his hands he could make a worth-while life of beginning things and now, perhaps, finishing some of them. Maybe Myra was right in a way. He had felt at times like a god who could control matter and form, and had dared to think he could determine his own future. Wasn't that what the Greeks called *hubris?* Perhaps the accident was an accident only in human terms. Well, at least he had finished one thing, and it made him feel lighter, younger; he had gotten Myra out of his system.

As he walked out onto the street, remembering Myra standing there naked in the dim light of his studio, threatening him with the chisel, he suddenly realized how funny it was, and he began to laugh. She would find stronger gods to contend with in Africa. A fat old lady leaning out of the window of the building next door saw him laughing and waved to him. He waved back.

2

Laura Bradley's voice, when she came to visit, carried clearly It was not as if he were cut off from the outside world. through the laundry chute, and he enjoyed hearing her try to convince Karen to have him committed to a mental hospital. As long as Karen kept her sensible independent attitude, he was safe. As long as their savings held out, Laura Bradley had no leverage. But he listened closely for any sign that Karen might betray him. When that time came, he would know what he had to do.

His only pleasure now was working down here in the dim light of his studio. His distance vision had faded, but he could see up close and worked mostly by touch. He was making babies again—not in the sentimental way he had done before, but in all their newborn ugliness, umbilical cord still attached, covered with blood and slime of the mother. All the possibilities—successes and failures. What was he seeking in these forms? Perhaps he would know when he found it.

Down here there was no time. The best way to live was alone, without worrying about today or tomorrow. And not yesterday, either (he was no fool!). He lived only in the making—in the form-shaping, mass-creating act in which reality was to be found. The way God created, in a void without yesterdays or todays or tomorrows, his mental energy concentrated on a bit of matter—dirt, clay—squeezing it, kneading it between his fat fatherly fingers until the shape came right, feeling it throb alive against his palms (squirming to get away from him, out of his hands into the firmament), but holding on to wipe off the mucus, and forming it to stand or walk or slither across the earth.

And he called it good.

Except these clay babies didn't live. Dozens of them, carefully shaped and modeled, but none of them right. Not one the way a baby should be. He worked until his eyes hurt and his hands were without feeling, and then he stumbled up to bed.

Usually, when he came up it was growing light and he scurried off to his resting place, afraid to face the day. And he sensed her sleeping beside him, sagging into the mattress with her heaviness.

It takes him a long time to sleep, and he keeps his face to the pillow, afraid of the light that may stab at his itchy, burning eyes. And there in the pillow he finds the images he was able to hold at bay while he worked. In the pillow there is no defense against the past. Soon he hears her waken, and he is pleased to have the bed for himself. As she groans her way up to a sitting position and then out of the bedroom, he stretches luxuriously, and he knows that between the comings awake from physical discomfort and nightmares, he will sleep, and he will not leave his bed, regardless of her complaints and protests, until he sees the darkness through the blinds. He will no longer come out of his bed except in darkness, when she is asleep. And he will no longer have anything to do with people who come and go in this house: not with men of milk, collectors of bills, Marchers of Dimes, or anyone else who comes here under the delusion that somehow he is still a member of this community, this nation, this race. They will have to accept the fact that having cast him out, they have made him something apart, a law unto himself, to eat or starve, vegetate or create, live or die—as the will moves him. And there is nothing they can do that will make him for one moment wonder what time it is in this world. Let fools slice up existence into segments to measure how much each day, hour, minute, second has passed away. He refuses to count his dying.

She knew he was sleeping too much. He would get sick spending all his time going from his bed to his studio and back again. If only there were some way to get him out of this withdrawal. She wasn't asking that he become involved with the preparations, but at least he could behave like a human being. She hadn't wanted to consider seriously what Mother suggested, but what if he did become violent? Did she have the right to put herself and the baby in danger? She would have to do something if he didn't come out of it soon.

It was wrong, she realized, to go down to his studio without his permission, but she felt it might give her some insight into what was on his mind. If it became necessary to have him put under observation, the doctors would certainly want to know what he had been working on these past weeks.

She suspected his strange withdrawal had something to do with Myra. She wasn't sure what had happened between them, and when Barney told her that day that Myra had packed up and left, she asked no further questions. She would not cross-examine him or judge him. Myra had, it appeared, returned and asserted her rights of prior possession, but the important thing was that she was gone now and Barney was still here. Nothing else mattered.

She went down slowly, holding tightly to the banister. It wouldn't do to trip now and have something happen. She had to be careful, Dr. Leroy had told her, especially during these last months.

She had expected to see the room filled with the work of these past few weeks since she had last been down here, but the studio was nearly empty. Over on the far side, on the rotating table, there was something under sheets; "The Victims" and whatever else he had been working on were gone. Several times she started back, thinking she had no business down here, spying on his work while he was asleep. Yet his work was part of his withdrawal—this sickness that was taking him farther and farther from reality, as if he were curling up in a cocoon. She felt the tenseness in her stomach, and waited for the baby to protest, but nothing happened. She pressed her hands against it.

"We have to look, Baby," she said. "We have to know what he's doing."

She forced herself to approach the circle of light under which the table stood, prepared for anything. Knowing his bitterness, his rejection of the world, she told herself one doesn't suffer without building up resentment. At least, he had a way of getting it out of his system. She pulled the sheet off, gently, noting how it had been draped so she would be able to put it back the same way.

It was the Venus. But oh, God! . . . The face was clearly hers this time, and the body was her pregnancy exaggerated so that her stomach was swollen up to twice what it really was, and her face and arms and legs were swollen too, to make her look as if she were ready to burst. What she couldn't make out at first were the small, animal-like objects piled all around the Venus. And then she saw that they were little bodies, lying on top of one another in a mound—twisted, the dead babies of her nightmares, piled one on top of the other, each deformed in some way: lobster claws, two heads, three arms, one eye, shriveled stumps for arms and legs—all maimed babies lying there dead (no, not all of them, some with eyes wide in pain), clinging to the mother figure. Some were at her breasts, and from between her legs another was in the process of being born.

But her eyes were staring with a dullness of death. Even in death, this monstrous Earth Mother kept giving birth to deformed babies.

She choked back a scream, and somehow managed to cover the sculpture with the sheet and head up the stairs. She lost her footing, slipped, and started up again, moving as if under water. She made it back to the living room somehow, and then the air seemed to close off. She felt the thickness of clay in her arms and legs, and, with the oddest feeling that Barney intended that she and the baby should die, she lost consciousness. . . .

When he discovered she had gone down and looked at his work, he was furious at first. It didn't take much to figure it out. She hadn't put the sheet back the way he usually draped his figures, and the moment he saw it, he knew she had been down there. But then he was glad. He hadn't wanted to know her reaction, but just knowing she had seen it gave him a feeling of triumph. It had been painful working for all these weeks with no one to share it (not that she could ever really share his creations), and to have someone know of its existence gave it reality—or is it the other way? To share its reality gives it existence! She looked —well—different to him these days. Frightened. It couldn't be the figures, he decided. They were harmless enough. He tried to explain to Karen that it was a kind of comedy of errors inspired by a French film he had once seen, in which some funny characters had created a machine to turn out some object and, instead, the machine turned out something else—he didn't recall exactly; it wasn't important—

but they didn't know how to turn the machine off, and the stuff kept popping out until it filled the whole damned room. And that had reminded him of the skit he'd seen put on with the boys from the neighborhood youth club, about the man who had decided to do his own delivery for his wife, and who finally, after quintuplets, called the doctor in horror and asked for instructions to turn it off. And he guessed that behind the impression was the memory of the fairy tale of the girl with the magic kettle, whose grandmother couldn't turn it off, and how the porridge filled up the whole town, choking the streets and threatening to smother the village. It was, he joked, a symbolic protest against the population explosion, showing an Earth Mother fertility image gone berserk.

But she didn't think it was funny, and he decided she was too close to the situation to appreciate it. It was, he insisted, a truly original idea. But he wasn't satisfied with the babies. He was able to sculpt them so they looked like babies, and he'd studied the medical books so he'd been able to give them the right kind of deformities. But somehow they still looked too human and lovable. One of his intentions was to show the imperfect creatures shaped by a suffering God.

But she didn't want to talk about it.

Why couldn't she understand that in creating these forms he had reached down into his unconscious and come up clutching memories of another place and time that could no longer be called the past if it existed here and now in his mind? If he could see those hunched, twisted, writhing figures—half human, half beast—didn't they exist? She didn't want to accept the reality of his imagination. She wouldn't admit he had stumbled onto something very significant. She had become too absorbed in her own selfish possession of the secret of life, and all she cared for was the here-and-now in her belly.

It was the kind of foolishness that makes people afraid to die, the belief that something is going to happen next week, or tomorrow, or a minute from now, and they're going to miss it. He tried to make her see there was no tomorrow for anyone, so why look ahead and fear death? The amazing thing was how closed she was to all reason, as if that thing inside her were so important it was worth clinging to, worth fighting the world for. Such precious cargo, he told her, was produced by millions of unskilled laborers all over the world (a drug on the market, exploding into populations that starved and died by the Ganges, wandered the jungles of Africa with fly bites on their eyes, came into the world deformed in body and soul—rest assured, he told her, his deformed babies were merely representations of the warped essence that masqueraded on earth in perfect bodies, but he could see how little she understood him. Her pregnancy had blinded her to anything beyond a few inches of flesh in her uterus.

He now believed that when an infant cried *in utero*, it was protesting death. Wasn't birth really a beginning of dying? And weren't all their clocks made to guide them through the labyrinth of hours to death? Man was a walking radioactive isotope with a variable half-life, decaying a little each second of each day. And why let their seed be born to die?

He would make her see. Involved as she was in this process of creating within herself, she would be made to understand that the only meaning in creating such a form was in its destruction. He hadn't put it to her that way yet (she wasn't ready for the creative leap); but he would show her how every person was torn between the commonplace egotistic urges to play God and breathe life into your little Adams and Eves and scold them for being disobedient and send them out of the garden-home into the polluted world to decay every second of every day, solely because you created them and made them extensions of yourself; torn between that and the beautiful ideal (God's other way) of destroying that which one creates.

She would understand and accept these new insights he was able to offer her, and when the time came she would

want to save their baby from this contaminated world. And
he would help her. He would show her how to do it.

He picked up one of the small deformed clay figures and
threw it against the wall.

She was relieved that he wasn't angry with her for looking
at his work. She realized it was foolish of her to think she
could keep it a secret from him, but he didn't seem to mind.
In fact, he seemed pleased, which was strange, considering
how excitable he usually was about things like that. It was
foolish of her to get so upset about the deformed figures,
but, as he said, he had merely externalized the mental and
spiritual deformities that all of them were born with, and
in that sense she shouldn't have been surprised that he
would use that kind of figure to show it. After all, it was on
both of their minds these days.

Despite his bitterness, she believed he would come to
accept and eventually love their baby. He had always wanted
a child, and that was something you didn't lose in seven
months. When the time came, nothing else would matter—
for him as well as for her.

But time went so slowly now.

When she heard the sound from downstairs, she thought
he had dropped something. Then it sounded as if something were being smashed. Again and again she heard
loud noises and then Barney shouting something incoher-
ent. She was terrified that someone might have gotten into
the studio and was beating him up again. She called to
him. There was a silence, and then the sound of laughter.
The most frightening laughter she'd ever heard, his voice
at high pitch, as if he were in pain and being tickled at
the same time. Slowly she went down the steps to see what
had happened.

Barney was sitting on the floor in front of his sculpture,
spotlighted in the circle of light. The sheet was on the
floor, and the work had been smashed in several places.

The head had been knocked off the Venus and was lying on the floor; the arms had been broken off. And all the deformed babies had been smashed in various parts of the studio, as if someone had thrown them against the walls. In the center of the debris, Barney sat, no longer laughing now, but stunned and frightened, as if he were about to cry, as if he wanted to cry but couldn't.

"Come upstairs," she said softly. "Come up and lie down for a while."

He seemed not to hear her, fighting back the tears that were brimming in his eyes. When she took him by the arm, he let her raise him to his feet and yielded as she led him upstairs. He was still silent and docile, and she had the feeling she could have done anything with him at that moment, and it was frightening. She led him up to the bedroom and put him to bed, and all the while the look in his eyes faded, as if he had successfully fought back the urge to cry, and left a blankness with only a trace of sadness. If only he would cry, let it all out, it might help.

She put the cover over him, turned out the light, and closed the door.

3

Odd how there were times when the world became unreal, when all days seemed very much like each other, and then there came a day when the whole thing seemed upside down and inside out, and you felt as if you'd stumbled through Alice's mirror to where nothing followed the rules.

Lying here in bed, he was in a world where everything he touched was destroyed; everything he brushed against became contaminated. It was the Stark Touch. He saw himself touching all the things in the house, trying to find something to give him a handhold in reality, but all the things decayed into white dust whipping up into a dust storm in the living room, settling into little piles in corners (he flattened against a wall, screaming without sound for someone to help him), until the men in white coveralls and hoods came with their dustpans and paper cups and scooped it all away.

What was he, that some dust rubbed off a man's feet in his car, rubbed off onto his jacket and hands, could have led to all this? Why were the dead cars on his father's lot always covered by gritty dust? Rust is red and flour is white, but radioactive dust has nothing but the color of pain.

How could he contaminate the dead as well as the unborn?

Although explanations hovered around the corner of his mind, he shrank from putting them into words or even thought-pictures because he knew that some meanings were worse than none. Was he a coward? Or did that word have meaning any more? Who was there who could give him a reason for living?

She didn't know he could watch her as she came and went from the bedroom, blurry and faint as if through a fine lace handkerchief. She spoke to him and was upset when he didn't answer her questions. Why couldn't she hear his thoughts? Why didn't she know he was begging her to reach out and pull him back before he was swallowed? He would have told her all this, but talking required great energy, and every time he started to speak he felt it slipping from between his lips, like some precious fluid he must keep inside in order to exist.

Why did she blame him for what had happened? It was Prager's fault. It was National Motors' fault. It was her fault for being there to receive it from him. What did he ever have to do with radioactive isotopes? He had never even taken physics in high school, and he flunked Chemistry II. So where was the sense to it?

What was God trying to prove?

Lying there silently, he was surprised at how she had

become self-sufficient in the face of this hopeless situation. He had to give her credit for holding out against her mother. If Laura Bradley had her way they'd have put him into the nuthouse for sure. But he knew she was holding out against them. Maybe she didn't want to add an insane husband to the curses she already carried.

The clock. He had told her a thousand times that he didn't want a clock in the bedroom. She had hidden the Fertility Clock somewhere, after he had smashed its face, but he could hear another one ticking, somewhere close by, as loud and insistent as the beating of his own heart. Time and again he would be dreaming with his eyes open, sinking slowly into himself, when suddenly he would be caught up, hearing her voice, and she would be in the middle of saying something, as if she had been talking to him for a long time, and in the background would be the incessant ticking . . . ticking . . . ticking . . . until her voice was lost in the ticking of some infernal clock, until he put the pillow over his head to shut out the sounds. . . .

He saw some of the neighborhood boys down at Crawford's Creek, swimming bare ass, and he was with them. Muddy, slippery banks to crawl up and flop down into the water, splashing and kicking water into each other's faces. And Waxy O'Brien was standing on the grass with his dick in his hand, shouting, "I've got the biggest one of all." And then they had a measuring contest to see whose was biggest, and it was a tie between him and Waxy. Then they had a pissing contest to see who could piss farthest, and Waxy won. He came in third and was embarrassed. And then they had a contest to see who could come the fastest. And he was scared because he had never done it before. And George Wilkins had a watch and was timing it, and Vincent came first. "One and a half minutes!" shouted Vincent. And then Lester Vittolo came next, all over the grass (he almost got it on George, who told him to watch out, you bastard). Two minutes. And Waxy came third with four

minutes. And he kept trying but nothing happened, and
they all started to laugh because nothing came out. George,
holding the watch in front of his face, was saying, "Come
on, Barney, come on, you can do it, Barney. You can do
it." And then it went limp in his hand as if it died, and
they were all laughing, and he dived into the creek and
swam to the other side where his clothes were and got
dressed and went off home. And there at home that night
in the bathroom he tried and nothing happened . . . and
every night in his bed he tried . . . and nothing . . . and
. . . nothing . . . until one night when he woke up late
in the darkness, he knew he had become a man.

"Barney!"

Her voice dimly through his liquid darkness.

"Barney, please get up!"

Ignore her. He didn't want to listen to her. He wanted
to remember. . . .

"Barney, something's wrong! I need you. . . ."

The strange thing about it was growing to learn that being fast wasn't the thing at all. A man had to be able to
control himself, so there would be time. . . .

"Barney, try to get up. The pains are coming. Something's wrong."

And the time his old man caught him at it in the bathroom. He had locked the door, and he couldn't understand
how the old man knew what he was doing, but he demanded that he open the door, and when he told him
just a minute, I'm not through, he shouted at him.

"Just a minute," he said. "Just a minute."

"I can't reach Dr. Leroy. The waters have burst."

He told him just a minute, but his father pushed against
the bathroom door and the little hook came out and he
caught him, and he was shouting. "What are you doing
there?" "Going to the toilet." "Let me see what you're doing there." "Nothing, Papa, I swear." But he pulled him
off the toilet seat and saw it spring erect, and he screamed,
"I wasn't doing anything, Papa. I didn't touch it. I wasn't
doing anything. It just got like that by itself." But his

father hit him with his fist, so that he fell against the bathtub. "You pollute yourself in this house? It makes you crazy. It makes you blind."

"Barney . . . labor pains . . . Barney, wake up. I need you, Barney. Labor pains have started. Please, for God's sake, get up."

He seemed to be swimming up from a great depth, past the mocking faces in Crawford's Creek, and the sound of laughter and screams, and the feeling of his father's fist against his head, to the edge of knowing it was Karen's voice calling him. He was so sleepy, he didn't want to come awake. What had he to do with this world or the people in it? What did she want of him now? Why not leave him to the memory part of his brain? In the present there was only pain; in the future there was only emptiness.

"I need you, Barney. You've got to get up and help. We've got to get to the hospital. I think I'm going to lose the baby."

And then he was back, beached on the shore of consciousness like an exhausted swimmer, trying to understand what she meant, and then understanding when she shoved the clock into his hand. It was blurred, and he held it close and saw it was seven o'clock.

"The labor pains have started."

"When?"

"About ten minutes ago. Thank God you're awake, Barney. I'm scared."

"Okay, I'm here now." He touched her forehead and felt it wet and clammy. "Let me get you a damp cloth."

He stumbled out of bed and made his way to the bathroom, feeling his way for a towel and wetting it under the faucet.

She was in pain again, and he checked the time—twenty minutes after seven—and he rubbed her back to ease the labor. When it subsided, she fell back again, clinging to his hand like a child at a dangerous crossing.

"You'll be okay," he said. "I'll call the hospital and tell them we're coming. And I'd better get your mother too."

"I tried. There's no answer. You can take care of me, Barney. Just you. Your hands feel good." She sighed as he rubbed her back. "I'm lucky you have such strong hands."

He worked the small of her back, rubbing and kneading her tight muscles, which yielded under probing fingers, up past the delicate wings of shoulder blades, to the soft slender neck. It would be easy, he thought, to end it for all of them, but he kept gently massaging the neck muscles until her head rolled comfortably limp. He forced the idea out of his mind. He could kill himself if he wanted, but not her. He had no business with her future. Her past, yes. But she had forced him to become involved with the present to study the minutes between spasms, a strange measurement of time.

She groaned as a contraction seized her.

"Still thirty minutes," he said. "Okay, now . . . easy . . . easy . . ."

"I think I'm going to die."

"No, you'll be all right. Just hang on."

"Hold my hand, Barney."

He waited with her, to time the pains, rubbing her neck, wiping the perspiration from her forehead, wishing there was a way to ease it for her, but after each spasm, she lay exhausted, and he wondered why life should be born so hard when death came so easily. The time between contractions decreased to twenty-five, and when he told her, she looked frightened and said it was time to get started for the hospital.

He finally got through to Dr. Leroy's home, and his wife said he was delivering a baby at the Elgin City Hospital. When he called the hospital, the switchboard operator said that he was still in the delivery room with a difficult case.

"My wife's in labor," said Barney. "He's supposed to deliver our baby."

"Well, bring her to the hospital," the voice at the other end said. "By that time, perhaps—"

"You don't understand. My wife is scheduled to go to

the Downtown Central in Detroit. He couldn't possibly get there in time if he's still in the delivery room."

"I don't know what to tell you, sir. But you should get your wife to the hospital. If Dr. Leroy doesn't make it, there will be other doctors who can deliver the baby."

The phone was close to the bed, and she heard. "No other doctor," she said. "Only Dr. Leroy. Only him, Barney." And then she muffled a cry and grabbed the sheets as another pain came.

"Look, do you have space available there tonight?" he said. "This is an emergency."

"Just a moment. I'll transfer your call to admissions."

The nurse in admissions said yes there was a bed available because someone had canceled just this morning.

"Fine," he shouted. "Leave a message for Dr. Leroy. We'll be right over."

"Now what name was that?"

"Karen Stark."

There was a pause, "Just a moment please," and he had the impression she had covered the phone with her hand. A moment later she came on again. "I'm sorry, Mr. Stark, but I made a terrible mistake. That bed has been taken. It must have happened when I was on my relief, and—"

"Don't give me that crap!" he shouted. "That space was available until I told you who we were. I'm bringing her in."

"What's the matter, Barney?"

"Nothing! I'll take care of it," he shouted. And then, into the phone, "Did you hear what I said. The waters have burst, and she's having labor pains every twenty-five minutes now. It's going to be a premature baby, and I can't get to Detroit in time. You're close by. You've got to take her in."

"I'm sorry, Mr. Stark. There's no room."

"The hell with that. Tell Dr. Leroy we'll be there."

"But, Mr. Stark—"

He slammed down the phone.

"Barney, I don't want any trouble."

"Afraid we'll contaminate their goddamned hospital."

"Barney, I don't want it to be this way. Please don't lose your temper. I . . ."

"Easy now. That's twenty minutes after the last one. Come on. Let's get you into the car."

"How are you going to drive? You can't see well enough. It's dangerous."

"I can see light," he said. "I'll follow the taillights of cars in front of me. You tell me when I've got to make turns. All I've got to do is keep distance between me and the rear lights of another car. Between us we'll make it."

He helped her out of bed, and it was only when she leaned on him, going down the stairs, that he realized how weak his own legs had become. It was always surprising to discover weakness in his body. But he couldn't afford weakness now. He had to get her to the hospital, and there was going to be trouble.

When he got her and the suitcase into the car, he went back to take the shotgun out of the hall closet. He made sure it was double-loaded and stuffed a handful of extra cartridges into his jacket pocket. When she saw it, she pleaded with him to leave it behind, but he ignored her and started the car carefully out of the driveway.

"We're going to need it," he said. "The word will get around that we're coming. Some of them may try to stop us. I don't think I'll have to use it, but I may have to show it."

She started to protest again, but another pain made her arch back against the seat. "It hurts, Barney. It hurts."

He hunched forward close to the windshield, hoping nobody was driving without lights. He would be making it all the way following taillights only. She guided him as he drove slowly, telling him when they were coming to a stop light, when to turn a corner, when to stop for a pedestrian. A couple of times he cut it too sharply and went on the sidewalk, shaking her up badly, but it seemed as if he would be able to get her to the hospital in time.

But what would happen when they got there? The nurse

would have reported it to the doctors and maybe told some of the officials about it, and word would spread quickly that they were coming. It was just a question of how strong the feeling was running against having them there —and whether there would be time for hysteria to build up.

That lousy article. Except for that, the whole thing might have died down enough to let them ignore her presence in the hospital. It had started the fear all over again, as if there'd been another accident. And the reporter had clearly left the implication that there was plenty of radioactive dust around that Tracer Control had not been able to find.

Someone would probably try to block them from entering the hospital. In which case he would have to threaten to use the shotgun. But would he be able to pull the trigger? He thought he would. He reassured himself that if there was an angry mob, he would have no compunction about shooting. And it wouldn't be from hate (that had been worked out of him), it would be for her. He would get her inside, and it wouldn't matter what they did to him afterward. The only thing that was important now was that she should be admitted to the hospital.

His own feelings about the baby were no longer important, either. Somehow, through her pain, she deserved to have it. She had earned it out of suffering, or out of patient waiting, or out of some deeper pattern he couldn't understand that enabled her body to fashion a human being from multiplying cells. She had created—was still creating—and now, unfinished, the new life was threatening to burst out of the kiln of her body too soon. And whether it was perfect or imperfect, she had the right to finish her work.

She sobbed and twisted back, and he knew it was bad.

Please, dear God, she begged silently, let us get there in time. Please, dear God, let me not lose the baby. I promise to love it no matter what's wrong with it. I'll love it and care for it and be a good mother. Only let it be born. I

know I haven't been a very religious woman, and there
have been times I've denied your existence, but I don't
now, dear God. I believe. I believe. Only let me not lose
my baby. I'll believe in you forever. I promise, dear God,
only let . . . only let—uuhhhhhh! Why must it hurt so
much, God? Why so much pain?

Poor Barney couldn't bear to see her suffering, she thought.
He could take it for himself, but he crumbled at the sight
of her in labor. He was a good man. She didn't condemn
him for what had happened between him and Myra (he
had always loved, always wanted Myra, but she was gone
and he was here), and she knew she could depend on him.

"Barney, that car!"

He swerved sharply to the curb and jammed the brakes
as someone cut in front of them. He sat there gripping the
wheel as if he wanted to break it, shaking, the sweat
streaming down his face.

"It's all right, Barney," she whispered. "Just some thoughtless kids. It's all right."

His grip relaxed. He sighed and sank back limply.

"We'd better keep going now, Barney. There isn't
time. . . ."

He nodded and pulled out carefully, straining to see the
taillights of the car ahead. But he drove too slowly, and
horns began honking. Then another car passed, and someone shouted, "Wake up, you jerk!" And then another, and
another, and more honking, until suddenly Barney accel-
erated.

"Don't let them bother you, Barney."

He pressed down on the gas pedal.

"You're going too fast."

"I know what I'm doing," he said, bearing down on
the last car that had passed him.

"Barney, you're tailgating. If he stops short . . ."

"He can be my seeing eye."

But about half a mile from the hospital the car ahead
signaled for a right turn and swung sharply out of their

way. Without taillights to guide him, Barney had to slow down again.

"Put your hand on the wheel," he said. "Right here, against mine. You can steer with me until you get another spasm."

She moved closer to him and helped keep the car centered on the road until she saw the lights of the hospital ahead.

"It's all right, Barney. We're there. It's all right now."

As he swung around the traffic circle the tires screeched against the curb.

There were about a dozen men in front of the main entrance, and they moved to block the steps when the car pulled up.

"Get out on your side," whispered Barney, pushing the door open for her. And when she hesitated, he nudged her. "Go ahead."

She got out on the side near the hospital. The men stood there blocking the path, and behind them on the other side of the glass doors, she saw some men in white— doctors or interns—and nurses and a few other people looking on from the lit-up lobby.

"You'd better get back into your car, Mrs. Stark," said Oscar Verne, from the service station. "No sense starting any trouble here."

"But I've got to get to my doctor. I'm having a baby."

"Sorry, Mrs. Stark, but my wife is there too."

"And my daughter!" shouted Martino, the hairdresser. "And I don't mean to have her and my grandchild get any of that radioactive dust."

She thought she would faint but braced herself against the car fender for the contraction that was about to come. She gasped and doubled over, and one of the men started forward to help, but stopped when he remembered. And then Barney was at her side holding her, and she realized he had the shotgun.

"Ten minutes apart now," he said.

"Mr. Stark, you ain't going to do nothing with that shotgun," said one of the men, and she recognized Mr. Peterson, from two doors down, whose dog had picked up some contamination from their front lawn.

"No? Think about it," said Barney. "It's you or her. I've got nothing more to lose. You think I'd worry about killing all of you?"

There was a murmur of protest as some of the men realized he was serious, but Martino shouted, "He's bluffing."

"This shotgun has two barrels. Each one will spread the shot wide enough at this range to get most of you. And I can reload pretty damned quick. You're outlined beautifully against that light from those glass doors. I warn you, I'm desperate. If you're not out of the way by the time she has her next pain—another few minutes—I'm going to stop thinking and just spray that entrance. I told you, I've got nothing to lose. But let me say something else. You're all scared of something that doesn't exist. Sure we were both contaminated, but the radioactive dust is all gone now. They cleaned us and our house up, and they did a complete job of it. What we're both suffering from is the effects of that radiation, but neither you nor your wives are in any kind of danger. Unless you try to stop us now."

They stood there, looking at each other as if deciding what to do, and then she felt the pain coming. She was terrified that he might shoot. She didn't want the spasm to come and make him pull the trigger. She tried to hold it back, and when she saw it couldn't be, she tried to keep from showing it. She clenched her teeth, swallowing the moan, trying to stand erect so that he wouldn't see it. But Verne saw it and gave her away.

"She's having it," he said, and moved aside.

But the others didn't move.

"Please, Barney, take me away from here. I can have the baby in the car. Other women give birth in cars on the way to the hospital; maybe I could." But even as she said it she knew she was far too weak, and a premature baby wouldn't live.

For a moment she thought he was going to shoot, but he didn't. He lowered the rifle and shouted. "All right, I won't hurt any of you. That would be too good for you. But you're not getting off this easy."

He swung the shotgun around and pointed it directly at her abdomen, off to one side, pressing it against her.

"We're walking past you, and anyone who tries to stop us will trigger both barrels. Kill her and the baby if you want to. If you want to murder her, you'll have to do it here and now."

It was a desperate bluff. She knew he would never do it. Yet his finger was on the trigger, and it wouldn't take much to fire the shotgun. But he had to be bluffing.

"Go ahead," he said to her, nudging her with the barrel. "Walk very slowly."

"Don't let them pass," shouted Peterson.

"Stop them."

"I can't. If I grab him, it'll set the gun off," said Verne.

"He won't do it."

"He's out of his mind."

"My finger is on the trigger," said Barney, "and anyone who pushes against me will be a murderer. Now move aside, you bastards, and let us pass."

They moved aside as she came up close to them. One of the nurses opened the door, and they went into the lobby. The doctors and interns who had been watching what was going on stepped back to make room. They went up to the reception desk, and Barney said to the nurse, "Emergency. Get Dr. Leroy. The contractions are about ten minutes apart."

The strain of the past few minutes caught up with her. She suddenly felt her legs give way. One of the interns caught her, and she saw Dr. Leroy's face just before she passed out.

He wondered if he would really have killed her if they had tried to stop him. He couldn't ever be absolutely sure, of course, what he would have done. Maybe he would have turned it on them after all, or maybe on himself, or maybe he would have done nothing. But when he and Karen started toward those steps he had every intention of taking her life, because if they hadn't been allowed to pass, what good would life have been? Hers? His? That poor thing inside her? He would never know the answer.

They found her a private room so as not to upset the other women in the maternity ward, and he stayed with her, hearing her suffer, barely able to see her face behind the white mound that looked like a bag of laundry, holding onto her straining hands when she grabbed him instead of the bedrails. Each scream, each spasm and lurch of her body went through him, and he felt peculiar when he thought that he had been the cause of this too. He had, in the beginning, wanted a child more than she.

He wiped her forehead with one of the towels and tried to ease her mind. She was more afraid than she had ever been, thinking of death, her own, the baby's. And he had to promise her she wouldn't die.

"And do you want the baby now?" she whispered, hoarsely.

"Yes," he said, not sure if he was lying or not.

"And you'll love it, no matter what it's like? No matter what's wrong with it?"

"Yes. I'll love it and care for both of you. I'll go for treatments. I'll get better. We'll have a life together."

But a contraction broke it off, and she clutched his arm so hard he thought the bone would break. She leaned forward, twisting like a hooked fish, and then fell back as the wave receded. She motioned for him to wet her lips with the damp cloth.

Dr. Leroy and a frightened nurse came in. She drew a curtain around the bed, and he waited near the doorway, from where he could see shadows of passing figures. A few seconds later two interns brought a stretcher. They helped Karen out of the labor bed into the stretcher and passed him. She had a sheet up to her neck, and he thought, if she dies in there the sheet will be over her face when they bring her back, but she will be as flat and slender as before.

He waited in the "Father's Room" for nearly two hours, trying not to think back or ahead, trying to keep his mind focused on the waiting, trying to imagine what she was going through in that delivery room. Once he imagined her dead, but he erased the picture from his mind.

Finally, Dr. Leroy came out, still wearing the pale-green gown and cap, and he flopped into a chair.

"She's going to live," he said. "But the baby was dead." He was silent for a moment, lit a cigarette, and puffed at it thoughtfully. "Perhaps just as well. It was only partially formed—mutated. Probably had been dead for days."

"But she felt it move the other day."

"Her imagination. It's been dead awhile, and it never would have survived anyway. She'll be coming out of the delivery room in a few minutes. She'll be very sleepy; I've given her a sedative. She had a very bad time in there."

He waited in the corridor, and they wheeled her stretcher up to him and paused.

"How are you?" he asked.

"Fine. Did Dr. Leroy tell you about the baby?"

He nodded, and bent over to kiss her cheek.

She closed her eyes, and for a moment he thought she had fallen asleep, but then she opened them. "Barney, I love you."

"I love you too."

"What's going to happen to us?"

"We'll put things together and make a life."

"I wanted a child."

He thought for a moment. "Even if we can't adopt children through normal channels, we can become foster parents. We'll take in children to care for even though they can't be our own. We don't have to own them. We'll care for children no one else wants."

"They won't let us Barney. Not here."

"We'll move away and change our name. I want to change my name back to what it was. I've been thinking about that. Would you mind very much being Mrs. Bronislaw Szutarek?"

She smiled. "It's a lovely idea."

As they started to wheel her away, she raised herself up on one elbow and whispered sleepily. "Babies no one else wants," she said. "War orphans hurt and deformed. . . . Children who are alone and suffering. . . . The way ours would have been."

He nodded and patted her arm. "It's a lovely idea."

She smiled and lay back on the stretcher as they wheeled her away.

Barney went back to where Dr. Leroy was sitting. "I want to see the baby," he said.

"There's no point in upsetting yourself."

"I have to see it."

Dr. Leroy shrugged and motioned for Barney to follow him into the delivery room. It was hard for Barney to see, but he strained and squinted to bring the blur into focus. A nurse in a blood-spattered gown was cleaning up and preparing to remove a small basin covered with a cloth. She looked surprised when Dr. Leroy asked her to uncover it, but she put it back on the table and carefully removed the covering.

Barney bent over close and studied the small, inert form. It had no arms or legs, merely stumps that ended at the shoulders and upper thighs. Its eyes were sealed and its head was curled forward, as if asleep. Of all the fetuses he had modeled, he had never created one like that. He touched the slippery protrusion where an arm should have been. He had never thought of one like that. And seeing the unliving creature lying there in the basin, he felt something come up from deep inside himself, a wave, a spasm, a contraction that would not be held back, dry at first, but then it broke, and the tears streamed down his cheeks as he cried for his only son.